The screaming stopped as abruptly as it had begun, but the reverberations seemed to bounce around the dark bedroom like Ping Pong balls. Theo waited a few seconds for his adrenaline to ebb, then threw back the covers and scrabbled on the bedside table for his bifocals. He was tying the belt of his bathrobe when the door opened and Dorrie slipped in, her arms wrapped around herself as though she could suppress the shivers and convulsive twitches of her body, which she obviously could not. Her ashen face was streaked with black lines of mascara, and water streamed from her sodden hair. She wore a terrycloth jacket, although it had been buttoned by hasty negligent fingers. Her feet were bare.

"Oh, Uncle Theo," she said. . . . "Oh, Uncle Theo . . ." She toppled over backward and stared at the ceiling through glazed, unblinking eyes

A Theo Bloomer Mystery

THE DEADLY ACKEE

Joan Hadley

BALLANTINE BOOKS • NEW YORK

Library of Congress Catalog Card Number: 87-29929

ISBN 0-345-35900-3

This edition published by arrangement with St. Martin's Press, Inc.

Manufactured in the United States of America

First Ballantine Books Edition: May 1990

This one's for:
TK, Ray, Becky, Terry, John, and Carolyn,
who graciously consented to accompany me to Jamaica
and assist with the research. They also helped me
survive a long, hard year and I love them all.

1

"Theo? I do hope I'm not interrupting, but I simply must discuss a rather minor situation that has arisen. Minor, but, well, slightly major."

Theodore Bloomer stared at the telephone receiver in his hand, perplexed by his sister's wheedling tone. It was unlike her to even consider the possibility she might be interrupting him, which might imply his time was of more value than hers. Unthinkable.

"I was in the greenhouse, checking on seedlings," he admitted cautiously. "The tomato hybrids seem to be coming along nicely."

"Really? Charles, Dorrie, and I do so enjoy your little offerings each summer. But I have a problem, Theo, and I must resolve it briskly. I have a bridge game at the club, and Pookie's picking me up in less than five minutes. Do you have any vital social engagements next week?"

"The horticulturists' club is planning a tour of the local azalea gardens," Theo said, still eyeing the receiver uneasily. "I had considered the wisdom of repotting several of my—"

"Well, that much is settled. I fear I must ask a small favor." Nadine Caldicott took a deep breath to recover from what must have been a painful sentence. "The whole thing

1

is quite my fault; I accept full blame for it. But you know how very headstrong Dorrie can be, a trait I often suspect might have been inspired, if not blatantly encouraged, by her doting Uncle Theo.''

"This involves Dorrie? What has she done now?''

"She and a group of her friends have arranged for a villa in Jamaica for their spring break next week. There will be Dorrie, her fiancé, Biff, a friend of his named Beachy or Sandy or something like that, those adorable red-haired Ellison twins, and one of Dorrie's suitemates from Wellesley. Let me think . . . Biff's at Amherst, the Whitcombe boy's at Annapolis, Mary Margaret Ellison is with Dorrie and the Bigelow girl, and her brother is between schools at the moment, I believe. You may have met some of them at the house; they're forever hanging around the pool when they're not at the club. They absolutely romp through the wine cellar, which drives Charles crazy.''

"I can imagine,'' Theo said. "I'm sure Dorrie and her friends will have a lovely time in Jamaica. However, I hear water running in the greenhouse, and I'd better check on it. If you'll excuse—''

"All of them come from very good families, of course, and the villa is fabulous, simply fabulous. Four bedrooms, fully staffed, private pool, view of the Caribbean. It's going to be a delightful little vacation. Doesn't it sound delightful, Theo?''

"Delightful,'' Theo echoed obediently. "But I fail to understand how it involves me, Nadine, and I'm afraid I must hang up now. I must have left the hose running in the greenhouse, and—''

"I need you to chaperone them.''

"Out of the question. The last time I accompanied Dorrie, I was blown down a mountainside by Israeli terrorists. It was most distressing, and I have no intention of—''

"It was quite good of you, Theo. Have I ever properly thanked you for retrieving Dorrie from that dreadful communist cell?''

"No, nor have you allowed me to complete one sentence without—"

"Oh, dear, Pookie's honking in the driveway and she is utterly impossible if she's kept waiting. I'll have Dorrie call with the travel information. I shall insist on paying for your expenses, although I might point out that you'll be having a lovely vacation while the rest of us are literally sloshing through Connecticut slush."

"I am not going to chaperone Dorrie and her—"

A dial tone buzzed in Theo's ear. Sighing, he replaced the receiver and returned to his greenhouse, where the hose had flooded the concrete floor. He moved several clay pots out of the water, picked up a trowel, then put it down with another sigh. His sister, Nadine, was a force that required more resistance than he could usually produce. She had teethed on the Junior League, then moved through charitable fund-raisers to the fully ripened post of president of the Hospital Auxiliary. She had not done so by evincing weakness. On the contrary, had she been the *Titanic* (not an improbable analogy), the Atlantic would have been dotted with crushed ice.

Theo was still puttering in the greenhouse when the telephone once again disturbed him. He went into the kitchen to wipe his hands on a dish towel, then warily picked up the receiver. "This is Theo Bloomer."

"I'm so glad I caught you, Uncle Theo. I absolutely have to go to the library and do a midterm paper; I've put it off for months now, and all of a sudden it's due tomorrow. It's as if Simmons gave us all this time to perspire over it, knowing perfectly well we'd have to stay up all night to get it finished. *C'est-à-dire*, having it dangle over my head has made my life a living hell."

"I'm sorry to hear that," Theo said mildly.

"Thank you," Dorrie said, graciously accepting the perceived sympathy. "Did Mother call you about Jamaica?"

"It's out of the question, Dorrie. I am sixty-one years old, and far too old to spend a week on a Caribbean beach with a group of college students. I have appointments next week, and some very time-consuming chores in the greenhouse to prepare for the planting season. I'm sure you and your friends can find another chaperone for your trip."

"But we can't. Mother agreed to go along, but then she realized that a year ago she had promised Pookie they would play in the women's pairs in the Greater Connecticut Bridge Tournament that very same week. We'd already mailed in the nonrefundable deposit at that point."

"There are several of you going," Theo pointed out, "and surely one of the other parents could accompany the group."

"Not one of them. We've absolutely pleaded with them, but they're all being totally beastly about it. But it's all right, Uncle Theo. We'll forfeit the deposit—which rivals certain Third World countries' gross national products, I might add. I'll just spend the week studying in my dorm room. With everyone else off on meaningful trips, the building will be a dark, dusty, creepy old mausoleum, and I can work on a term paper or something equally thrilling. Perhaps I'll try a strawberry rinse on my hair, or a new shade of fingernail polish . . ." Several delicate sniffles ensued as she envisioned the scene.

Theo was not impressed. "Come now, you don't have to spend your vacation in the dorm. You can stay at home, and spend the time with your friends."

"If the trip collapses, I won't have any friends. I realize it's my senior year and my last spring break ever, but I truly don't mind that it will be the most wretched week of my entire life. Please don't waste a single second worrying about me, Uncle Theo."

"Why don't you go without a chaperone, my dear? After all, you're all college seniors and quite capable of taking care of yourselves. You'll have a much better time without a gray-haired nursemaid to remind you to eat your vegetables and—"

"This is hardly the sixties. We have standards now, and it

simply wouldn't look right for a group of very attractive singles to stay in a villa in a foreign country without a proper chaperone. It could lead to all sorts of tacky gossip at the club. Biff's grandmother would be so appalled she might change her mind—and her will—and let his younger sister get her pudgy little hands on the Hartley sterling collection, which was probably made by Paul Revere or someone like that.''

"Then hire someone to accompany you.''

"We need a proper chaperone, not a Kelly Girl.'' A paper rustled, and a sly note crept into her voice. "There are more than three thousand varieties of flowering plants in Jamaica, and eight hundred of them are found nowhere else in the world.''

"Dorrie, as much as I would like to chaperone you and your friends, I cannot leave during the spring planting season. I'm testing a new tomato hybrid that is purported to be blight-resistant, and it's almost time to put in snap beans and peas.''

"Two hundred species of wild orchids. Sixty of bromeliads, and five hundred fifty of ferns.''

"Two hundred species of wild orchids?'' Theo heard himself saying, despite his better sense.

"Yep. You can do almost thirty a day, Uncle Theo. I'll personally go to the botanical gardens with you and make appreciative little noises over each and every blossom, even if it means sacrificing peak tanning hours on the beach.''

She continued to extol the botanical treasures found exclusively in Jamaica as Theo gazed through the glass doors at his greenhouse. Even if deprived of water for a week, he suspected his tomato seedlings were made of sterner stuff than he. Then again, very few species were Caldicott-resistant. Science was not yet that advanced.

Sangster International Airport was crowded with tourists, porters, businessmen clad in lightweight suits, and small children darting about like water skimmers. Weary parents pleaded without success as the omnipresent public address system crackled without clarity. It was, Theo decided, precisely like every other international airport he'd been in, despite the proximity of romantic Montego Bay. The humidity, noise, litter, flies, and grime were not romantic.

The crowd milled around him as he stopped for a moment to slip off his jacket and carefully fold it over his arm. No one gave a second glance to the tall, balding man with the neatly trimmed beard and bright blue eyes behind thick bifocals. Had anyone bothered to study him, he would have been categorized and dismissed as the essence of mildness, a genteel retiree, perhaps inclined to bore listeners with a harmless hobby or two. Cats, African violets, model trains. Certainly nothing too eccentric, exotic, or expensive. Theo had discovered many years ago that his nondescript demeanor served him well, and he took pains not to contradict the image.

His niece and namesake, Theodora Bloomer Caldicott, was hardly nondescript. She was a tall, graceful girl, equipped with wholesome preppie enthusiasm and a goodly dose of Connecticut snobbery. Her long blond hair usually bounced around her, but today it was up in a ponytail as a concession to the heat. Theo watched her fondly as she strolled through the airport. Caldicotts looked neither left nor right, nor at the floor, where one might inadvertently see something rude. They looked straight ahead, ever mindful of posture. The less fortunate were expected to move out of the way. For some inexplicable reason, they did.

Dorrie stopped abruptly and clapped her hands. "Isn't that quaint?" she demanded of no one in particular. "A little band of local musicians playing island music! It is so completely cute I cannot believe it. Give them a dollar, Biff."

Biff (a.k.a. Bedford James Hartley II, reputed to be Dorrie's fiancé) smiled indulgently. "Now, Dorrikin, we don't want to disrupt the island economy by passing out American dollars to every native who can pound some obscure instrument or dresses in polyester print."

"But they're playing calypso, just like Harry Belafonte. I think it's absolutely quaint, and I think we should encourage them to maintain their traditions. It's terribly important in a depressed economy for the natives to have a continuity with their heritage. It helps them keep their minds off poverty and things like that."

A blond-haired boy retraced his steps to join them. "Don't be an ugly American, big guy," he said to Biff, punching him in the arm. "Give them some change and let's find our luggage. I'm ready to do some beach and brewskis."

Alexander "Sandy" Whitcombe was Biff's oldest and dearest friend, Theo had learned on the flight, although somewhat of a pariah since he attended the U.S. Naval Academy at Annapolis rather than one of the more traditional ivy-coated schools. Dorrie had mentioned that said midshipman's father was some species of admiral and very adamant about family traditions, and that personally she found uniforms appealing. Well, not on doormen, of course, and only if they were dress whites and not khaki, which was primitive, especially if one were to perspire. Not that she meant chinos, obviously, since they were de rigueur in the summer. Or unless one was doing Kenya, in which case one simply had to wear those darling safari outfits from Banana Republic, complete with pith helmets, no matter what havoc they wrought on one's hair.

It had been a long flight. Dorrie had insisted on sitting with her darling Uncle Theo to keep him company since he was being such a super good sport to come with them. The fact that Biff had sat with another of the girls had warranted not a few catty comments interspersed in the nonstop chatter. A very long flight, indeed.

Even before boarding the plane (weeks ago?), Theo had noted that Sandy's hair was more closely cropped than the norm, and his posture reminiscent of the military, which was hardly surprising. His freckles were neatly aligned. Biff, on the other hand, had aristocratically elegant features, stylishly shaggy dark hair, and the slouch that seemed to accompany the burden of old money. However, they were dressed identically, from their sockless loafers through their madras shorts to the discreet little alligators on their knit shirts. The uniform to end all uniforms.

As Biff hesitated, visibly aggrieved, Theo took out a dollar and dropped it in a hat in front of the band. "I enjoyed the music," he murmured.

The four black men gazed back. "No problem, mon," the guitarist said, flashing white teeth.

"Now look what you've done!" Dorrie said to Biff. "The others have gone ahead, and I don't see any of them. If you hadn't pulled this silly little Scrooge routine, we wouldn't have lost them."

Biff's ears turned the precise shade of pink Theo hoped the fruit of his hybrid tomatoes might prove to be. "If you hadn't stopped to behave like some undergrad sociologist, we wouldn't have lost them, either."

Sandy draped arms around the combatants' shoulders. "Children, children, let's not get blown out over this. We're on spring break. We're supposed to relax, enjoy ourselves, work on those tans, and bask in the moonlight of Montego Bay. We'll catch up with the rest of the gang at the luggage terminal. Then right on to the limo, the villa, and the beer!"

Dorrie tucked her arm through Biff's and fluttered her eyelashes contritely. "Dorrikin didn't mean to snap at Biffkin. She's sorry."

Biffkin kissed Dorrikin's sweet little nose.

Theo trailed after the three as they went through the airport. The small spat between his niece and her fiancé was disturbing, and he wondered what had provoked it. He then dismissed it from his mind. With six young adults under his supervision, he suspected they had only just begun.

The other three were waiting for their luggage. The male half of the "adorable Ellison twins" was leaning against a pillar, a cigarette dangling from his lips in true Bogart fashion. He had carefully styled red hair and hooded green eyes that seemed more closed then open. He arched an eyebrow as Dorrie, Biff, and Sandy joined him.

"Trouble in paradise?" he said, smirking at their flushed faces. "Is it possible Ken and Barbie will not discover bliss under the tropical stars?"

"Stuff it," Dorrie said. She wheeled around and took refuge with the distaff half of the adorable Ellison twins. Mary Margaret raised an eyebrow, but it took her quite a while longer to manage the effort. Her red hair was lighter than her brother's, and tumbled down her back in artistic disarray. Her body was voluptuous enough to catch and retain the eye of every male in the area. Superglue could not have been more effective than her brief white shorts and translucent blouse.

"Is Trey being abominable?" she drawled. "Hardly surprising."

The final member of the sextet appeared from the direction of the ladies' room. Bitsy (Elizabeth Angelica O'Conner) Bigelow was petite, from her pert little nose to her pert little feet. Her short brown hair jiggled with each step, as did parts of her anatomy. "Trey once modeled for a Yeti poster," she said, smiling sweetly at the object of her barb. "They couldn't use it, though. Too gruesome."

"You flatter me," Trey said.

"Were that remotely true, which it is not, it would also be completely unintentional." Bitsy proved that she, too, could raise an eyebrow.

Theo took Dorrie aside. "Is this bickering the standard behavior among your friends? We haven't even officially set foot in Jamaica, and it's already growing tiresome."

"There is a tiny amount of tension between Trey and Bitsy," Dorrie said in a low voice. "They were engaged last semester. It was announced in *The New York Times*, which was quite a coup considering that her father made his money in pet accessories. *The Times* is leery of nouveau, if you know what I mean. Well, to make an excruciatingly boring story short, Trey pulled something intolerable, and Bitsy was forced to call the whole thing off—the very next day after she'd had the first fitting for her wedding dress. It was dreadful.''

"I can imagine."

"The lace was obviously synthetic, and the hem length unsuitable for her height. I don't know what came over her. We all almost expired when she showed us a picture of it, but not a soul in the dorm dared breathe a word of criticism.''

"But if they have this unpleasant history between them, why did either of them agree to come on the trip?'' Theo asked, aware he would never grasp the delicacies of dorm demeanor.

"Bitsy pointed out that her family and the Ellisons belong to the same country club, and the mothers to the Symphony Guild. It simply isn't feasible for them to feud, not with the Memorial Day tennis tournament in a couple of months and the scads of club functions and parties this summer. Everyone would have been obliged to take sides and ostracize one or the other of them. Guest lists are hellacious enough as it is, without having to remember which camp people are in. It does put a damper on the divorce rate, though.'' Dorrie chewed on her lip for a moment. "It's terribly sensible of Bitsy, don't you think?''

"I suppose so, in a cold-blooded way. Perhaps she didn't take the engagement seriously.''

"She spent thirty-seven hundred on the dress, Uncle Theo. It sounded pretty darn serious to me.''

Before Theo could respond, the conveyor belt rumbled to life and luggage appeared through the rubber curtain. Within a few minutes, all the bags had been loaded on carts, wheeled through customs for a perfunctory search, and piled on the sidewalk by obliging porters with broad grins and convenient palms.

Trey was the last to amble through the door. He gazed at a long, lumpy bag. "I say, that looks like a body bag. Did someone sneak a corpse through customs? Are we to have the pleasure of someone's dear, departed great-auntie every afternoon for pickle juice cocktails?''

"Golf clubs," Sandy said. "There are some excellent courses.''

"I would have thought golf was too, shall we say, plebeian for you military chaps," Trey said, flicking cigarette ashes on the bag. "I thought you spent your idle moments spitting on your shoes or assembling weapons while blindfolded.''

"Leave him alone," Biff said. "I brought my clubs, too.''

Mary Margaret put her hand on Biff's arm and gave him a lazy smile. "Trey's just being vile because he's a wretched golfer. His handicap qualifies him for protection under the Equal Employment Act. I'm not bad myself. In fact, the pro at the club said I was very good.''

"He was simply mad about her grip," Trey added. "He told everyone in the locker room that it was outstanding.''

Mary Margaret kept her eyes on Biff. "But I could always use a lesson or two. I hope you'll help me with my backswing.''

Theo heard Dorrie's well-bred growl, but could only close his eyes to avoid viewing what he feared was about to transpire. He opened them as an alarmingly pink station wagon stopped in front of them. A woman with daffodil-yellow hair leaned across the seat to roll down the window. Her lipstick matched the flamingo hue of her wagon, as did the several undulations of eyeshadow.

"Caldicott party for Harmony Hills villa?" she asked. When Theo nodded, she climbed out of the station wagon and came around to the sidewalk. She was nearly as tall as he, and moved with a professional briskness that sent him back a few inches in an instinctive retreat. Her dark brown eyes and broad smile did much to soften her squarish, blunt features. She was, Theo concluded, not unattractive.

"You look tired from your flight," she announced. "I'm Geraldine Greeley, the leasing agent with whom you've corresponded. The villa's ready, so why don't you pop all your luggage in the back and pile in the station wagon.''

The group gaped at her as if she'd suggested selecting a wardrobe on the basis of sixty-second blue light specials. Theo sighed, introduced the stunned group, then said, "I'm Theo Bloomer, Ms. Greeley. For reasons that now seem obscure if not insane, I'm the chaperone. Might it be possible to persuade a porter to load the luggage?"

"Call me Gerry, honey." She turned shrewd eyes on his charges. "It'll be a tight squeeze, but the villa's only a couple of miles away. You can survive, can't you?"

"Certainly," Mary Margaret said, her fingers still wrapped around Biff's arm. "We'll just snuggle in like little old peas in a pod. You don't mind if I sit on Biff's lap, do you, Dorrie?"

Dorrie shot Biff a bright smile as she moved toward the front door of the station wagon. "Why on earth would I mind? You two little sweet peas can snuggle your little pods out."

"I am not sitting on his lap," Bitsy said, indicating Trey with a flip of her chin. "I'd rather walk."

Trey flipped his cigarette over his shoulder as he gave her a facetiously sympathetic look. "It might not be a bad idea, Bitsy. It might even take a few ounces of cellulite off those buttocks."

"My cellulite is none of your concern! I, for one, fit very nicely in my pantyhose."

Sandy took Bitsy's elbow and pulled her aside for a whispered conversation. By the time they returned to the car, the luggage had been arranged in the back. Dorrie sat between Gerry and Theo in the front seat, her jaw extended to its utmost and her lips clamped. The others had managed to find adequate space in the backseat. Gerry turned around as the final door slammed.

"Everybody comfy?" When she received no answer, she started the engine and pulled into the line of traffic inching out of the airport parking lot. "I hope you find the villa pleasant. Your cook's name is Amelia. You may find her attitude a bit difficult, but she's worked with my firm for over ten years and does an excellent job, especially with island specialties. The maid is—''

Dorrie interrupted with a shriek. ''You're on the wrong side of the road, you madwoman! We're about to have a head-on collision!''

''It's the British influence, dearie. You won't get used to it in a week, but you'll be able to open your eyes in a few days.''

Theo opened his eyes to a squint. ''Aren't we driving too fast for this . . . ah, road?''

''It's an island tradition to drive like a bat out of hell. The Jamaicans put a dozen bodies in a little car and take off as if it were the opening of the Indy 500. Your car is at the villa, but I suggest you take great care until you've had a chance to observe the road conditions and customs. Eli will be available to drive you wherever you wish, or run errands for you. He's the lawn and pool boy, and has separate quarters in a room under the pool.''

''A veritable troll,'' murmured Trey.

''If you say so,'' Gerry glanced at him in the rearview mirror with a vague smile.

''Trey's an authority on trolls,'' Bitsy contributed. ''It was his major until he was tossed out of school for the fifth time. Or was it the sixth?''

''Darling, I didn't know you cared enough to count.''

''At least I can count.''

Theo gazed out the window at the lush green foliage of the landscape, wondering not for the first time why he had consented to accompany the house party, which held little promise of being the least bit ''delightful.'' Two hundred species of wild orchids would not compensate for seven days of sniping, bickering, snarling, and whatever else arose. It was, however, too late to do much about it.

The road curved up into a sloping mountainside of villas, each protected with a high fence and gate. The yards were manicured stretches of green, shaded by towering poinsettias and royal poincianas, palms and tamarind trees, shrubs thick with bright orange flowers and explosions of scarlet. A few cars with tourists crept along the broad streets, while dark-skinned women walked purposefully, baskets balanced on their heads.

They arrived at the gate of the villa with only a few more muffled gasps. A black man who appeared to be in his early twenties unlocked the padlock and pulled back the gate, then gave Gerry a deferential nod as she drove through and up the steep driveway.

"That was Eli," she said, parking beside a short flight of steps that led to a terrace. "This is your home for the next week, and I do hope you have a lovely time. Amelia has purchased enough supplies for a day or two, then you can make a list and have Eli take her to the market. The fruit and vegetable truck will come by daily, and the fish truck every few days. You can purchase live lobsters from them if they have any after the hotel and restaurant rounds."

"And the brewski truck?" Sandy asked as he helped Bitsy out of the backseat. "Every hour, I hope."

"You'll find a complete selection of liquor in a cabinet in the kitchen and several cases of chilled beer in the refrigerator," Gerry said. "I've been at this job for twenty years, and I know what our visitors want in their first five minutes."

Dorrie snorted as she joined Theo in the driveway. "Some of our visitors seem to prefer physical contact, particularly with men who have forgotten preexisting relationships."

Gerry introduced Eli, who had followed the station wagon up the driveway, and instructed him to unload the luggage. Theo picked up his suitcase and followed the group into the villa, which seemed to consist of at least three levels. The door from the driveway led to the main floor, with a kitchen in back and a dining room with wide french doors that opened onto a terrace. A few steps down from the terrace was a crystal blue pool surrounded by a deck. The bedrooms were presumably upstairs; the living room was on a lower level beyond the dining room. By the time Theo assimilated all the steps, the group had assembled in the living room.

"Can you believe this?" Dorrie whispered in a thoroughly awed voice. "This is a movie set, right? Early bordello— right down to the red velvet, the fringe on the drapery swags, and that absurd loveseat just begging for a hooker to sprawl across it. Mary Margaret, you are going to be in your element."

"Dorrie," Biff began reproachfully, "you shouldn't speak to—"

"Let's get the bedroom situation arranged," she continued. "I really must wash my face. Some of you may have less hygienic goals, but I can already tell this humidity is going to cause all sorts of problems with my complexion, not to mention my hair. I can almost hear my ends splitting. Come along, everyone; let's get this over with."

There were three bedrooms upstairs. Dorrie, Bitsy, and Mary Margaret took the master, which had three beds and a small balcony overlooking the terrace. Biff and Sandy took the bedroom beside the girls', and Theo found himself relegated to the smallest. Trey agreed to the room off the living room, murmuring that he did not believe in roommates unless they were also sprightly, imaginative bedmates. No one volunteered.

Theo unpacked his suitcase, hung his shirts in the closet, aligned his shoes in an esthetically pleasing formation, arranged his toiletries to his satisfaction in the minute bathroom, and then went downstairs. Dorrie joined him as he crossed the dining room, her face ominously composed. Gerry was waiting on the terrace beside the pool. A dark, thin woman with a dour expression stood beside her, a notebook in her hand.

"This is Amelia," Gerry said. "She has a list of the provisions already purchased, and will sit down to do menus whenever you wish. However, she has prepared a Jamaican chicken recipe for tonight, if that's acceptable to you."

Dorrie had spent more time with the help than she had with her parents. "Let me check the invoices against the provisions and get it done with," she said, holding out her hand for the notebook. "I'll do menus tomorrow morning after breakfast, Amelia. I dread things dangling over me."

The cook slapped the notebook in Dorrie's palm. "You find everything will match, miss. I don' cheat like some of the trash I know."

"Well, of course not," Dorrie said, shrinking back for a second as Connecticut protocol deserted her. Connecticut help did not challenge their betters—if they wanted steady employment. "I wasn't suggesting any such thing. It's simply basic procedure, like counting the silver after a dinner party."

"You can count forks if you want, miss. I got better flatware at home than they keep here." Amelia strode toward the kitchen.

Dorrie's eyelashes fluttered as she stared at the departing back. "My goodness, she's rather temperamental, isn't she?"

"But she's a marvelous cook," Gerry said. "I'll go to the kitchen with you and help you get started, then perhaps we might have a pitcher of rum punch by the pool while we discuss your plans for the week. I have brochures, maps, information about the train, names and telephone numbers for charter boats, and all that sort of thing. We'll meet your uncle out by the pool in a few minutes."

Theo agreed to the plan and went down the steps to the patio surrounding the pool. He pulled a chair under the shade of a slightly tattered umbrella, took off his bifocals and polished them, then put them on the nearby table and leaned back, his eyes closed.

When he opened them, he found himself looking at two large, white, unfettered breasts. The nipples, he noted in confused alarm, were precisely the purplish shade of the *cattleya violacea*, a rather common orchid that he had, before his retirement from the florist industry, used in many a corsage.

2

Mary Margaret smiled smugly as she picked up a towel and covered herself. "My deepest apologies, Mr. Bloomer. I presumed you were asleep. I never dreamed I might embarrass you."

"I was indeed asleep," Theo managed to say, suddenly realizing the necessity of again polishing his bifocals. "Although it was more of a catnap. At my age, I find a few moments will often refresh me, and I must admit the hours on the airplane were tiring. I had no idea that you—ah, you were preparing to sunbathe in a . . . a natural state. Please don't think for a second that I was perpetrating a vulgar ruse in order to . . . to behave in an ungentlemanly fashion."

"Never in my wildest fantasies, Mr. Bloomer." She picked up a straw basket and strolled toward the far side of the pool. She spread out a second towel, then lay down to expose her bare back to the sun. Her rounded rump was covered, albeit unsuccessfully, by a very small black triangle. Theo assumed it was intentional. He was not especially surprised when her hand did something mysterious and the black triangle was discarded. He admired the clarity of the water in the pool, then challenged himself to name the plants in the yard. All of them, one by one.

He had identified a cestrum, a malpighia, and a climbing

vine he suspected was a cissus when Dorrie and Gerry came across the terrace and pulled up deck chairs on either side of him. Behind them, a short black woman carried a tray with a pitcher, an ice bucket, several glasses, and a plate of crackers. Gerry introduced her as Emelda, the maid.

"Hope you like my rum punch, Mr. Bloomer," she said, her round face wrinkling as she smiled at him. "I make the best punch on the island, or so they tell me."

"I'm sure it will prove excellent," Theo said. Once she had gone, he looked at Dorrie. "Everything under control in the kitchen, my dear?"

"I suppose so, although we're having peculiar things for dinner, and I'm not sure what the others will think. Callaloo, chocho, peas and rice, and a chicken dish that actually may have potential." She gazed at Mary Margaret's inert form, then turned to Gerry. "It is vital, however, that I do menus immediately. I do think we'll be safer with lobster, shrimp, steaks, and that sort of thing."

"But you ought to sample the Jamaican food while you're here," Gerry said. "I'm sure Amelia will prepare ackee and salt fish for breakfast, along with fried plantains, bammies, and boiled green bananas if she can get them."

Dorrie gave Theo a look reminiscent of a lab bunny facing a twelve-inch hypodermic needle. "I'd better speak to her at once," she said as she scrambled out of her chair and hurried toward the house.

Theo took the proffered glass of rum punch from Gerry. "In one sense, Dorrie is terribly sophisticated, but in another she's as provincial as a native who's never left the island. Her parents have taken her to Europe several times, but they always stay in American hotel chains where they can count on English-speaking waiters to serve bacon and eggs for breakfast. Her father almost had a stroke when first confronted with a continental breakfast."

"Tell me about this group, Theo. They are somewhat younger than most of my clients, and they seem awfully uptight for a bunch of college kids on spring break."

He took a moment to recall what he could of Dorrie's commentary on the airplane. "Well, Sandy, the blond-haired boy, attends naval academy. His mother is solid Baltimore money, his father a stern, harrumphing sort who stresses discipline and personal sacrifice. Sandy and Biff are old prep school chums, with lots of holiday visiting and yachting in the summer."

"And Biff belongs to the red-haired girl?"

"That seems to be an issue at the moment," Theo confessed. "Biff is reputedly engaged to my niece, Dorrie, although I don't believe it's official yet and no dates have been discussed that I'm aware of."

Gerry stared at the figure across the pool. "Oh, dear, I could see the fireworks going off, but I wasn't sure why. The redhead has the moves of a hungry tigress; I can understand why your niece is storming around the kitchen."

"It's actually her normal behavior." He then explained the volatile situation between Trey and Bitsy, which earned a few ill-disguised snickers of laughter from Gerry, who was clearly amused by the complexities of the house party. "I merely intend to survive the week," he concluded stiffly.

"Marie Antoinette said the same during the French Revolution, Theo. But for now, let me show you the brochures concerning the boat and train rides, the beach parties at the hotels, the great houses and gardens, and all the touristy things in the area."

They were discussing botanical gardens when Biff, Sandy, and Bitsy, now dressed in bathing suits and carrying towels, suntan lotion, magazines, and other necessary paraphernalia to battle the sun, came out of the house and down the steps to the pool deck. Sandy and Bitsy continued around to the table with the pitcher and glasses, but Biff, after a furtive peek at the terrace, turned the opposite way and sat down next to Mary Margaret.

When Dorrie returned to the terrace, she stopped to stare at the two whispering together, their faces no more than a foot apart. For a moment, Theo thought she might stomp her foot or even snatch up an ashtray to hurl at the treacherous duo, but she gained control of herself and glided down the stairs with a serene smile. Caldicotts avoided public displays, relying on more subtle forms of vengeance. Nadine had produced more than one nervous breakdown through strategic manipulation of seating arrangements at dinner parties.

Once Dorrie had a glass of rum punch in her hand, she crossed her legs and looked at Gerry. "I had a discussion with Amelia about the breakfast menu. Are you aware that this ackee thing is poisonous if not handled properly?"

"That's what we're having for breakfast?" Sandy said from his chaise in the sun. He grasped his neck and produced a gurgling noise. "I'd rather croak with a decent tan so Mummy can have an open casket. Can't we wait until the last morning for the fateful dish?"

"I read of this ackee in the travel guide," Theo said. "It is known as the *blighia sapida* and is now considered endemic to Jamaica, although it was introduced from Africa by slave ships in the late eighteenth century. It is only dangerous in its unripened stage, when ingestion leads to what is called the vomiting sickness. There is no known antidote. Once the pod has split, it's safe. In fact, it's the national dish of Jamaica."

Dorrie shook her head. "Amelia showed me one, and it's utterly gross-looking. The interior resembles eyeballs with shiny black centers. It was disgusting, which is by far the kindest thing I can say about it."

"It sounds scary," Bitsy said, her eyes hidden behind oversized sunglasses that gave her the appearance of a curly-haired insect. "I don't see any reason to take chances with it. The cook may not know how to judge whether it's ripe or not, and I for one have no intention of dying outside the continental United States."

Gerry chuckled. "It is the national dish, and Amelia has prepared it all her life. The white flesh is boiled, then chopped and cooked with salted codfish imported from Canada. It tastes very much like scrambled eggs."

''Then let's just have scrambled eggs.'' Bitsy took a bottle of suntan oil from a denim bag and began to apply it to her legs. After a moment, Sandy took the bottle from her hand and assisted her amid little squeals of protest and giggles when his hand strayed.

''What do you think, Biff?'' Dorrie called across the pool. ''Shall we have poisonous fruit for breakfast, or would you prefer to live dangerously in other ways?''

Biff glanced up guiltily, then stood up and came around the pool to pour himself a glass of punch. ''Whatever has put you in this tedious snit, Dorrie? It is not attractive.''

''What can you possibly be talking about, Biffkin? I was inquiring in all innocence about everyone's preferences for breakfast tomorrow morning. One of us has to deal with the help, after all, and let them know what we expect of them. The little chore has cut into the peak tanning hours already, but someone has to do it. Now that it's settled, perhaps I'll change into my string bikini and wallow around on the deck like a half-naked albino walrus.''

''Dorrie, that was a totally gross thing to say, and—''

''Is it time for martinis?'' Trey called as he appeared on the stairs that led to the front lawn. ''I have explored the territory and can claim it as my own. However, I am absolutely arid, and it is after five o'clock in the afternoon somewhere in the world.''

Dorrie turned away from Biff. ''Yes, darling, although we're all having rum punch. Shall I pour you one?''

''I never touch anything with fruit juice in it. My body is unaccustomed to anything remotely connected with vitamins. It drove Mummy wild. She used to tell me bedtime stories about sailors with scurvy, rickets, and zits.''

''I'll run up to the kitchen and have Emelda fix up a pitcher of martinis just for you,'' Dorrie said. ''In the interim, you can join the discussion about the breakfast menu. We're considering having this thing that's poisonous.''

''I never eat breakfast, so you may all spread cyanide on your toast if you desire. And tell the woman that martinis are shaken, not stirred." Trey flopped into a chaise and gave the others a boyish smile. "I'm sending the pool boy to the hotel shop for suntan oil and a copy of *The Wall Street Journal*, by the way. If any of you chaps need anything, you'd better hop off your fannies and catch him before he leaves."

All turned their heads as a beige car roared down the driveway and squealed around the corner.

Biff gave him a withering look. "You might have let us know ahead of time, Trey. I might need something, too."

"I doubt they have cold showers in the shop at the hotel. The rooms, probably, but not the shop. Too public for words."

"Biff," Mary Margaret called, "would you be so kind as to bring me a glass of punch and help me oil my back? I can tell I'm going to turn bright red if I miss one little centimeter of flesh. I'd just die if I burned my back on the first day."

"Because you're planning to spend so much time on it at night?" Trey called back in a genial voice.

Biff glared at him, then at the terrace door through which Dorrie had vanished. His hand shook as he filled a glass with the red punch, but he managed a smile as he went around the pool and knelt next to Mary Margaret. Taking the plastic bottle, he began to dribble oil on her back.

It was intermission time. Aware that the second act would not begin until Dorrie returned, Theo looked at Gerry. "You mentioned that you've been with your firm for twenty years. You must enjoy it."

"It's amusing," she said. "We handle nearly fifty villas in this development, and lease to parties for anywhere between one week and three months. Some of the families have been coming as long as I've been here."

"And before that?" Theo inquired.

"I was a real estate agent in New Jersey. The climate here is so much more civilized, and the pace more suitable for this middle-aged body. It can be frantic when I have several groups descending the same day, but for the most part I do correspondence in the office, work in my garden, or run up to New York for travel fairs and conventions.''

"I went to Jersey once," Trey said. "It was more than enough for a lifetime. Princeton, of course, but it turned out to be one of the country's most boring institutions. Where did you live?''

"Not too far from New York City. You didn't like Princeton?''

Bitsy sat up. "He was booted for what he called a practical joke. I believe the police referred to it as a second-degree felony." She oiled her forearms, then lay back.

"I didn't realize you'd transferred to the Harvard Law School," Trey said, his voice hinting at anger for the first time. "But I might have guessed, since your literary taste leans toward epics like *Love Story.*''

"At least I can read.''

Theo decided to intervene. "So, Gerry, you have a garden. Tell me, have you tried tomatoes here, or do you find the climate too hot?''

"I garden in a very modest way, Theo. I have a few bougainvilleas, azaleas, and simple things like that. I'd invite you to inspect my efforts, but I can see you'll be very busy this week.''

Theo spotted Dorrie on the terrace, a pitcher in her hand. She was staring down at the couple on the distant side of the pool, and he could see the pitcher trembling. Mary Margaret was prone and glistening, but Biff stared back with a coldly defiant expression. Trey was snorting under his breath, Bitsy's latest barb seeming to have found its target. Bitsy's mouth had a self-righteous curl. Sandy was gazing at the ocean.

"Very busy, I fear," Theo agreed with a sigh. He decided to consult his travel guide for the perimeters of the hurricane season. It might provide a divertissement.

Dinner was strained, but the group had been through years of nannies, etiquette classes, parental lectures, and prep school rules, and the conversation was determinedly polite.

They gathered on the terrace for coffee to allow Amelia and Emelda to clear the table. One was always considerate of the help.

Sandy took one of the brochures Gerry had left for them. "There's a beach party at one of the big resorts tonight. All the booze you can drink, wet T-shirt and limbo contests, non-stop reggae music. It sounds outrageous. Why don't we check it out?"

"It's open to the public?" Dorrie said doubtfully.

"I think it's sounds marvelous," Mary Margaret said. "Don't you think it sounds marvelous, Biff? If Dorrie's too tired, I'm sure she can stay here and try to get a good night's sleep." She switched her smile to Dorrie. "You look like a raccoon, with those old dark circles under your eyes. Did all those drinks on the flight give you a nasty hangover?"

"Your concern is so totally sweet, but my mascara must be smudged. I'm not the least bit tired. I was wondering if you'd prefer to stay here and try to do something about your hair, which must be causing you no end of depression. We can thank our lucky stars that Mr. Robert isn't here to see it, can't we? But I think the party sounds marvelous."

She and the other two girls went upstairs. Biff said to Theo, "We'd be delighted to have you come with us, sir. The music may be loud, but I'm sure we can find a table toward the edge of the crowd so it won't be unbearable for you."

"How kind of you, but please go without me," Theo said hastily. "I would prefer to sit by the pool for a while, then retire at a reasonable time. I assume my presence as a chaperone is more an honorary position than a relentless responsibility. You will take care of the girls, I trust?"

"Very good care, sir," Sandy said earnestly. "As Dorrie mentioned, it is open to the public, and there is an undesirable element on the island."

Trey, who had been noticeably quiet at dinner, managed a nod.

The girls came down half an hour later, now in sundresses. Sandy announced that Eli would drive them over and wait, which meant they could all get looped, paralytic, twisted, wasted, and wrecked. It did not sound particularly appealing to Theo, but he wished them a pleasant evening and carried the coffee cups and pot to the kitchen.

Amelia snatched the tray from him. "Emelda supposed to clear the table. That be her job."

"I was on my way upstairs," Theo lied, "and it was no problem at all. Have you and Emelda made arrangements to be picked up once you've finished in here?"

"We walk to the bus stop at the bottom of the hill. Am I to fix ackee and sal' fish tomorrow morning or not? If not, I can go to the market before I come here, but I'll be late and won't have breakfast ready on time."

"I truly don't know," Theo said glumly. "I suppose you might as well fix the dish, as long as there's plenty of toast and coffee for those who are a bit squeamish."

"Whole bunch of them are squeamish," Amelia muttered. She dumped the coffee cups in the sink and splashed water on them. "Real squeamish."

"Indeed." Theo went upstairs to find his travel guide, then returned to the terrace and sat down to reread about the ackee tree and its potentially lethal fruit. After a short while, Amelia and Emelda went out the kitchen door and walked down the driveway, talking loudly to each other. Although their English had been fine earlier, Theo could understand nothing of what they said between themselves. He flipped to the section on island dialect.

The chapter was enlightening, but not enough to prevent his eyes from closing and his chin from falling against his chest. He was blissfully dozing when something caused him to open his eyes. He first suspected his unruly charges had returned home, but the house was dark and the driveway vacant. As he wrinkled his forehead, he heard voices from the villa next door.

"I'm absolutely booked solid tomorrow. I'm having lunch at a private estate in Ocho Rios. The woman has been asking me over for an intimate little luncheon for six weeks. If I simply show her a little affection, as distasteful as it may be for me, I can take her out next week for a long, profitable cruise should I encounter our friends on the high seas. However, I'm going to have to spend some time with her—even if it bores me to death.'' The voice was male, irritated.

"Then don't do it,'' a second male voice said, although it was so low Theo had difficulty making out the words. Male, definitely, and more composed than the first speaker. "I don't like this business.''

"And you think I do? I'm sick of pseudo-reggae music, lunches with pudgy white ladies from New York, escorting the same to dinners where I almost puke every time I look across the table—''

"I never knew gigolos were so sensitive,'' interrupted the second voice.

Theo realized he was eavesdropping, an act he permitted himself only when he deemed it necessary. He coughed to announce his presence, then flipped open his book and rustled the pages. The voices stopped, although he could not help noticing a few whispers before a door closed on the far side of the fence. Within ten minutes, headlights flashed on the palm trees and a car rumbled down the driveway and into the night.

Seconds later, a car pulled up the driveway adjoining the terrace. For a moment, Theo thought Gerry might have returned with more brochures, but noted the car was a tame beige. He put down his book, wondering why a reputedly tranquil paradise seemed to have so much traffic. Eli climbed out of the car and stopped by the entrance to the terrace.

"I left the kids at the beach for a while. I'll go back for them around midnight.''

"Are you sure they'll be quite safe, Eli? This is their first night in Jamaica, and they're not familiar with the local customs.''

"No problem. I could see they familiar with the drinking and dancing customs. The red-haired girl was onstage trying to limbo when I left, and one of the boys had puked twice out by the water. Jamaicans don't go to the hotel parties, anyway. We go to our own places where the music is better and the rum cheaper." Eli displayed perfect white teeth. "You want to come with me some night? I can show you a good time, with lots of pretty women."

"No, thank you," Theo said, trying to imagine himself in such a place. "If nothing else, I have gathered that the political situation is causing unrest between the major parties, and a certain amount of resentment against the tourists."

"Not around Montego Bay, Mr. Bloomer. There be trouble in Kingston, where they had the gas riots couple years back. They have the demonstrations, the riots, all the fun. Here in MoBay, we just serve rum and make music for the tourists. Then we take their dollars and drink rum and make music for ourselves. No problem in MoBay."

"That's comforting to hear, Eli."

"Okay, mon. Was Mrs. Greeley here looking for me just before I came back? Sometimes she wants me to mow yards at the other villas, but I think these college kids are going to keep me busy all week."

"No, it was someone visiting next door. Mrs. Greeley intends to stop by tomorrow with tickets and information; I shall remember to tell her that you're concerned about the schedule."

"Thanks, mon." Whistling, Eli went partway down the driveway and into his quarters below the pool. After a few minutes, Theo heard reggae music drifting through the window. The music was quite pleasant to listen to as he looked at the streak of moonlight glittering on the Caribbean. After a while, the reggae was replaced with the faint strains of a Mozart concerto. If only, he told himself, he had come without Dorrie and her friends, it would have been as delightful as Nadine had promised. He caught himself wishing her ill luck in the women's pairs in the Greater Connecticut Bridge Tournament. On that petty thought, he went to bed.

* * *

The ackee argument of the previous evening proved a waste of time, since Theo was the sole diner at the breakfast table. He tasted the concoction carefully and determined that it was much like scrambled eggs. It was also quite tasty, and he said as much to Amelia as she came to clear his plate.

"What about the others?" she demanded.

"They were out very late last night, and will most likely want only coffee for breakfast. The coffee is excellent, by the way."

"Come from special plantations in the mountains. I'll bring you a pot on the terrace, and fix some more for the others should they decide to get up. I don' know when Emelda's going to clean bedrooms if they stay in bed all day."

"Surely many of the tourists who stay here overindulge," Theo said, unsure why he was defending the group. "They're on vacation."

"They drink too much, party too much, and climb in the wrong beds with the wrong people. I've even had married couples here that switched bedrooms every night. Emelda about went crazy putting on clean sheets every day."

"You don't see us at our best, do you? These kids are all college students in tough schools, and I suppose they do go to extremes when they're on vacation."

Amelia snorted as she went to the kitchen. Theo carried his coffee cup to the terrace, and was gazing at the bright flowers along the street when the pink station wagon honked at the gate. Eli appeared, went down to unlock the gate, then closed it and retreated as Gerry drove up the driveway.

She joined Theo at the table. "I just stopped by for a moment on my way to the office. I understand your group made it to the beach party last night and had quite a time."

"I was already asleep when they returned, so I've not yet heard anything about it." He studied her amused expression. "You must have heard something, however."

"Mary Margaret Ellison is well on her way to becoming an island legend. It seems she entered the limbo contest and made it to the finals. At that point, she realized her dress was impeding her performance. A limbo champion and a legend in her own time, our Miss Ellison.''

"She refused to allow her dress to interfere with her limbo performance?'' Theo said, dismayed. "That is to say, she felt obliged to remove the impediment on a stage and in front of a large crowd?'' When Gerry nodded, he sank down in his chair. "I am failing to fulfill my duties, and I am ashamed of myself. I declined to attend this party with them last night, never considering the possibility that my absence would permit any of them to indulge in regrettable behavior. I should have gone.''

"I assumed you did, but I didn't hear any gossip about a tall man in bifocals and boxer shorts attempting the limbo.''

Theo pulled himself up. "Hardly. But how did you hear the gossip about Mary Margaret so quickly? It's only past nine the morning after the unfortunate incident.''

"The servants' grapevine is remarkably efficient. Some of the drivers observed the limbo finals and passed on the information in villa kitchens over coffee this morning. Maids talk over the fences while hanging out laundry. The produce men go from house to house, bargaining with the cooks in the driveways. By noon, the incident will have been analyzed for maximum amusement in every Jamaican café in MoBay.''

"Oh, dear. I suppose I shall have to have a word with Mary Margaret, but I have no idea what I shall say to her. This really ought to be handled by a woman, who can offer the girl sensible female advice.'' He looked at Gerry. "I don't suppose . . . ?''

For a moment, she looked startled, then broke into laughter. "I'm a real estate agent, not a surrogate mother, Theo. If the rumors about the quantities of rum consumed by the Harmony Hills villa group are also true, I doubt you'll be able to have any words with anyone until late in the afternoon.''

"They had too much to drink?''

"Of course they did. Everyone there did; it's standard behavior and the only hope to salvage the poor girl's reputation. Most of those present won't remember much this morning."

Dorrie staggered across the terrace and plopped down next to Theo. Her face was puffy and swollen, her eyes pink, and her robe was buttoned in a haphazard fashion that left a bumpy path up to her neck.

"Coffee, please," she croaked in a hoarse voice. "And make it snappy. I feel as if I've been put through a wash-and-wear cycle and hung out to dry."

Gerry rummaged through her bulgy straw purse and produced two tablets. "I'll get a cup from the kitchen, along with soda water so that you can take these. They're prescription, and ought to help."

"I am beyond help."

"They can't hurt," Gerry said as she started for the kitchen. "I'll be back with the soda water in a minute."

Dorrie gazed at Theo. "She meant to say Perrier, didn't she? Please don't make me drink generic soda water, Uncle Theo. I am in no condition to deal with it."

"Perhaps your palate will excuse it this once," Theo said drily. "You do not appear to be at your peak of discernment this morning."

"This is not the time for weak attempts at humor. One more little joke and I shall throw myself over the railing."

Theo did not point out that she was likely to survive the three-foot fall. When Gerry returned with an empty cup and a glass of soda water, Dorrie obediently downed the pills with only a brief flicker of distaste. She then took her coffee cup and retreated to a shady corner of the terrace to mutter under her breath. Gerry promised to return later and gave Theo a gay little wave as she left. He did his best to reciprocate, but Dorrie merely raised a finger.

"Gerry was telling me about Mary Margaret's impromptu striptease act," Theo said once the pink station wagon reached the foot of the driveway. "I am most distressed that she would engage in that sort of behavior."

Dorrie produced a prim sniff. "Well, I wasn't surprised.

Her father may own an entire insurance company in Hartford, but Daddy swears he cheats on the golf course and everybody knows he's perpetually behind on the club dues. Her mother checks into quaint little rest homes about three times a year, the kind with barbed wire fences so no one can see you while they dry you out for the next charity ball. And Trey has been always a complete wastrel, from the age of eight when he was booted out of Miss Pipkin's cotillion class to his arrest last summer when he stole John David Irwin's boat and abandoned it three miles down the coast. He said he got bored and decided to find a local pub. John David dropped the charges, but let me tell you, it made for some fabulous conversation during the Labor Day tournament.''

"Why are they tolerated, then?"

"Oh, everybody's used to them, and we are talking zillions of dollars," she said, shrugging. "Is this interrogation absolutely necessary, Uncle Theo? My head is on the verge of a godawful explosion. I doubt the strain required to answer all these questions is exactly beneficial.''

"I still feel obligated to have a word with her," Theo said. "Even if her parents are as uncivilized as you claim, I must insist she behave in a more decorous manner while under my supervision.''

"Have at it, Uncle Theo. But you'll have to find her first.''

Theo felt a twinge of alarm. "She's not upstairs?''

Dorrie held out her hand to study her shapely pink fingernails. "I had a manicure two days ago, and there's already a chip. It's incredibly difficult to get value for one's money these days.'' She curled in her claws and fluttered her eyelashes at Theo. "Mary Margaret didn't come home with us last night. The last we saw of her, she was going off with a veritable platoon of drunks. Wherever do you think she can be?''

3

To Theo's heartfelt relief, Mary Margaret appeared at the bottom of the driveway shortly before noon, looking slightly disheveled but intact. He came onto the terrace in time to see her wave at a blue car as it sped down the hill. She then tugged at the strap of her sundress and paused to arrange a nonchalant expression before strolling up the driveway to the terrace.

"Good morning, Mr. Bloomer," she said. She sat down across from him and reached for the coffee pot.

"Good morning, Mary Margaret," Theo replied primly. "I fear you will discover the coffee is quite cold by this hour."

"Well, it must be time for Bloody Marys, then. I'm going to tell the cook to make me one. Would you like one?"

"No, thank you. I would like a word with you, however, once you've asked Amelia to make your drink."

"No problem," she said as she departed through the terrace door. It was well over ten minutes before she returned, now dressed in shorts and a T-shirt. Her hair was pulled out of her face by a barrette, and her face scrubbed to an innocent sheen.

"I was disturbed this morning when I learned you were not upstairs," Theo began in what he hoped was a sternly avuncular tone. It had yet to be successful with Dorrie, but he felt that he should make the attempt. "Also, I have heard reports that you created something of an uproar at the beach party."

"It was a stitch and a half," she agreed.

"It was hardly appropriate behavior. Should your parents learn of it, they would be upset, to say the very least. It has been made clear that I have been remiss in my duties as chaperone. I should have accompanied the group to this party in order to provide a stabilizing influence."

"I'd have done it anyway, and it wouldn't have been all that entertaining for you—since you've already seen the prime points of my anatomy." She wiggled her eyebrows at him, then took a long drink of the Bloody Mary. "Haven't they heard of Tabasco in this place? Don't worry about my parents finding out about your dereliction of duty, Mr. Bloomer. Trey probably called this morning to tell Daddy all about it, if he could get the words out through his brays of laughter."

"You do not worry that they will be upset and perhaps demand that you return home at once?"

"Why would they do that? Mummy's in Switzerland to have her thighs vacuumed and Daddy's probably got his current girlfriend tucked in the master bed. Anyway, it wasn't as though I was at the club in front of their stodgy old banking friends. I kept my bra and panties on, for God's sake."

"And where did you sleep last night?" Theo persisted, although it was becoming obvious that she was not the least bit remorseful.

She gave him an ingenuous smile. "I'm really not sure who owned the place—isn't that a total panic? I met these guys from Dartmouth, of all places, and we went to a divinely quaint native bar, literally packed with all these black men wearing funky braids and absolutely glaring at us as if they thought we were slumming. When that got to be stifling, we piled in the jeep and drove all over the mountainside looking for a party one of the guys had heard about."

"You and your . . . friends crashed a party?"

"As far as parties go, it was a dud. Just this older man

with buck teeth and a few of his friends. Once he heard our woeful story, he let us in and gave us martinis, and everybody ended up skinny-dipping in the swimming pool. A couple of the guys had pretty quick hands, but I am capable of dealing with that sort of thing after hanging around Trey's friends all these years. I passed out in a chaise beside the pool toward morning; I suppose the flight yesterday drained me.''

"Oh, my dear," Theo murmured, at a loss for further avuncular words of admonishment.

Before he could decide how best to proceed, Dorrie and Bitsy came out on the balcony. "Welcome back," Dorrie called down to Mary Margaret. "Did the boys from Dartmouth make you an honorary member of the fraternity after they'd all . . . made you?"

"You know more about the initiation procedure than I do, honey." Mary Margaret looked at her watch. "Where the hell is everybody? I'd like to hit the beach by one o'clock to do some sun. I for one do not intend to go home with a horrid white line across my back. Some people may enjoy the zebra effect, but I find it totally gross."

Bitsy smiled sweetly. "And heaven knows you're an expert in the area of total grossness. Trey and Biff are still in bed. Sandy's in the living room knocking golf balls into a plastic glass. By the way, if you wanted anything from the shops, it's too late. Dear, thoughtful Sandy sent Eli out to pick up ice, limes, and a newspaper without bothering to check with any of us. Oh, but he couldn't have checked with you because you just got in from your little drunken orgy, didn't you? How silly of me." She glanced over the fence at the villa next door, then did a discreet double-take. "Look at that example of the male species," she said, jabbing Dorrie with her elbow. "He is to absolutely die for, isn't he?"

Dorrie's mouth fell open. "Call the executioner."

Theo heard a splash, which he presumed indicated the existence of a swimming pool on the far side of the fence. The girls' expressions indicated they were observing more than a neighbor taking a dip, but he could see nothing beyond the healthy bougainvillea thick with orange flowers.

Mary Margaret pushed back her hair and, in an irritated voice, said, "Do you think it's just a tad impolite to goggle and stare at the neighbors? I swear, you two are sweating and twitching like a pair of hypoglycemics in a candy store. What time will Eli be back with the car? Has anyone decided which hotel beach to use today?"

Dorrie shook her head, her eyes still directed over the fence. "I don't know when they'll be back, Mary Margaret. Why don't you call your buddies from Dartmouth and see if they'll give you a ride?"

"I don't even know which hotel they're staying at. Besides, Biff swore he'd show me how to toss a Frisbee. He was a teensy bit worried that you might object, but I assured him that we're all too adult for that sort of petty, childish behavior. Why, you wouldn't throw a tantrum out of sheer jealousy, would you?"

"Heavens no," Dorrie said distractedly. She whispered a few words to Bitsy, who went into the bedroom and returned seconds later with a small pair of binoculars.

"I may barf," Mary Margaret said, glaring at the balcony and the two girls taking turns with the binoculars. "I really may barf."

Theo retreated to his room.

They were having lunch on the terrace when Gerry's pink wagon pulled up the driveway. Conversation had been desultory, due to the various levels of hangovers evident on the faces around the table. The girls seemed to have recovered more quickly, but out of empathy restrained themselves to a few barbs. Trey had all the liveliness of the broiled fish on his plate, and his eyes the same blankness. Sandy and Biff had eaten a few bites, although neither had produced more than a grunted reply.

Gerry joined them at the table. "I noticed nobody was awake for ackee and salt fish or boiled green bananas this morning," she said as she accepted a glass of white wine from Sandy.

Biff's face turned the greenish-yellow color of the green swan orchid (*Cycnoches chlorochilon*). "Maybe another time," he managed to say as he pushed back his chair and stumbled across the dining room for the stairs.

"Poor baby," Mary Margaret said, watching him with a smile.

"It's totally tragic," said Dorrie. "Why don't you toodle upstairs and hold poor baby's head while he tosses his cookies all over you and the bathroom floor?"

"That's disgusting." Bitsy looked at Gerry. "Who is that divine man who has the villa next door?"

"An old friend of mine, Hal D'Orsini. He's been on the island as long as I have, although he spends his summers on the Continent. He says he cannot abide the heat here, but the Riviera is hotter. I suspect it's more the influx of tourists in the off-season. The rates drop by half, and those who can subsequently afford them are not quite his crowd. He flees in a panic from the rabble into the comforting arms of the filthy rich."

Trey pulled himself out of a trance. "D'Orsini? Haven't I heard of him? Did he go to Harvard with Uncle Billy, Magsy?"

"Would you like an unripened ackee shoved down your throat?" she responded without rancor. "Call me that name one more time."

"I don't know about your Uncle Billy," Gerry said, "but I do remember something about Andover, followed by Harvard. He's merely rich and idle now."

Mary Margaret gazed speculatively at the fence. "Why, if he's an old school chum of darling Uncle Billy's, we really must have him over for a drink. He's practically family. We'd be downright remiss if we didn't give him a neighborly greeting over the fence, wouldn't we?"

Sandy looked at Bitsy, whose expression was as speculative as Mary Margaret's. "I'd hardly imagine him a candidate for the family album, Mary Margaret. We don't know all that much about him, and we don't want some elderly sort hanging around all week.'' He flushed as he caught Theo's eye. "Not you, sir. We're all delighted that you offered to come with us.''

"We certainly are," Dorrie inserted acidly.

The others began babbling assurances that they certainly were, but Theo was not touched by their avowed, eternal gratitude. He waited until they ran out of avowals, then said to Gerry, "Sandy does have a point. What does Mr. D'Orsini do when not idling?"

"Count D'Orsini, actually," she said. "I really don't know, Theo. He has a yacht that he takes out quite often, and entertains when the right people are in residence.''

Dorrie gave Bitsy a conspiratorial smile, then turned to Gerry. "Perhaps it might be more appropriate if you invited him for a drink. You could mention Uncle Billy; I'm sure he'd be fascinated to meet the niece and nephew. They are so completely clever.''

"I'll stop by later in the afternoon and ask if he has plans for the cocktail hour. Where are you going this afternoon? Have you decided on a beach, or are you going to stay by the pool? If you venture out, you ought to have Eli drive you there and wait.''

"I sent him on an errand," Sandy said.

"You and Trey seem to consider him your personal chauffeur," Dorrie said. "He spends a great deal of time doing errands for you two. Had you mentioned it to me, I would have asked that he pick up six and four.''

"Six and four?" Theo murmured gently.

"Suntan lotion, Uncle Theo. I have plenty of sixteen for my nose and two for my back, but I'm going to have to use six on my shoulders until I've picked up some color. I want to risk four on the backs of my legs, although I may live to regret it.''

"Are you using eight on your forehead?" Bitsy asked.

They commenced a long, serious conversation about numbers and anatomy, and continued it as they went upstairs. Mary Margaret announced she was going to change for the beach, and if Eli didn't get back damn tout de suite, she was going to be livid. Trey and Sandy wandered away, leaving Theo and Gerry across from each other.

Theo frowned as he considered the conversation he'd overheard the previous night. Something about it had sounded— well, a bit off. It had disturbed him, although he could not quite put his finger on the cause of his uneasiness. He lectured himself into a more charitable frame of mind.

"You say this D'Orsini is an old friend of yours, Gerry? You're familiar with his family and history?"

"He swears he can trace his family back to Caesar Augustus and then some, and the title to the sixteenth century. I don't believe more than a fraction of it, but I do know he's basically harmless, charming, and always willing to accept a free martini. He's also way too old for these college girls."

"I'm not sure they agree with you. They were watching him earlier today while he was swimming, and they seemed to be interested in what they observed."

"He is attractive, and insists on doing laps in the nude. But please don't worry about him, Theo; he'll be impeccably dressed in time for cocktails. Shall I suggest that he drop by at six this evening?"

"I suppose so," Theo said, tugging at the tip of his beard as he looked over the tops of palm trees to the delphinium blue of the Caribbean. He was not delighted at the prospect of meeting Count D'Orsini, but he suspected he had little choice.

Gerry said she would call later and went to her station wagon. Before she could get in, Eli drove up the driveway in the beige car. She motioned for him to join her in the shade of the house.

"You seem to be spending quite a lot of time fetching ice from the store," she said in a cool voice. "Amelia and Emelda could pick some up in the mornings on the way to work; their bus stop is next to a store."

"I'm just doing what this group tells me, Miz Greeley. They say go here, Eli, go there, Eli, go get newspapers and suntan lotion, Eli. They have enough suntan lotion to slide this villa right down the mountainside and into the water. But I'm supposed to do what they say, right?"

"You'd better keep your nose clean if you want to keep this job. There are plenty of boys who'd gladly take over your quarters and cushy duties. You're still in a probation period, Eli, and you need to pay attention to your work. Count D'Orsini mentioned that you were skulking around his yard earlier this morning, but I see you didn't mow."

"I was working in the flower bed down by the fence, and I didn't get to it, Miz Greeley," he said with an obsequious smile.

"And in the flower bed beneath his living room window?"

"I just raked out the leaves, Miz Greeley. But no problem about mowing the grass. I do it late this afternoon, once everybody back from beach."

"See that you do. In the future, whenever you work in Count D'Orsini's yard, knock on the kitchen door and tell the cook that you're there. I will not tolerate this skulking nonsense." Gerry got into her station wagon, slammed the door, and backed down the driveway at what Theo felt was a perilous speed.

"Why, sho' nuf, Miz Simone Legree," Eli said sourly. He glanced up and winced as he saw Theo on the terrace. "Just joking, boss; she's a nice lady, real nice. When you think the boys and girls be ready for me to drive them to the beach?"

"They're upstairs changing now," Theo said. He noticed Eli's hands were empty. "Did you find whatever Sandy needed from the store?"

Eli stuffed his hands in his pockets and scuffled his feet nervously in the gravel. "No, he want today's copy of *The Wall Street Journal.* I went all the way into downtown MoBay, but all I could find was day before yesterday's. He sure is hot to see today's paper. Is he some kind of stockbroker, Mr. Bloomer?''

"He's still in school, although I have no idea about his major." Theo blinked through his bifocals at the grinning boy. "Did you go to a Jamaican school, Eli?"

"Yes, sir, I went all the way through eighth grade in MoBay. My mammy was real insistent that all her children learn how to read and write."

Amelia came through a side door, a bulging plastic trash bag in her hands. "You a liar," she said without turning her head.

"You a tight-assed old island woman," he said.

"I know your mammy, and I know about your school. All the way through eighth grade? Ha!" Amelia went back into the villa, allowing the door to bang closed like a crack of gunfire.

"She don' know nothing," Eli said to Theo. "I better get ready to take the kids to the beach now."

Once again, Theo found himself alone on the terrace. He was not bored, however, since he had several intriguing little puzzles to think about. Not that he presumed any of them held particular significance, but old habits died slowly, and at a certain point in his past he had been trained to notice discrepancies. There were almost as many as there were orange blossoms along the fence.

The outing to the beach required a series of shuttles. Although Theo would have preferred to visit a garden, or even to simply sit on the terrace and read, he forced himself to change into Bermuda shorts, a rather splashy floral-print shirt Dorrie had brought him from Hawaii, and a canvas hat to protect the hairless circle on the top of his head. Which was growing, he noted glumly as he went into his private bath to fetch the sole bottle of suntan lotion he owned. The bottle was dusty, and unnumbered.

When he arrived in the driveway, he found Bitsy, Sandy, and Dorrie waiting in the shade, a formidable collection of baskets and towels piled beside them. Bitsy was on her tiptoes, trying to see over the fence. Sandy looked as though he were in dire need of a nap, his eyelids drooping and his face slack. Dorrie, on the contrary, was not the least drowsy.

"I cannot imagine why we invited those insufferable Ellisons to come with us," she was saying to Bitsy as Theo approached. "They may receive their weekly allowances in Krugerrands, but they have the manners of. . . . of some subspecies of primates! Not to insult the baboons, of course."

Theo deduced that Dorrie was not pleased with the seating assignments of the first shuttle. He was not especially pleased, either, although he doubted Mary Margaret would have adequate time to stir up mischief at the beach before he arrived to keep an eye on her. Whether she might have time to stir up mischief with Biff he could not say. Nor did he see any reason to ask the opinion of his tight-lipped niece.

Amelia came to the door. "I am planning to leave early tonight for church service. Emelda will stay to clear the table."

"That will be fine, Amelia," Dorrie said, her petulence replaced with a tone more suitable for dealing with the help. "Are you perfectly clear on the menus for tonight and tomorrow? I do have a few minutes if you want to go over them again with me."

"I ain't fixing ackee, miss." The door slammed.

Bitsy acknowledged that she could see nothing of interest, and sank down with a disappointed sigh. "As adorable as the petite fashions are, I do sometimes wish I were taller."

"To get a basketball scholarship?" Sandy said. "Maybe you can find a doctor to slip you some drugs, like hormones or something."

Bitsy shot him a frosty look. "No one in my family ever takes so much as an aspirin. You might consider adopting the same policy."

"This is a vacation, Itsy-Bitsy," he said. He leaned back against the house with a muted thud, crossed his arms, and made a face. "For once, I thought you might be over our old buddy Trey and ready for a little relaxation. But you pant after him so damn hard I'm surprised you don't stumble over your tongue.''

"That was uncalled for," she began. Before she could elaborate (or simply berate), Eli drove up the driveway. Minutes later they were driving down the hill, swerving to avoid potholes and errant tourists, honking at dogs and children, and keeping Theo in a state of silent hysteria. He did not release his breath until they squealed to a stop in front of a sprawling resort hotel.

Dorrie was out of the car before the dust settled. "Where is the pathway to the beach?" she demanded of Eli. Her face was pink, but not, Theo presumed, from the previous day's sun-bathing. Eli gestured at a walkway, and she marched away with the expression her mother used when faced with a glaring error at the bridge table. It was not a pretty sight.

Theo followed Sandy and Bitsy down the walk, across a patio with a fountain, and over an expanse of sand to a shady area under a clump of palm trees. Trey was on a chaise, his face hidden by a straw hat. Dorrie stood over him, her hands on her hips.

"Rouse yourself from this coma and answer my question. Where are they?" she demanded, kicking the leg of the chaise for good measure.

"Magsy has always wanted to parasail, so she talked Biffkin into checking out the prices with the black chap on the far side of the cove. Maybe the line will snap and she'll end up chopping sugarcane in Cuba. Then Dorrikin and Biffkin can be snuggle bunnikins."

"Don't call me that." She stalked away to a nearby chaise and dropped her beach bag in the sand. Theo watched as she methodically oiled her body with five different preparations, settled her sunglasses firmly on her nose, and took a thick paper-back from her bag. "Parasailing is infantile," she announced as she flipped open the book.

Theo found a chaise and moved it to the far edge of the shade, where he could have some protection from the bright sun, the Frisbee games, the geranium-red children armed with lethal-looking shovels, and the conversation of his charges. He then arranged his towel and book to his satisfaction, ascertained that beverages could be purchased from a concrete stand not too far away, and announced he would be delighted to bring drinks to those who would care for one. When no one replied, he strolled along the beach bypassing the stand for the moment, in order to see if Mary Margaret was, as suggested by an unreliable source, engaging in an innocent diversion. For once.

The beach of the adjoining cove was covered with loose rocks and the remains of coral formations. There was a group at the far end, milling around a motorboat that bobbled in the shallow water. He saw Mary Margaret's red hair in the center of the group. After a few minutes, the crowd retreated and the boat roared into motion. It pulled away from the shore in a wide, curling line. Then, like a primeval jellyfish, a yellow parachute rose from the water and soared into the sky. Dangling from it was a decidedly flimsy apparatus supporting a red-haired passenger. Theo could hear her shrieks from where he stood, but he felt no flicker of empathy. She could not, he concluded, get into trouble at a hundred feet above the surface of the water.

As he turned away, a black man with shoulder-length braids nudged him. "You want to buy some ganja, mon? Super sinsemilla from the best producer on the island, but for you a special price."

"Ah, yes, *cannabis sativa*," Theo said. "In the States I believe it is better known as marijuana, isn't it?"

The man grinned. "Yes, mon, they call it grass, pot, weed, dope, Maryjane, all kind of name. Sinsemilla is the very best, though, and grown to be very, very strong. You want to buy a nice little package?"

"Cultivation is illegal in Jamaica, as is possession. Do I look the sort to commit a felony while a guest on your island?"

"No problem, mon. The cops don't bother nobody for a

little ganja, especially not tourists. Taking it back through customs is another matter, another matter if I do say so. But Jamaican Gold sell very well in the States, and if you get it home, you could afford to buy yourself some nice new clothes.''

Theo glanced down at his hibiscus-covered chest. "Thank you very much for the suggestion, but I do not believe I wish to purchase any ganja today. Perhaps another time."

He bought a cup of watery punch and returned to his chosen spot in the shade, pondering the casual encounter with the dope-seller. His travel book had mentioned the ease with which one could, if one chose, acquire the illegal organic matter in Jamaica, but he was somewhat surprised that he had been approached within his first few minutes on the beach.

He was nearly asleep when he heard Mary Margaret's high-pitched voice drawing near the cluster of chaises. She was describing the absolutely incredible thrill of parasailing, how she simply had never had such an experience, how it was almost sexual. Theo did not open his eyes. He did, however, when she added that she had met a divine man and everybody simply had to meet him or she would be devastated beyond belief.

Praying it would not be the braided dope-seller, Theo sat up and turned to look over his shoulder at Mary Margaret's new friend. The man, in his fifties or perhaps a bit older, had shaggy white hair, bushy eyebrows, and a florid but affable face. His nose was red, from either the sun or the availability of rum punches on the beach. He wore baggy khaki shorts, a T-shirt that suggested an obscene activity, and a wrinkled beach jacket. Darkly tinted sunglasses masked his eyes.

"Dorrie Caldicott, Bitsy Bigelow, Sandy Whitcombe, my despicable twin brother, Trey, and Theo Bloomer, who's our chaperone," Mary Margaret said, making the rounds with the ease of a hostess at a cocktail party. "You met Biff over by the boat. Everybody, this is Jackson Spitzberg. He's a movie producer from the West Coast, down here to scout locations for a wonderful new movie he's going to shoot this summer. Isn't that exciting?''

Bitsy and Sandy agreed that it was exciting. Trey muttered an acknowledgment of the introduction, but Dorrie merely fluttered a hand without looking up from her book. The producer came across the sand toward Theo, his hand extended.

"Jackson Spitzberg's the name. Nice to meet you, Bloomer," he said in a hearty voice thick with Hollywood warmth.

Theo ignored the hand. "What in blazes are you doing here?" he growled so that the others could not overhear.

"Scouting locations like the little girl said. I've got a dynamite concept for one of those old-fashioned epics, with ripped bodices, romantic rape scenes under the tropical stars, a slave revolt, a slobbering pirate or two for color, and maybe a hurricane for the climax. It's a hell of a concept, a real slam dunker if I say so myself. Don't you think the cinema public is ready for a return to the golden days of filmmaking, Bloomer?''

"You are full of it," Theo said coldly. "Perhaps the beach public is ready for the information that you're CIA, Sitermann. Perhaps I'll ask the gentleman with the motorboat to tow a banner across the sky. On the other hand, bellowing those three magic letters may just do the trick. Shall we conduct a small experiment?''

"Hey, Bloomer, don't get all riled up. Why don't we find a quiet place at the bar inside and do a rum punch or two? We'll shoot the bull about the good old days together on the kibbutz, then—''

"The good old days when my niece was accused of murder? The good old days when she and I were blown down the side of a mountain by a duo of sociopathic terrorists?'' Theo shook his head. "I don't think we're thinking of the same time period, Sitermann, nor do I think I wish to shoot anything, including bull, movies, or even a Magnum, with you over a rum punch. I prefer the concept of leaping to my feet to point an accusatory finger at you while shouting 'CIA?' in mock disbelief.''

"Be a good sport, Bloomer. I'll tell you as much as I can; I swear it on my grandpappy's Swiss bank account.''

Theo took off his bifocals and polished them with a corner of his shirt. Once he had replaced them, he looked up with a disillusioned smile. "Oh, Sitermann, you spies are all alike.''

4

Although he might have enjoyed the spectacle of Sitermann's public exposure and subsequent embarrassment, Theo realized Dorrie was flipping the pages of her book at an improbable rate and was apt to look up at any moment. He mentioned the possibility to Sitermann, and they retreated to the bar inside the hotel.

Once they were seated, Theo gazed across the table at the spy. "Why are you here, Sitermann? You are not a movie producer any more than I'm the winner in a J. Edgar Hoover lookalike contest."

"Vacation, old boy. Even the pricks heading the Organization allow us a couple of weeks a year to relax, and I opted for sun and fun."

"While undercover? You'll hardly return with much of a tan. The trenchcoat, you know."

"Very amusing, but what if I'm not undercover? How do you know this isn't the real me?"

"There is no real you," Theo said, shaking his head. "But I am most distressed to find you here, and I want to know exactly what you're up to. The coincidence is unnerving. You are not, and I repeat, not here for sun and fun; you are here on assignment and I insist on knowing what it is."

"But it is a coincidence—a bloomin' coincidence, if you'll

excuse my little pun." Sitermann downed his drink and beckoned to the waiter for a refill. "You haven't touched your drink. Chug-a-lug and I'll spring for another—expense accounts being what they are. God bless the American taxpayers."

"I don't believe you. I wouldn't believe you if you were giving a eulogy at your grandmother's grave," said Theo. The customary mildness was gone, and the ensuing steeliness seemed to unravel Sitermann enough to wipe the amiable smile off his face. He tugged on his nose as his eyebrows met to form a bushy white hedgerow.

"Okay, okay, I can tell you want to play hardball. You've been in my shoes and you—"

"I beg your pardon. I can assure you that I've never been in your shoes, and I resent the presumption."

"Sure you do, Bloom. That's why there's a ten-foot gap in your résumé when you apparently fell off the face of the earth. I swear, one of these days I'm going to nail the agency that will admit having used you for some damn fool covert operation."

"I wish you success. Would you please continue?"

"Yeah." Sitermann sighed. "You know damn well that I can't breach security, but maybe this much will help. I'm on loan via the DEA to assist the Jamaican boys in doing a little something about the drug scene. The locals are downright ambivalent about cutting off the flow, since dope ranks right after tourism in feeding the economy. It's the number one cash crop and the number one export; rum doesn't even come close. Nearly one hundred percent of it goes to the U.S., and the street value's probably more than two and a half billion dollars. There are some plantations back in the mountains, complete with irrigation systems and private runways, that would blow your mind. I'm surprised they haven't formed a growers' association to lobby for protection."

"And this has nothing to do with my presence on the island—or my niece's?"

"Not unless the two of you are planning to smuggle a

couple of pounds of sinsemilla back to the bridge club in Connecticut. I swear on my hypothetical grandmother's grave that I had no idea you were in Jamaica, Bloomer. There was not one mention of it in the briefings I received.'' Sitermann blinked with great earnestness. ''When I saw you on the beach, I was as startled as a virgin in the backseat of a '57 Chevy, but as she was reputed to say, you never know what'll pop up. What are you doing here, old man—seeking your lost youth?''

Theo reluctantly explained his presence. ''But,'' he added once Sitermann stopped laughing, ''why are you pulling this nonsense about being a movie producer? I think I preferred you in the role of Hopalong Cassidy on the Israeli range.''

''Potential starlets. It's amazing what soft young things will do for a bit part in a movie. Their honey-colored eyes just brim with gratitude when I promise a screen test back in L. A., and they can't do enough to thank me for even considering them. Why, that red-haired girl squealed louder than a BMW when I told her about the epic. I'm thinking about calling it *Desire Under the Palms*, but I seem to think it's been used. What do you think, Bloom?''

''I think it's a wonderful title,'' Mary Margaret said as she suddenly sat down in the chair between them. She propped her elbows on the table and gave him a soulful smile. ''When will you start filming, Mr. Spitzberg?''

'Call me J.R., honey. The 'J' stands for 'just' and the 'R' stands for 'rich.' I can't say for certain when we'll go into production, but the bottom line is pretty damn quick if we want to impact the Christmas releases. I talked to Raquel's agent last night, but she's tied up with another project, very hush-hush. Mia refuses to leave the East Coast, Jane's not quite right for the concept, and I'm leaning toward someone with a little more pizzazz than Meryl. Someone with hair the color of the Caribbean sunset, with eyes the sultry emerald green of the tropical rain forest, with bazooms that just don't stop. Someone Travolta can sink his teeth into, if you're with me on this, honey.''

Mary Margaret was having difficulty breathing. "That sounds totally fascinating, J.R., totally. Why don't you tell me all about your problems, and I'll rack my brain to help you out?"

Theo stood up. "Thanks for the drink, old boy. I'm going back to take a little nap in the sun while you two try to think of a way to persuade Mia to migrate. But I will keep your earlier comments in mind, and if I ever learn you were not telling the truth, I'll rack my brain, too. Or hire a skywriter. How much can three letters cost?"

As he left, he heard Mary Margaret issuing an invitation to Sitermann-Spitzberg to come by the villa for a drink that evening. To his regret, but not his surprise, he heard an acceptance. He was not convinced that Sitermann had been truthful, but there was no action dictated until he learned otherwise. Except for warning Dorrie, of course, who had met the CIA agent under less tropical conditions and would recognize him as easily as she could identify a single drop of designer perfume. From fifty feet, upwind.

He saw Dorrie standing knee-deep in the water, with Biff nearby to protect her should some presumptuous sea life endanger her petunia pink toenails. They were talking in what appeared to be a friendly fashion, which gave Theo a fragile hope that they had resolved the Mary Margaret issue and might cease the squabbling. He returned to his chaise longue and dusted the sand off his book. He could not, however, engross himself in the description of the bromeliads indigenous to the island, and he found himself observing his niece and her fiancé with a small frown.

When the two came out of the water, Theo gestured for Dorrie to join him. "Have you and Biff arrived at an understanding?" he asked quietly.

"He says he was just being polite. I pointed out as nicely as possible—considering certain appalling recent events—that he was being obsequious and snively and oblivious to my presence. After all, I am supposed to be the center of his attention. He has no business oiling anyone but me." Dorrie permitted herself a brief smile. "He had no choice but to agree, since it was perfectly clear who was right, and he swore he would do better. We're going dancing tonight at some tremendously expensive place so that he can attempt to make amends. He also mentioned a darling little necklace that I've had my eye on for some time, so I suppose I'll be magnanimous this one time. After all, we're practically engaged."

"Congratulations. By the way, a most astonishing thing happened earlier, and I wanted to warn you, my dear."

"Mary Margaret repented, enrolled in a convent—and they took her?"

Theo told her. After a pause, Dorrie gave him a sharp look. "Did you believe him, Uncle Theo? I don't want to say anything tacky about your friend from the CIA, but I found him most unreliable. Do you recall that ghastly plaid cowboy shirt he wore one evening? And those gold-plated chains that he must have ordered from the back of a comic book? Really, he did not seem the least bit credible last summer, and I see no reason why you ought to believe him now."

"Then what would you have me believe?"

She flipped her hair back and sighed. "Good point. I certainly don't want to consider the possibility that I shall go through life being tailed by a spy in a polyester cowboy shirt."

"Nor do I," Theo said. "Mary Margaret has invited our pal Sitermann, who's currently using the alias J. R. Spitzberger, to the villa for a drink this evening, and I would imagine he does not want his true identity announced to the group. I suppose I shall comply."

"As long as he doesn't wear a leisure suit, I won't expose him. But I think you ought to keep an eye on him, Uncle Theo. There's something about him that makes me feel he's not to be trusted."

Uncle Theo agreed.

* * *

Eli shuttled them back to the villa in time to shower and dress for their guests. When Theo reached the terrace, he noted that all three girls had spent considerable time with their hair and makeup, in honor of either the count or the Hollywood producer. Or both. On the contrary, Sandy and Biff were in shorts and T-shirts, barefooted, and totally uninterested in the cocktail party, if one were to believe their pointedly bored expressions. Trey was slumped in a chair, engaged in what appeared to be an unsuccessful attempt to get an itsy bitsy spider up a waterspout.

Theo poured himself a glass of rum punch from the omnipresent pitcher and took a seat in a shady corner. He was relieved when Gerry's station wagon honked at the foot of the driveway. Eli appeared to open the gate, but before he could reclose it, a slim man with strikingly thick white hair came around the corner and up the driveway. His tanned face was in sharp contrast to his white suit, pastel blue shirt, and pale gray tie, and he walked with the air of an explorer in a cinematic jungle. His nose was sharp, his forehead high, his cheeks concave, and his smile perfectly shaped to convey the appropriate combination of charm and wry amusement. All three girls gulped. The boys settled for sneers that went unnoticed by everyone but Theo.

The apparition joined Gerry as she came up the steps to the terrace. "This," she announced, "is your neighbor, Hal D'Orsini. He is a rogue and a scoundrel, and the only reason he's not a pirate is that he doesn't want to risk ruining the crease in his trousers." She went around the group, murmuring names.

"I am delighted to meet you," he said with a small bow that produced three more gulps from the distaff faction. "I hope I shall have the pleasure of your company often during the week, and that you will feel *mi casa es su casa*. And Mr. Bloomer, how kind of you to take time off to chaperone the group. They are quite fortunate to have the benefit of your company."

His voice was carefully melodious, with a vague Bostonian undertone and a dash of British upper class. It was the voice Theo had heard, well . . . overheard, the previous evening. The voice of the man accused of being a gigolo. Theo acknowledged the introduction with a nod.

Trey roused himself to light a cigarette from the butt in his hand. "So you were at Harvard with Uncle Billy, old chap? I've heard some truly inspirational stories about the good old days and some of your pranks."

"Indeed." Hal sat down and accepted a glass from Dorrie, whose eyes were brighter than those of a stuffed animal. "Billy Bob and I had quite a time, but that was years ago when we were mischievous boys. You must tell me how you find our island paradise. Have you had an opportunity to explore the ghetto dubbed MoBay, or have you idled away your hours on the beach?"

Mary Margaret began to describe her adventure on the parasail, not failing to mention how it was, if one could imagine, almost sexual. In the midst of her breathless recitation, J. R. Spitzberg strolled up the driveway, but unlike his dashing predecessor, he was panting as he reached the terrace and his nose would have rivaled a chrysanthemum (Dark Flamingo) for redness.

Mary Margaret arranged the chairs so that she was between the two guests. She introduced her divine new friend from the West Coast, then leaned back and crossed her legs, very much the cat eyeing a bowl of cream. Or, Theo amended, the same cat eyeing a pair of plump little chipmunks. Dorrie lifted an eyebrow at Sitermann's seersucker jacket, but produced a polite smile before turning back to study Hal D'Orsini.

"Have you made any plans for tomorrow?" Gerry asked. "I was going to suggest you use the company's van for an outing to Ochos Rios. You can see Columbus Bay and climb the Dunn's River waterfall, and there's a large open-air market."

"Climb?" Dorrie echoed, zeroing in on the pertinent word. "As in scrambling up a bunch of rocks while water and moss and God knows what else drips on your head? That sounds physical.''

Hal leaned across the table to pat her hand. "It's terribly touristy, but there are guides to help you and it's quite safe. I suspect you've got a firm little body under that charmingly delicate surface.''

Biff growled, but Dorrie squelched any potential comments with a stern look. "I was the captain of the field hockey team at school," she allowed in a modest voice. "For three years in a row, actually. I protested, but everyone absolutely insisted and I was forced to accept the position. I do enjoy the right sports, but I'm not at all sure I want to climb places where snakes and lizards congregate.''

"Or slime," Bitsy added, wrinkling her nose.

Hal gave Dorrie's hand a squeeze before settling back. "I'll tell you what, children. I've got an appointment over that way tomorrow, and I was thinking about running over in my boat. I could pick you up at the pier later in the afternoon and give you a lift back here.''

"Oh?" Bitsy, Mary Margaret, and Dorrie said in unison. The three gulps brought the total to nine thus far.

"What about the van?" said Sandy. Biff and Trey nodded savagely, as if someone else's property constituted their major concern in life. Theo knew better, but he was intrigued by the new twists in the plot. As was Gerry, apparently.

"Don't worry about the van," she said. "Eli can take you to the pier, then bring the van back and wait for you here.''

"What kind of boat do you have, D'Orsini?" Sitermann-Spitzberg asked suddenly.

"Nothing special, just a little seventy-foot runabout. Sleeps eight, but it's crowded with any more than that. I use it for fishing, or to flee when I feel inundated with tedious people.''

"How far can you flee?"

Hal stared across the clutter of glasses on the table. "It's hardly the *QE II*, but it's adequate for my simple pleasures. Are you thinking of picking up one for yourself?''

"Yeah," Sitermann-Spitzberg said, finishing his drink and pouring another. He drank half of it, made a face, and put down the glass. "Just a little runabout to do Catalina when the mood strikes. My office at the studio can be a madhouse. The writers, the directors, the actors, the endless stream of agents, lunches, openings, the whole crazy Hollywood scene—it can be migraine city, if you follow me on this one."

"Really?" said Hal, still staring.

There was an uncomfortable moment of silence. Mary Margaret swiveled her head like a weather vane, then clapped her hands. "Well, it's all settled! We'll do this waterfall thing, shop, and come back on Count D'Orsini's boat. I think it'll be fantastic."

When Dorrie and Bitsy agreed, the boys seemed to accept the inevitable. Theo, determined to keep a prudent eye on Mary Margaret murmured that it did sound like a pleasant outing.

"Then it's a date," Hal said, standing up. "I must run along now, but I'll pick you up in Ochos Rios at four. We'll nibble on caviar and crackers, sip a little champagne, and perhaps catch the sunset on the way back. If there's anything I can do in the meantime, feel free to toss a note over the fence or give me a buzz. Until tomorrow, ciao."

Gerry excused herself and went with him to the foot of the driveway. Theo watched them as they halted near the curb for what appeared to be a slightly unhappy exchange.

Dorrie gave Biff a piercing look. "Well, shall we change now so we can leave as soon as we've finished dinner?"

Mary Margaret wrenched her eyes off the figures below. "Where are you going?"

"The biggest hotel we can find," Biff said, oblivious to Dorrie's darkening expression. "We thought we'd hunt up some calypso music and dance the night away. Why don't you all come along?"

"Biff," Dorrie began, "I thought—"

"Come on, honey, we'll have more fun if everyone comes along for the ride. It'll be a blast. Trey?"

"Sure. I can't think of anything more amusing than watching Magsy pick up men in a bar. Once she graduates, she's going to open the Miss Magsy School of Seduction."

Bitsy smiled at him. "At least she'll graduate, which is more than I can say about others of us. But I guess I'll go along for the ride."

"I'm going to pass," Sandy said. "My head's still blown out from last night, and I'm going to have to pace myself if I want to get in any golf this week. Beddy-bye for this boy."

"Pooper," Bitsy said, pursing her lips. "I don't think that's very nice. But if you're going to stay here, maybe I will, too. I never go to bars without an escort; it's utterly gauche."

"Why, I'd be delighted to be your escort, Miss Bitsy," Trey drawled. "In fact, I'd be downright honored if you would allow me to have the pleasure of your company. But if you're afraid you'll have too much champagne and start crawling all over me again, you'd better stay here."

"Crawl all over you? I wouldn't even walk on you if they flattened you with a bulldozer and carpeted Tiffany's with you."

Trey wiggled his eyebrows. "So you say, Miss Bitsy, but I hear the doubt in your voice, the little whisper in the back of your mind that you might not be able to control yourself around me."

"I refuse to be manipulated by your crude remarks. I have decided to go dancing, but don't flatter yourself that you'll get within twenty feet of me. I think I'll follow Mary Margaret's lead and pick up men in the bar. As long as they're not total pigs, they'll be preferable to you!"

"Hey," Mary Margaret protested, "let's leave moi out of this."

Dorrie sniffed. "If only we could."

Sitermann gave Theo a look of deep sympathy. "See you around, Bloom." He told Mary Margaret he would get back to her pronto about their little agreement, then gave the group a mock salute. "Ciao."

WIth a sense of envy, Theo watched the spy amble down the driveway. Sitermann had the freedom to spend a quiet evening with a book, or to sit in solitude and watch the stars above the dark water. He could seek out a companion for conversation, engage in a hand or two of pinochle, or even enjoy an early retirement.

Theo, on the other hand, was going dancing.

It was no more dreadful than he had anticipated, although certainly no less so. With some amount of grumbling about the tight squeeze, they managed to fit in the little car. Eli drove them to a mammoth pink hotel with a tile roof and well-lit palm trees. The bar was outside, which helped him to survive the band. Calypso it was not. Dorrie patiently explained the premise of heavy metal, then jiggled away with Biff most of the evening. Mary Margaret settled for dancing with a group of boys at the next table, but faithfully returned to both her drink and Theo's relief. Bitsy and Trey sat at opposite ends of the table, producing cold smiles and cheap shots with sporadic indifference.

By midnight the group agreed to leave. Biff went to the parking lot and returned shortly to say Eli was not waiting for them.

"But I'm ready to go right now," Dorrie said. "He was supposed to wait for us; that is what he gets paid for, isn't it?"

"I suppose we could call," Bitsy said, wrinkling her nose. "We'd have to wake Sandy, but he won't mind. After all, we can hardly walk to the villa. It's uphill."

Dorrie picked up her purse. "You call, Biff. We'll wait in front of the hotel." She then herded everyone across the patio and down a sandy sidewalk. Within a few minutes, Eli appeared in the beige car.

"Sorry, folks," he said, grinning at them, as he got out.

"You might reread your job description," Dorrie muttered as she climbed in the car. Biff came out of the hotel and obediently leapt in beside her, murmuring apologies for whatever sin he might have committed.

"Oh, I know exactly what I'm supposed to do," Eli said. "And I've been working real hard, miss."

As the others got in the car, Theo studied Eli, who beamed back with an immensely smug expression. "You haven't indulged in any substances that might impair your ability to drive, have you?" Theo asked, prudently.

"No problem, Mr. Bloomer. I'm as pure as the day my mammy birthed me. This boy doesn't do drugs." His face sobered. "I realize that drugs are a serious problem here in Jamaica, and I hate to see kids and grown men wasting their lives with tokes of ganja. Even the Rastafarians, who claim ganja is a part of their religious rituals, get a little too mellow."

"Uncle Theo, we are waiting," Dorrie said from the backseat. "I may develop serious circulation problems in my right leg if we sit here much longer. Good Lord, Mary Margaret, have your thighs always been this flabby?"

Aware that he was putting his life on the line, Theo ignored her. "I, too, am aware of the problem, Eli. For the moment, we should allow these kids to retire to their beds, but I would be most interested in continuing the conversation when we have the opportunity."

"No problem," Eli said, once again grinning as he opened the door for Theo. "And now, home, Jeeves. Park Avenue South, here we come."

Theo closed his eyes for the drive home.

The following morning they began to gather on the terrace after breakfast. Theo had equipped himself with a guidebook that explained the geological significance of the limestone that formed Dunn's River Falls, although he had little hope anyone would be particularly interested. He took his coffee to a corner to reread the section.

Dorrie came out on the balcony. "Uncle Theo, did you tell the help that we'll be out all day? Once they've cleaned, they have no reason to hang about idling. You might as well give them the afternoon off.''

"Very thoughtful," Theo answered. "I shall do so before we leave.''

Dorrie bent down, then stood up with a black plastic circle in her hand. "Whatever can this be?''

Trey squinted up at her. "A Ritz cracker with gangrene or a lens cap from a camera, I would guess. Have you girls been snapping photos of the chap next door— for *Playgirl* magazine?''

Bitsy looked up from a magazine. "You are disgusting. Count D'Orsini, on the other hand, is a gentleman, and we would never invade his privacy. Where did that come from, Dorrie? Has someone been in our room?''

"Let me ask Mary Margaret if it's hers.'' Dorrie went inside, then returned with a worried expression. "Mary Margaret didn't bring a camera. Neither did I, for that matter. It would disrupt my lines. Could this be yours, Bitsy?''

"Cameras are à la bourgeoisie. I wouldn't be caught dead with one. There are people who actually sit around living rooms drinking beer and looking at other people's slides, but I'd rather wear generic than bore people to death with such nonsense.''

Dorrie frowned at the lens cap. "Well, it wasn't here before we went to the hotel last night, because I came out for a moment to towel-dry my hair. Mr. Robert seems to think excessive blow-drying is responsible for these insidious split ends, so I've been avoiding it whenever remotely possible. Where did this come from? Do you think someone was on the balcony last night?''

"That's a thoroughly icky thought,'' Bitsy said. "Do you think some sleazy sort was lurking out there to take photographs of us while we undressed?''

Sandy came through the doorway from the dining room. "Can I see the proofs?''

Dorrie held up the lens cap. "Is this yours? I found it on

the balcony, and we're trying to decide if someone might have been prowling last night while we were gone."

He shook his head. "No, I didn't even bring a camera. Why should I waste my precious time taking photographs of trees and flowers, when I could utilize the time drinking?"

Theo saw no reason to mention his camera, since he was confident that the lens cap was in its proper place. He was as curious as Dorrie, however, about the mysterious appearance of the object. Looking at Sandy, he said, "You were here last night. Did you happen to hear anything out of the ordinary?"

"No, sir, not a thing. I had a couple of beers by the pool, then took a magazine to bed to study the centerfold. All quiet on the Caribbean front, so to speak."

"And the gate remained locked until we returned at midnight?"

"I guess so, sir," Sandy said, shrugging. "I didn't hear anything or see any headlights in the driveway."

"You were here the entire time?" Theo persisted. When Sandy nodded, he closed his book and stood up. "I am disturbed that someone might have gained access to the balcony. I think I shall question Eli about the key and the security arrangements, and I suggest all of you check your belongings to ascertain if anything might be missing. I shall also call Gerry and report the incident, although I imagine she can do nothing."

Dorrie again went for the pertinent word. "Missing? I didn't think to look through my jewelry! What if someone took my dinner ring or the locket Biff gave me? I would have a coronary, literally, and Daddy would be furious." She was muttering about escalating insurance rates as she disappeared into the bedroom.

Mary Margaret, Bitsy, and Sandy departed to do as Theo suggested, all three looking upset. When Biff came onto the terrace, Theo told him what had transpired.

"Good God," Biff said, staring at the balcony. "I brought a camera at Dorrie's insistence, since she wanted a few shots of herself on the beach and so forth, but I was just putting in a new roll of film and my lens cap was there. Why would someone be on the balcony, anyway? The view's okay if you like that sort of thing, but it hardly seems worth the risk simply to shoot the ocean.''

"And at night," Theo said, equally puzzled. They sat in silence until the others joined them. No one reported anything missing.

"It couldn't have been a burglar," Dorrie said. "He would not have overlooked the diamond dinner ring Daddy gave me for my birthday last year. I don't know how many carats it is, but it weighs an absolute ton."

"Maybe it was a sickly burglar," Trey said. "Maybe he forgot to bring a crane to lift the thing, and was so devastated that he simply took a photograph of it for his album and slithered away."

"Or maybe he thought it was paste," Mary Margaret said, yawning. "I know I did the first time I saw it. Are you sure it's not a rhinestone, Dorrie?"

"Mary Margaret Ellison, are you insinuating that I am incapable of recognizing a diamond when I see one?"

Theo held up his hand. "Please, girls, we must decide what action, if any, we intend to take. Eli should appear with the van at any moment, and I will discuss the key situation with him. However, since nothing has been stolen, we may have to simply forget about it."

"What about that so-called gold chain you wore last night?" Dorrie said to Mary Margaret. "Are you going to claim it's anything but tinted aluminum foil?"

"I didn't want to bring any of my good stuff."

"I thought you hocked the family jewels to bail out that Hell's Angel you were so fond of," Trey said. "I did stumble across a bundle of pawn tickets one morning."

"While pawing through my underwear drawer?"

"However did you guess?"

Bitsy banged down her purse. "That's disgusting. I'm beginning to find your remarks too tacky for words."

A van pulled up the driveway before Trey could manage a counter. Theo went to speak to Amelia and Emelda, who accepted the afternoon off without argument. He then went to question Eli about security.

"I've got a key, and the office has one," Eli said. "I made sure the gate was locked behind us, and there's no way anyone could get inside the fence. But what's this about, Mr. Bloomer?"

"There was some indication that someone was prowling here last night, which is distressing for all of us. Sandy said he heard no one, yet the evidence is clear that someone went to the second floor and entered the girls' bedroom. Did you happen to come back to the villa while we were at the hotel?"

"No, sir, I just went to visit some friends. What's this evidence you mentioned?"

"A lens cap was found on the balcony. It really is puzzling, since it implies someone was taking photographs in the dark. Otherwise, the lens cap would have been noticed and retrieved. One would need a very expensive lens, but that would be a peculiar modus operandi for a cat burglar."

"You're right," Eli said, frowning at the balcony. "You seem to know quite a bit about playing detective. I thought I heard one of the kids say you were some kind of florist."

Theo took off his bifocals to polish them. "Yes, but I'm presently retired." He did not elucidate.

The others came outside to get in the van. After several minutes of jostling and acerbic comments about preferred seats and flabby thighs, Eli backed down the driveway and turned toward the coastal road that led to Ochos Rios. Theo noted, before he closed his eyes, that he seemed to be smiling to himself. Curious.

5

The road curved along the coastline, cutting through villages that evoked shudders from the backseat of the van, then veering back to the rocky beaches dotted with swirls of deflated algae, birds, decaying fish, yellowish foam, and splintery skeletons of abandoned boats. A voice from the rear commented that the hotel beaches were the only raison d'être for the island; another pointed out that these beaches were open to just anyone and what did one expect—Cannes?

Potholes were abundant, as were subcompacts and buses packed to the roof with Jamaicans. Speed limit signs seemed to serve only as targets for mud balls and spray paint. Chickens and children played at the edge of the road. Dogs lay in the dust, some resting for the moment and others resting for all eternity. Eli kept up a cheerful stream of chatter despite what Theo felt were brushes with death every forty-five seconds or so.

They stopped at Columbus Park to gaze at rusty cannons amid the flowers. Theo had found the pertinent page in the guidebook when Dorrie announced she was hot, thirsty, and not especially interested in a bunch of corroded war toys. Sighing, he followed the group back to the van, reminding himself that Caldicotts were intrigued with history only when it related to the trunk of the family tree. Columbus may have happened onto the continent, but the passengers on the *May-flower* were much more relevant at the monthly DAR meetings.

Dunn's River Falls did merit a few appreciative murmurs, however. Surrounded by a verdant hillside park dotted with flower beds, ice cream stalls, and souvenir shops, the water splashed and glittered as it spilled down a series of limestone pools. Snaking lines of tourists picked their way up the rocks, led by muscular black guides whose chests were invisible under dozens of cameras.

The girls assessed the situation and all agreed they had no intention of climbing anything, for any reason, at any time in the foreseeable future. Mary Margaret announced that she was going to the ladies' room or would simply explode. Theo joined the other two girls on a bench, while the boys went down wooden steps to the bottom of the falls.

"I cannot understand why Biff insists on this sort of reckless behavior," Dorrie said, "and I find it excruciatingly childish. If something were to happen to him, I would be left in the lurch socially all summer, and the idea of hospital visits is appalling; the ghastly shade of pea green and all those medicinal odors make me quite ill to my stomach. Anyway, I thought machismo went out with the seventies, along with pet rocks and Democrats."

Bitsy watched a plump woman in a floral print tent waddle past, then said, "Well, I cannot understand why that real estate agent thought we ought to come here, for that matter. We could have spent a perfectly civilized day shopping and having lunch at a nice hotel, but now we're stuck here for what may be hours. The people here are too tacky for words, and there are probably mosquitoes and snakes under every leaf."

"She may have overestimated your inclination for athletics," Theo said. "The climb doesn't seem all that challenging; many of the participants are less than perfect specimens, but all of them seem to be enjoying themselves."

Dorrie dabbed her forehead with a tissue. "I don't see

how they could possibly enjoy anything in this heat. They're bound to perspire, no matter how frigid the water is. Bitsy's right. This Gerry person is a loon for suggesting this trip."

"She seems quite sensible to me," Theo protested.

"Oh, she's divine. I especially like the pink eyeshadow. Have you noticed the size of her feet, Uncle Theo? She could rent out her shoes for deep-sea fishing trips."

"And that quaint little mustache," Bitsy added, "reminds me ever so much of Groucho Marx. Or perhaps Adolf Hitler."

"Don Johnson," Dorrie said, giggling.

Bitsy shook her finger. "But we mustn't be tacky. One couldn't help noticing her shoes are Gucci and that silk blouse she wore yesterday must have cost two hundred dollars. I picked up a pair of sunglasses exactly like hers in Rome for absolutely billions of lire. Daddy about died until the storekeeper did the arithmetic. You must concede she dresses well for someone who is employed." Dorrie took up the financial appraisal of Gerry's wardrobe.

Theo was nearly asleep when Dorrie tapped him on the shoulder. "Bitsy's gone to get sodas," she said, "and I want to ask you something while we're alone. I know Sitermann told you that his presence was a coincidence, but I was wondering if he might have been responsible for the lens cap I found this morning. It is rather spyish."

"That's a legitimate observation, my dear. I contemplated the same possibility, but I can't seem to resolve the problem of access to the villa. Eli says there are only two keys, one of which is always with him and the other at the real estate office. How would our CIA pal get hold of a key—and why would he be taking photographs from the balcony?"

"It was only a thought," Dorrie said crossly. "I'm much too hot to deal with details. Maybe he wanted a particular view of the moonlight and needed to get up high. Having seen the fence earlier, he bribed Eli to loan him the key. Eli left the parking lot because he knew he couldn't drive us to the villa until Sitermann brought back the key."

"The latter makes some sense, but I doubt the view from the balcony is any more spectacular than from other locales on the hillside. One could walk up the hill and achieve the same effect—without bribery, stealth, and the very real danger of getting arrested for burglary."

Dorrie shivered at the reference to unnecessary ambulation. "Then you tell me why someone was taking pictures from the balcony. If it had been light and Count D'Orsini had been doing laps, I could understand. In vino veritas. I might have snapped a few myself, although I'll deny ever saying that if you breathe so much as a word of it."

Theo gravely assured her he would never breathe a word of it. "I will speak to Eli once more about his key," he continued, "and try again to reach Gerry about the office copy. She was out of her office this morning. I don't think our visitor was Sitermann, though. For one thing, he has no motive, and for another, he's too well-trained to leave equipment behind. The CIA doesn't tolerate sloppiness, except perhaps in bookkeeping matters and expense accounts."

"CIA?" The bushes behind them rustled, then Bitsy appeared with three cans of soda. "Then he's not really a hotshot Hollywood producer? Mary Margaret will just die when she finds out she's wasted all that drool over a counterfeit."

"Oops," Dorrie said under her breath.

It took Theo nearly ten minutes to convince Bitsy that she should not tell Mary Margaret, or anyone else, the truth about J. R. Spitzberg, sham movie mogul extraordinaire. Visibly disappointed, Bitsy at last agreed to save the revelation for a future time, when the information would not jeopardize the drug investigation operation.

"Where is Mary Margaret?" Dorrie asked after Theo had elicited a final, solemn vow. "Are there any vans with mattresses and curtains in the parking lot?"

"You don't think . . . ?" Theo said, dismayed.

"There she is!" Bitsy said, pointing at a line of waterfall climbers coming into view. "She's between Biff and Sandy.

I hope the water doesn't pull off her bikini; it wouldn't take much.''

Dorrie scowled, then abruptly forced a smile as Biff waved to her. ''That bitch has gone too far,'' she said through clenched teeth. ''And look at the way Biff keeps helping her up the rocks, as if she were some frail invalid. No one with thighs that thunderous is remotely frail. Enough is enough. This is more than anyone should have to tolerate.''

Beside her, Bitsy was nodded savagely. Theo opted for a sigh.

Within an hour, they had regrouped at the van. Dorrie was smiling as she asked Biff about the climb, but her eyes were gray and her voice suspiciously bright. Mary Margaret interrupted to say that it was, if one could imagine, almost a religious experience. Theo waited for his niece to produce a scathing comeback, but to his surprise, she merely said she would have thought it was more, well, sexual than religious. If one could imagine.

Eli drove into Ochos Rios and parked across the street from the open-air market. He warned them about the higglers who would pester them unmercifully, then said he would wait near the van while they shopped. Dorrie seemed more cheerful as she led the expedition into the jungle.

Two hours later Theo followed the group back to the van and helped them unload armfuls of shirts, straw baskets, wood carvings (including an obscene one that Trey swore had cost next to nothing and would look perfect on the mantel next to Mother's needlepointed family crest), two steel drums, and a variety of other native crafts, despite labels mentioning various Asian countries. The girls seemed pleased with themselves, although Theo could see Dorrie was still simmering. The boys punched each other and bragged of the number of times they had been approached to buy ganja. According to them, the vendors had been nonstop.

''I hope you didn't actually purchase anything,'' Bitsy said.

"No problem," Trey said, pulling out of his pocket a plastic bag filled with dried green leaves. "We don't have to buy generic. This is designer quality, guaranteed to blow off your ears and the top of your head."

"Hey, mon," Eli said. He grabbed the bag out of Trey's hand and threw it in the van. "It's not cool to flash stuff on the street. You wouldn't like the local prisons."

"Trey would fit right in with the rats and lice," Bitsy said as she climbed into the van. "Think of all the little friends he could make."

"And we could pack a lunch for him," Sandy said. From a bag he took our several reddish objects and tossed one to Trey. "Perhaps they'll ripen during the trial, old man. If not, at least you won't languish in prison for the rest of your life."

"How thoughtful of you to worry about moi's baby brother. Let me see one," Mary Margaret said.

Before she could take one of the ackees, Eli grabbed the bag. "You kids are courting disaster. Ganja's not cool, and neither are unripened ackees. You sure you want to live till the end of the week?"

Theo took the ackee from Trey and handed it to Eli. "I think we need to dispose of these in a prudent manner," he said firmly.

"I just bought them for a lark, sir," Sandy said, sounding more contrite than he looked, "but I'll trash them as soon as we get to the villa. I wouldn't want one of us to nibble on one as a midnight snack. Not even good old Trey, who'll eat anything when he's stoned."

Dorrie picked up the plastic bag and, with a sniff, dropped it in a corner. "I didn't realize people still fooled around with marijuana, but some of us never quite grow up, do we? I am ready for adult pleasures, such as the yacht, champagne, and civilization. Are the rest of you planning to goggle on the sidewalk like a bunch of freshmen rushees, or are you going to get in here so we can go?"

They went.

* * *

The pier was lined with boats of all sizes, most of them adorned with glossy hardwood, polished brass, expansive white decks, colorful canopies, coy names, and jovial sailors dressed in the precisely correct degree of casual elegance. Count D'Orsini's craft was no exception, nor was he, in white slacks, a silk shirt with a cravat, and a blue captain's hat. *Pis Aller* was painted on the bow in elaborate curlicues.

"Welcome aboard," he said, offering a hand to Dorrie. "Please make yourselves at home on my humble boat. The champagne is chilling, and the sun preparing itself for a spectacular display. You look especially lovely this afternoon, my dear. Do be careful with that step; I would be devastated if you turned one of those shapely ankles."

Dorrie acknowledged the obvious with a smile. "This is so kind of you, Count D'Orsini. If we had been forced to drive back on that ghastly road, I don't know what I would have done—but it wouldn't have been a pretty sight." She climbed onto the boat, producing a small girlish shriek as the deck rocked beneath her foot, and finding it necessary to steady herself with a hand on the count's shoulder.

Biff landed behind her. "Come on, Dorrie, you've sailed since you were six years old. Remember that little Sunfish we used to run around the island with? We won the junior division the first year we entered."

"That primitive thing?" Dorrie laughed. "It would have fit in the hull of this. Why, I do believe your new boat could fit down there, too, and leave room to stack a few cases of champagne."

Theo nudged Bitsy and Mary Margaret to climb aboard before Biff could offer his opinion about relative sizes. Sandy followed them, as did Trey. Theo then stepped onto the deck and shook Count D'Orsini's proffered hand. "This is indeed kind of you, sir," he said. "We are all looking forward to the cruise back to Montego Bay."

"You are quite welcome. Before we cast off, may I offer you champagne or would you prefer Perrier with lime?"

Dorrie had rediscovered her balance. "Perrier? Thank

God. All we've been able to find the entire trip is some obscure local stuff. I told Bitsy I would rather die of dehydration than actually drink it.''

"What a dreadful loss that would be," Count D'Orsini murmured.

Dorrie shot Biff a smile, but he had moved to the stern with Mary Margaret. As he made a low comment, the redhead's laughter caused several of the nearby sailors to stare over the rims of their martini glasses. Dorrie's jaw twitched, but the smile held steady in true Caldicott tradition. "Could I have just a sip of Perrier before we open the champagne, Count D'Orsini?'' she said through an onslaught of eyelash flutters.

Theo retreated to a deck chair. The others arranged themselves for maximum comfort and visual effect, then permitted a cabin attendant to serve them champagne and toast triangles piled high with caviar. As the crew began to back the yacht out of its slip, Theo gazed at the jostling crowd at the edge of the market area. In the shadow of a stall was a figure with binoculars trained on the *Pis Aller.* The sun bounced off the lenses as they tracked the movement of the yacht, sending back a glare that caused Theo to squint in discomfort.

He waved at the figure, then settled back and accepted a glass of chilled Perrier and a triangle of toast. Sitermann. Sitermann showing an unnatural interest in Count D'Orsini's boat. Or in the count—or in a member of the crew—or in one of the passengers. Sitermann, who had sworn on his hypothetical grandmother's grave that he was on a mission completely unrelated to Theo and his sextet of preppies. Then again, Sitermann lied. Like a rug.

Wondering if any of the others had noticed the spy skulking in the shadow, Theo studied the group. Mary Margaret and Biff were still in the stern, shoulders a centimeter apart, laughing at some private joke while they gobbled down caviar as if they anticipated the advent of an unseasonal Lent. Trey was asleep in a chaise longue. Sandy was listening intently to the captain in the bridge above the deck. Bitsy lay on a mat, supine and oblivious to anything but the continually replenished crystal glass in one hand. And Dorrie was sitting next to Count D'Orsini, her face rapt with admiration and her hand serenely tucked in his. Every few seconds, however, her eyes darted to the stern with the stealth of a professional shoplifter.

By this time they were too far out for Theo to ascertain if Sitermann was still observing them. He saw no glints of sun on lenses, nor did he see a flash of white hair in the surges of tourists among the stalls of the market. Not, of course, that it meant the spy had not taken a different post from which to follow the yacht as it moved across the water toward the edge of the bay and the sea beyond.

"Oh, Sitermann," Theo muttered softly.

The following morning Theo sat on the terrace, coffee in hand. There were stirrings of life in the villa, but no one had yet appeared for breakfast. Which was fine with him. The previous evening had been spent beside the pool, and had passed pleasantly enough despite the verbal strafing, which was beginning to seem normal if not mandatory. Dorrie had been cool but polite; Biff had responded with more than one comment about her cozy chat with the count. Mary Margaret had announced that she absolutely had to have a boat just like the *Pis Aller*, that it was just the right size for fun little runs to Bermuda, et cetera. There had been a remark about the Bermuda Triangle and with luck—but Theo had exited.

Emelda brought out a fresh pot of coffee. "Eli says you all came back on Count D'Orsini's boat last evening. He's something, isn't he?"

Theo did not think it prudent to mention that the count was possibly a gigolo, probably a fraud, and clearly adept at wooing pretty young things for his own purposes. "He was kind enough to offer us the ride on his boat. I fear I am not yet accustomed to driving on the left side of the road, and I find it most unnerving, to say the least. We did not have to deal with that on the water, for which I was grateful. How long has Count D'Orsini lived next door, Emelda?''

''Oh, he don't live there. He's watching the house for the Bradfords, who are visiting their grandbabies in California for two months. The count watches houses for all sorts of folks. I don't know for sure if he has a real house on the island.''

''I hadn't realized that,'' Theo said.

Emelda wiped her hands on a dish towel. ''Ain't his boat, either. It belongs to this writer man who had to go home to England for surgery. The count's been using the boat for nearly a year, taking rich widow women out to deep-sea fish and get drunk on champagne. One of my nephews cleans the boat every week, and he says the number of empty bottles is a scandal, not to mention the ganja and cocaine they does in the cabin. Why, if—''

''Emelda!'' Amelia snapped, coming onto the terrace with a tray of coffee cups. ''Why are you here gossiping with Mr. Bloomer? Don't you know you have to polish the furniture today?''

''I do know,'' Emelda said in a dignified voice. ''I was merely answering some questions that were asked of me.''

''So you say.'' Amelia gave Theo a frosty look as she went into the dining room. Emelda followed slowly, making it clear she was not intimidated by the cook's criticism.

Theo held in a smile until the kitchen door slammed shut. The chat had been enlightening, in some ill-defined way. The resulting information, which served to confirm the gigolo theory, was analyzed, then stored away until such time that it might be deemed of value, although Theo could not have predicted when that might be. He was musing in serene solitude when Gerry's station wagon honked at the bottom of the driveway.

When Eli failed to appear, she parked along the curb and opened the gate, which had been left unsecured and slightly ajar. She stopped halfway up the driveway and vanished from Theo's view, presumably to speak to Eli in his quarters below the pool. When she subsequently reappeared and came up the steps to the terrace, her expression was grim.

"I must do something about him," she said as she sat down. "He seems to spend more time running around than he does attending to his duties, and he should have locked the gate when he left. But that's my problem, not yours. Have you made plans for today?"

"There was some discussion about a train trip into the interior," Theo said. "I myself was interested, since it might provide an opportunity to see some of the indigenous vegetation. A four-hour trip, I was told, with a visit to a native market and a rum distillery."

"The Governor's Coach." Gerry took out a brochure from her large handbag and placed it on the table. "It may be better if I make reservations for you. Are all of you going?"

"The others have not yet come down for breakfast, but I think there was general agreement that all six of them would come. The girls were intrigued by the promise of further shopping, and the boys by the idea of unlimited sampling at the distillery. No one mentioned bromeliads or wild orchids." Theo shook his head, then gave himself a terse mental lecture about self-indulgence. "If you think we need reservations, you may count on seven of us."

Gerry went inside to telephone, and returned a few minutes later with a faint frown. "Amelia is quite distressed this morning. I do hope I can keep the villa fully staffed the rest of the week."

"I must apologize," Theo said. "I am guilty of keeping Emelda from her duties by engaging her in conversation. If you think it will help to alleviate tension, I shall apologize to either or both of them."

"Amelia isn't upset at Emelda. She found several unripened ackees on the windowsill in the kitchen, and was concerned that one of your group might eat one for some inane reason. If that should happen, nothing can be done. It is fatal."

"So's my hangover," Sandy said, coming out to the terrace with a glass of water in his hand. "I'm going to stay away from rum for the rest of my life, or until this afternoon—whichever comes first. Did we really decide to go on a noisy, bumpy, jarring train into some primeval forest so the girls could stalk one-hundred-percent cotton skirts?"

"There was unanimous consensus late last evening, and Gerry was kind enough to make reservations for us," Theo said.

"You'll need to have Eli drive you to the train station in MoBay immediately after lunch," Gerry said. "This brochure has information about the time and route. I must run along to the office now; I have two groups coming in this afternoon, and I need to finalize the details. Have a pleasant trip, Theo."

"Thank you. Before you leave, may I ask you one small question concerning the security arrangements here?" When she nodded, he told her about the lens cap found on the balcony the previous morning and the implication that someone had gained access to the villa.

"I'm glad you told me," she said. "The office copy of the key is kept in a locked box, and no one could have used it. I was at the office most of the evening; I did have reason to check on another key, and I am quite sure the Harmony spare was in place."

Sandy cleared his throat. "I stayed in that night, and I didn't see anybody. But Eli's the logical suspect, isn't he?" He frowned at Theo. "What do you think, sir? I really don't like the idea of someone in the girls' bedroom. We could go down to Eli's room and confront him, but he's gone to the hotels to see if he can find me a *Wall Street Journal*. I play the market in a very small way."

Gerry looked at the balcony, then at the fence that shielded Count D'Orsini's villa. Her eyes narrowed appraisingly, but when she turned to Theo, her voice was light. "Did you ask the girls if they were doing a bit of surveillance?"

"We were all at the hotel that night, except for Sandy. Besides, Biff is the only one who brought a camera, and he certainly wouldn't have been using it in the dark to photograph our neighbor. I'm afraid there is a bit of jealousy involved. The count and my niece had a long, intimate conversation yesterday afternoon, and it did not sit well with young Mr. Hartley, whose nose was bent quite far out of shape as a result.''

Gerry laughed. "Oh, I don't think the boy has anything to worry about, Theo. Hal is strictly superficial charm and wit; he wouldn't know what to do if he found a girl in his boudoir.''

Sandy banged his glass down on the table. "Maybe Eli sneaked back here with a girlfriend for a little parallel parking.'' His face turned red as he noticed Gerry's mystified expression. "You know, ma'am, horizontal rumbling . . . or, ah, well . . .'' He gave Theo a look of deep panic.

"Hanky-panky," Theo interpreted obligingly. "Sex.''

"I am shocked, Ensign Pulver," Trey said as he came through the door from the dining room. "You'd better watch out if you don't want your lance to fall off, old boy. Animal life, diseases, petrification from lack of use. You never know, do you?'' As he waggled a finger, the girls came onto the terrace.

"You are disgusting," Bitsy said.

"No argument from moi," Mary Margaret added.

"And I am forced to agree, for once," Dorrie said.

"Make it twice," Biff said.

"Good-bye, Theo," Gerry said with the deeply sympathetic look the lions might have given the Christians before dinnertime. "Have a good day.''

Theo smiled faintly.

6

"I cannot believe I've survived this ordeal," Dorrie said as they stumbled up the dark driveway. "I mean, really—the idea of a four-hour train ride turning into a nightmare of such magnitude. An entire generation of mayflies could have been born and died in those so-called four hours. And the audacity of those people to call it the Governor's Coach! No one of any breeding or stature has ever set foot in that dingy car, much less allowed his name to be used in conjunction with it. Someone ought to report this scam to the American embassy."

Theo patted her on the shoulder. "There's no point in upsetting yourself any further, my dear. Trains do break down, even in the Washington–New York corridor, and—"

"For six hours, and in a place that could have provided the set for *Village of the Damned*? Even Baltimore's more civilized than that place. You know how I feel about poverty, Uncle Theo, and the locals acted as if they'd been invaded by minute green aliens in stainless steel quiche pans. It was hardly our fault that a hundred tourists were forced to sit around their so-called park for six hours!"

Biff patted the other shoulder. "But it wasn't that bad, honey. We had music and rum punch, and we didn't actually go into any of the little stores or have conversations with the natives. I rather enjoyed the dancing.''

"I'm amazed that you remember anything, considering the quantity of that vile drink you poured down your throat. Hawaiian Punch and hundred-proof rum is not my idea of fun. Nor is having Mary Margaret sit in my lap, although you seemed to enjoy it. Sandy certainly enjoyed having her in his lap all the way back, although I was worried it might leave him permanently disabled.'' She ducked from under his hand. "I presume you will have Eli fired, if not executed, Uncle Theo. His failure to pick us up at the station was the last straw. If you hadn't been able to unlock the gate somehow, we'd still be standing in the gutter like . . .'' Her voice broke as she struggled to maintain her composure. "God only knows what it's done to my hair,'' she added in a ragged whisper.

"It was unconscionable,'' Sandy said, his arm around Bitsy's shoulder to encourage her to keep moving. "Eli should have found out the change in arrival time and been there. The girls are exhausted.''

"My creases are simply spent,'' Trey said in a hollow voice, earning a dark look from Bitsy. "Sorry, darling, but it's the bitter truth. I hate to think what might happen if I even attempted to wear these trousers to the club on a Saturday night. Your mother would have a stroke.''

"At least we'd notice. As for your mother—''

"I shall speak to Eli,'' Theo interrupted. "The car is here, and Eli is most likely in his room. If he cannot give me an adequate explanation of his failure to pick us up, I shall report the incident to Gerry.''

Dorrie produced a cold smile. "The only adequate explanation is death—and it had better be his. If Amelia did not leave lobster salad for us, she can join Eli in the morgue. It is nearly midnight. I have had nothing to eat in the last ten hours except greasy potato chips, red liquified sugar, and unsalted peanuts from the first century. My complexion is screaming in protest. I honestly think there will be a blemish by tomorrow if I don't take decisive action immediately.''

"I'll look in the refrigerator while you shower," Theo murmured, hoping Amelia had done as directed. Dorrie was irritated enough to engage the firing squad and give the commands in person. The rest were grumbling, too, and clearly exhausted from the excursion. Theo, on the contrary, had rather enjoyed the forced delay in the small village while a second engine (reputedly equipped with functional brakes) was dispatched form Kingston, on the other side of the island. He had wandered into the forest, where he had happened to spot not only black and silver tree ferns (*Cyathea medullaris* and *Cyathea dealbata*, respectively), but also several epiphytes on a tree, including an orchid of the Oncidium family. The discovery had left him breathless for several minutes.

He had also struck up a conversation with a Jamaican boy, who, upon receipt of a few American coins, led Theo to an ackee tree so he might admire the upswept branches and dark green foliage that contrasted nicely with the reddish oval fruit. They had also chanced upon a streamer-tailed hummingbird and a flock of daffodil-colored parrots. All of which had been carefully noted in a small notebook for future reference. A satisfactory outing, although it had taken a great deal of fortitude to retain the edenic scene during the subsequent and incessant complaining during the remainder of the trip.

Eli's room was dark, and Theo's knock went unanswered. Theo went on to the kitchen, where he discovered a large bowl of lobster salad, several other salads, a bowl of fruit, and plates and silverware on the counter. He had transferred the meal to the terrace and was setting places when the others came back down from their rooms.

"What did Eli have to say, Uncle Theo?" Dorrie demanded.

"He was not in his room. He may have walked to a nearby

villa to visit friends, and anticipated returning in only a minute or two to let us in.''

Dorrie looked at Bitsy. "Did you check our room to see if anyone might have been prowling again? The very idea gives me a rash.''

"My jewelry was where I left it,'' Bitsy said, wrinkling her forehead as she considered the possibility. "I couldn't tell if your things were undisturbed, since you've literally strewn them all over the place. While we're on the subject, have you seen my lime green polo shirt under your clothes? I wanted to wear it this morning with the matching shorts and visor, but I couldn't begin to find it.''

Dorrie looked away. "I haven't seen your shirt, dear, but you ought to allow it to stay lost. Although it absolutely strickens me to say so, the green gives your skin a dreadfully sallow tint, as if you'd lost a battle to chlorophyll.''

"Do you think so?'' Bitsy flashed her teeth.

"Shall we open a bottle of champagne?'' Theo suggested. "It would go nicely with the lobster, don't you think? And we've certainly earned a bit of pampering after today's unscheduled delay.''

"Right on,'' Trey muttered. The others nodded.

They were eating when headlights flashed in the driveway next door. "I think we ought to invite Count D'Orsini over for a glass of champagne,'' Mary Margaret said. "I'll go ask him.''

Dorrie nodded. "He was so kind yesterday, and we really must reciprocate as best we can, despite the limitations of the local help. Biff, why don't you pop over the fence and see if he's busy?''

"Because it's after midnight, for one thing,'' Biff said. "And I'm not especially fond of popping over fences, for another.''

"You did quite a bit of popping this afternoon. You and Mary Margaret acted like two little kernels of popcorn in a pool of hot oil. It was too cute.''

"Oh, I'll wander over and invite him,'' Mary Margaret

said, pushing back her chair. She rearranged her hair so that it curled around her neck like a sinewy boa, then rewarded them with a complacent smile. "After all, he's practically family, since he and Uncle Billy were as tight as ticks during school. The stories Uncle Billy tells just leave me in stitches, if you can imagine."

"Religious or sexual?" Dorrie growled as Mary Margaret strolled down the driveway and disappeared through the gate. She dug into the hapless lobster, her fork clattering as she jabbed an errant mushroom. Her snort of satisfaction had its origins in the dawn of the species.

Several minutes later a figure came up the driveway, but it was neither Mary Margaret nor Count D'Orsini. Sitermann was in a tuxedo, his bowtie atilt like an ailing butterfly, his hair disheveled, his face more florid than an *allium giganteum.*

"Thank the celebrity showcase you're still up," he puffed as he came onto the terrace. "My car died a couple of blocks away, and I wasn't about to walk back to the hotel. I barely made it here without being run down by some maniac on the wrong side of the road, like my old buddy Jack in *Easy Rider.*"

"Poor baby," Dorrie said, handing him a glass of champagne. "But perhaps it'll make a good concept for a production."

"Good thought, sweetheart. I'll put in a call to the office tomorrow morning and let them toss it around, see if they can come up with anything." He gave her a guarded look, then sat back with a sigh. "You folks sure dine on the far side of midnight."

Theo related the highlights of the train trip. "It was frustrating to be forced to wait all afternoon," he concluded. "We did not have time to stop at the market and we had only a few minutes at the distillery. I suppose it was a disappointment for all of us."

"Then our driver failed to pick us up at the station, Mr. Spitzberg," Bitsy inserted. "One would almost suspect it was a CIA conspiracy to ruin our day. All that waiting, no shopping, a tiny paper cup of rum—and then kamikaze taxis back to the villa. Can you put that in your epic movie, Mr. Spitzberg?''

The spy glanced at Theo, who could only shrug in response. "I'll keep it in mind," he said at last. "What a great possibility you've got here. Can you visualize the camera doing a slow pan across the bay, then zooming in inch by inch for a lingering, erotic shot of the moonlight on the water?" He formed three sides of a rectangle with his thumbs and forefingers, and played camera for their benefit, making appreciative noises under his breath.

Dorrie was not interested in hypothetical camera sweeps. "What happened to Mary Margaret? She's had enough time to offer the invitation, do a striptease, and take on the entire fleet."

"That she has," Trey contributed. "I've timed her before."

Theo waited until Bitsy had deemed him disgusting, then stood up and tried to peer over the fence. There were a few lights visible, but no sound of either voices or music. "I'd better see if she . . . has, shall we say, been diverted," he said unhappily.

"Let me go, sir," Sandy said. "You might twist your ankle going down the driveway in the dark. It should only take me a second."

Theo agreed, since he wasn't sure he would be pleased with whatever he would find on Count D'Orsini's property in terms of behavior, dress, or some lack thereof. Dorrie and Bitsy exchanged sly smiles and wiggled eyebrows. With a few uneasy glances at Bitsy, Spitzberg continued to study possible camera angles through his hands, pointing out the superb juxtaposition of light and dark, of structure and nature, of purity and eroticism. Theo found it entertaining, if totally nonsensical. At least the spy was trying.

Sandy returned with Count D'Orsini, who appeared worried. "I say," he said to Theo, "did one of your gals actually say she was coming over to my villa a while back?"

"Mary Margaret went down the driveway about ten minutes ago to invite you over for a glass of champagne. It couldn't have taken her more than half a minute to arrive at your door. Are you implying she did not appear?" Theo stared at Sandy. "Could she have stumbled and fallen into the shrubbery at the foot of the driveway, perhaps hitting her head on a rock?"

Biff scrambled up. "I'll look, Mr. Bloomer. Good lord, she couldn't have gotten lost along the way. It's not more than a hundred and fifty feet down our drive and up the one next door."

"Mary Margaret is a gal of many talents," Trey said, covering a yawn. "However, she was booted out of Girl Scouts. There was something about the husband of the troop leader, a double sleeping bag, and a leaky pup tent. She was devastated when they took away her merit badge. She swore she had earned it through diligence, if nothing else."

Theo turned to Trey. "One more word from you, and you will no longer be known as an adorable Ellison. Is that clear?" After receiving a surprised nod, Theo told Biff and Sandy to take a flashlight and search the area between the two villa gates and all of Count D'Orsini's yard.

"But, Bloomer, old chap," the count said, rubbing his hands together as he paced the length of the terrace, "shouldn't we call the police or something? This makes no sense whatsoever. I know nothing of the young woman's propensities for melodramatic disappearances or practical jokes, but I really feel some sense of responsibility for her in that something might have happened to her on my property."

Theo realized he was rubbing his hands together as if in mimicry. Putting them in his lap, he said, "Let's give Biff and Sandy a chance to look for her before we take further action. I don't know her well enough to judge if she might be attempting to alarm us for her own amusement. What do you think, Dorrie?"

"I don't think she'd pull this kind of stunt. She doesn't have enough wit to think it up on the spur of the moment, and I doubt she would find it all that entertaining. Staying out all night at a party is more her style, Uncle Theo. Mooning people in the club parking lot. Leaping in the fountain at the mall. Wet T-shirt contests at the fraternity houses."

Sitermann/Spitzberg nodded. "From what she told me of her history, this doesn't seem like her idea of amusement, Bloomer."

"But how could she lose her way when her destination was less than two hundred feet?" Theo said, his voice level despite his growing sense of dread. "We heard no cries, no sounds of a scuffle, no cars in the street."

"Everything was peaceful when I walked up," Spitzberg said.

Count D'Orsini swung around, looking less boyish in the glare of the terrace lights and a good deal more battered by age. "I didn't see anyone when I returned home, and I didn't notice any unfamiliar or suspicious cars parked along the street. Mary Margaret did not knock on my door or ring the bell; I was having a brandy in the living room, and I surely would have heard her had she attempted to gain my attention in some way."

Biff and Sandy came up the driveway. Sandy shook his head in response to Theo's sharp look. "No sign of her, sir. We checked under every bush and tree, went all along the fence, looked all over the backyard and garden, and even walked down the street a block in both directions. What could have happened to her?"

"I cannot imagine, nor can I decide what steps we ought to take at this moment. Calling the police is an option, but I'm not at all sure what, if anything, they might be able to do at this hour. They will undoubtedly point out that she is old enough to wander off, and more than capable of doing so—based on past antics. If Mary Margaret has done this as a crude joke, and subsequently is located in a local bar drinking beer and dancing, then we will look quite foolish and the police will be less than amused. However, I am responsible for her so I fear I have no choice but to call the police and report this puzzling event.''

As he went through the dining room, Dorrie caught up with him. "Do you think Mary Margaret's disappearance could have anything to do with Eli's absence?" she asked in a low voice.

"I don't see how there could be a relationship between the two. We have not seen Eli since early this afternoon, when he drove us to the train station, and he is nowhere to be found. Are you thinking his absence might be involuntary—that whoever has detained him might also have grabbed Mary Margaret while she was between the villas?''

"I don't know." Dorrie sighed. "We do know that someone—and I still suspect Sitermann—was on my balcony two nights ago, using a camera for some obscure reason. A spy appears, Eli disappears, and now Mary Margaret disappears. There is something going on, Uncle Theo; I can feel it all the way down to my cuticles.''

"Indeed, my dear. Before I call the police, I think I shall check Eli's quarters once more to see if I might find some sort of clue to his present location.''

"What if his door is locked?''

Theo blinked at her from behind his bifocals. "I anticipate no problem getting inside, and the exigency excuses a bit of unauthorized entry. Would you care to accompany me? We might slip out the kitchen door and go around the back of the pool, simply to avoid arousing undue suspicion in the others, don't you think?''

They went across the kitchen patio, ducking under the ghostly fingers of laundry on the clothesline, and gingerly followed the rough flagstone path that brought them to the far side of the pool and the sloping lawn. As they came around the lower side of the pool, they heard those on the terrace conversing in worried voices. No one had yet produced a theory to explain Mary Margaret's absence, although Trey managed to introduce several possibilities that Bitsy, without missing a beat, found disgusting. Theo found them all alarming.

The door was locked, but as Theo had implied, it was not impassable. He took a small metal strip from his pocket, used it with a minimum of bother, and within seconds shooed Dorrie inside and closed the door behind them. He then took a penlight from his pocket and shined it around the room, with brief pauses on a rumpled bed, a braided rug that had been pushed partway under the bed, a pile of neatly folded shirts on a battered rocking chair, and a collection of liquor bottles. One of which was amaretto, he noted with a faint frown.

"Nice work on the door, Uncle Theo, but the window's open. We could have crawled through it rather than playing burglar."

Theo shined the light on an elaborate stereo system. "Look at this, my dear."

"Holy Reebok," Dorrie whispered. "How much do pool boys make these days? I may forget this sociology-degree nonsense and major in chlorine."

"He does seem to have done quite well, although I understood he has only recently taken this job with Gerry's agency." Theo moved across the room to a bookcase. "Christie, John D. MacDonald, Le Carré, Parker, Hess, a few Jane Austen novels, Thackeray, and Stowe, to name a few, all dog-eared and scarred from actual usage. He is well-read for someone who admitted to no more than an eighth-grade education."

"Shine the light over here, Uncle Theo. Look at this wardrobe. Brooks Brothers? Lacoste shirts? A Burberry coat? Pool boys in Connecticut do all right, since they know they're vital, but this is absurd. Honestly, how much skill does it take to vacuum the bottom of a swimming pool?"

"Apparently one commands a salary high enough to allow the purchase of some very expensive camera equipment," Theo said drily as he moved the light to a table in one corner. "This is an infrared viewing scope and costs well in excess of a thousand dollars. Here's a telephoto lens that would be extremely effective in low light, and a nocturnal lens that is decidedly state-of-the-art. A zoom, and another that is too complex for me to identify. A very nice tripod. What interesting hobbies our Eli has . . .''

"On minimum wage." Dorrie turned around slowly, her teeth cutting into her lower lip as she stared at Theo. "What does all this mean? Why would Eli have taken pictures from my balcony?"

"It is obvious that Eli is not the garden-variety of pool boy, but I'm not sure what sort of hybrid he might be," Theo said. He sat down on the edge of the narrow bed and let the penlight dance about the room. "I would very much like to speak to him. I have a vague idea of his true identity, but I must be quite sure before I say anything further. In the interim, we must do something about retrieving Mary Margaret."

"If you insist, Uncle Theo."

They went back to the kitchen and Theo placed a call to the local police station. Once he had made known the purpose of his call, there was a long silence, followed by an explosion of laughter and several comments about the unpredictability of tourists, especially the young female kind. Theo persisted, but at last replaced the receiver and turned to Dorrie with a wry expression.

"They are not impressed," he said. "I suppose it doesn't seem all that critical, and I do not blame them for that. Mary Margaret has been missing for less than thirty minutes; she was cheerful, physically fit, sober, and operating under her own power when she left the terrace. The sergeant said he would accept a report in the morning, but he seemed confident that our stray would be home and safe in bed by that time."

"In someone's bed, anyway." Dorrie chewed her lip for a moment, then shrugged. "We'd better tell the others. Then I, for one, would like to go to bed. This day has been absolutely dreadful, Uncle Theo. It's been worse than any of

Mother's charity cocktail parties, when I've been obliged to be polite to her boring friends who talk endlessly about worthy causes and starving children—over brie and crudités.''

''An ordeal,'' Theo murmured as they returned to the terrace. The group still looked worried, although they had polished off all of the food and managed to locate another bottle of champagne during the interlude.

Count D'Orsini met Theo in the doorway. ''Did you call the police? Are they coming over to initiate a search for the poor gal?''

''If she has not returned by the morning, the police have agreed to investigate, but for the moment they suggest we simply wait and see if Mary Margaret walks through the door.''

''Please let me know when she returns.'' He nodded at the others, then went down the driveway and through the gate.

Bitsy put down her champagne glass and looked at Dorrie. ''Are you going to condition your hair tonight? I'd like a few minutes in the bathroom before you lock yourself in there for three hours to squeal about split ends.''

Before Dorrie could answer, Biff patted her hand. ''Your hair is perfect, Dorrikin.''

''It's about time you noticed that.'' Dorrie then announced that any conditioning would be of a purely preventative nature, and left the terrace with a sniff. Bitsy followed, apologizing for the implication, and the boys drifted away in a murmur of good-night-sir's.

Theo realized Sitermann was sitting quietly in a shadowy corner, his bowtie undone and his hand wrapped around a glass of what appeared to be scotch, undiluted by water or ice.

''So what'd you find, Bloom?'' the spy said, his free hand gesturing at the blackness of the pool and yard below, the dim street, and the lights that dotted the hillside all the way down to the inky water in the distance. ''Did you search the errant girl's room for a little black book of island haunts?''

"Did you, or were you too busy devising camera sweeps for the future epic? Or perhaps you found a few promising sites in Ochos Rios, more specifically in the market?"

"I bought the damndest wood carving there. At first glance, you think it's an old codger playing a clarinet, but when you look harder, you—"

"Can it," Theo said without rancor. "Why were you keeping Count D'Orsini's yacht under surveillance?"

"Me? Oh, Bloom, you are a suspicious man. What if I were to tell you that I was shopping for gifts for my sister-in-law and her children?"

"I'd say that you were lying."

"That hurts, old man. It really does, right to my heart."

"They extracted your heart the day after they recruited you. Standard procedure, I would imagine, since I never met a CIA agent with the sensitivity of a rock. But if you're not going to tell me anything, let me see if I can make a wild guess or two." Theo formed a temple with his fingertips and smiled at the spy. "We know you're in Jamaica to help the local authorities with the drug situation, which is out of control. You're interested in not only the ganja growers, but also those who import more potent drugs from conveniently well-situated places, such as Colombia."

"The real thing, so to speak." Sitermann returned the smile.

"So to speak. Now, there are most likely two modes of transportation involved in the importation of cocaine—air and boat. Count D'Orsini, who is neither as aristocratic nor as wealthy as he would prefer to be, has a boat capable of extended jaunts into international waters, where he might, with foresight and planning, encounter another boat and transfer cargo without the cloying interference of the customs officials."

"His boat has a remarkable radar system for someone who professes to stalk only sailfish and marlin. It has a sonar device that could locate a chip of coral at two hundred feet down, a radio with which he could chat with his pals in Nice, and a fascinating storage compartment that requires a microscope to find.''

Theo nodded. "As I suspected. Now, if we accept the fact that you would like to meet the captain of this remarkable craft and perhaps have the opportunity to allow him to make a transaction that would end in exposure and arrest, then we might concoct a scheme in which you befriend a resident of the very next villa. That wouldn't be improbable, would it, Sitermann?''

"Gawd, you are a sly one. I sure wish I could get my hands on your dossier and figure out who your bosses were. I've eliminated the CIA, the FBI, Interpol, the British boys, and most of the resistance groups in World War II. It doesn't obsess me, but I do a little snooping when I'm not occupied.''

"I am delighted to know you have a hobby. But to return to the present, let's continue with my hypothesis, shall we? It seems that Eli, the so-called pool boy, has an incredibly expensive hobby of his own—photography. He doesn't concentrate on nature shots, or even shots of girls on the beach; his equipment is more suited for undercover surveillance, such as recording unsavory moments from a discreet distance. One wonders if he is employed by someone other than an innocent real estate agency.''

"You don't mean . . . ?" Sitermann polished off his drink, took a bottle from under his chair to refill his glass, then settled back with a brightly curious look.

"The local police, I would think. It's a very clever setup, actually. He goes undercover and takes a job at the adjoining villa in order to observe any possible drug deals taking place there. Only two nights ago, we obligingly left him alone so that he could sneak onto the balcony and take photographs of whatever was occurring between the count and a business associate. All these trips are most likely to his office for conferences, orders, and strategy sessions. Were you there, my friend?''

"Naw, I let the locals run this operation as best they can,''

Sitermann said expansively. "Gives them good experience, a chance for a little glory, and a reason to request sophisticated toys courtesy of our government. You're right about our boy Eli, of course; we even trained him in Virginia for undercover work. But what does this have to do with the red-haired girl's disappearance, Bloom?"

"I don't know. Do you have any knowledge of this, any little thing that might have slipped your eelish mind? If you do, you'd better spit it out, Mr. Spitzberg."

The spy held up three fingers in the traditional Scout salute. "All kidding aside, I swear I have no idea what happened to the girl. I didn't know Eli took pictures from the balcony a couple of nights back, and I don't know where he is at this moment in time. Look, I happened to hear the girl talking about the villa while she was waiting to parasail, and I recognized the location. I had no idea you and your niece were a part of the house party; God knows I would have run the opposite way as fast as these bony legs would carry me before I'd voluntarily tangle with *you* again."

Theo was not awed by the sincerity in Sitermann's voice, and he knew too many Scouts who'd mugged little old ladies. "Then what were you doing in this area tonight?"

"Classified, old boy, classified. Would you mind calling me a cab? I think I'll mosey back to the hotel and see if I can find any potential leading ladies in the bar."

Once the spy was gone, Theo instinctively carried the dishes back to the kitchen and rinsed them in the sink while he pondered Sitermann's avowal of ignorance. Afterward he climbed the stairs to the second floor and tapped on Dorrie's door.

Giggling, Dorrie opened the door a slit. "Are you going to bed now, Uncle Theo?"

"I am, yes. I wanted to be sure that you and Bitsy had found your possessions as you left them, and that nothing might be missing."

"It's all dandy," Dorrie said, still giggling although Theo

had found his comments less than humorous. "You run along to bed and don't worry about Mary Margaret. See you in the morning."

Theo walked on to his bedroom, unable to prevent himself from visualizing Mary Margaret in a variety of situations, none of which enhanced his role of chaperone. In a bout of whimsy, he considered the wisdom of telephoning his sister, Nadine, to tell her what a lovely time he was having and how he did indeed wish she were there, but dismissed the heretical idea as a symptom of exhaustion. He put on his pajamas, visited the bathroom, ascertained that the villa was at peace, climbed into bed, and snapped off the light on the bedside table. He lay awake for a long while, searching his mind for a rational explanation for Mary Margaret's evanescence, which had happened in less time than it took Dorrie to list her credit cards.

He finally put it aside and forced himself to visualize tidy green rows of sugarsnap peas and blossoming tomato plants, all sturdy, well-irrigated, and free from the slightest smudge of blight. Smiling, he snuggled into the pillow and closed his eyes.

Thirty seconds later the screams began.

7

The screaming stopped as abruptly as it had begun, but the reverberations seemed to bounce around the dark bedroom like Ping-Pong balls. Theo waited a few seconds for his adrenaline to ebb, then threw back the covers and scrabbled on the bedside table for his bifocals. He was tying the belt of his bathrobe when his door opened and Dorrie slipped in, her arms wrapped around herself as though she could suppress the shivers and convulsive twitches of her body, which she obviously could not. Her ashen face was streaked with black lines of mascara, and water streamed from her sodden hair. She wore a terrycloth jacket, although it had been buttoned by hasty, negligent fingers. Her feet, always shod to protect them from unsightly calluses, were bare.

"Oh, Uncle Theo," she said in an expressionless voice.

"What has happened, my dear? Here, sit down and let me bring you a towel so you can dry off. You must be thoroughly chilled."

"You would be, too," she said as she sank down on a corner of the bed, her fingers still digging into the softness of her upper arms. "I can't decide if I should scream, faint, or barf. Perhaps I ought to do all three, although I don't suppose I can do so in that order. Oh, Uncle Theo . . ." She toppled over backward and stared at the ceiling through glazed, unblinking eyes. A trickle of saliva ran down her cheek.

"Dorrie, you must tell me what happened. As much as I appreciate this melodramatic introduction, I must insist you explain what evoked those blood-chilling screams a few minutes ago."

She sat up, but immediately clamped a hand over her mouth and lurched toward the bathroom. Admittedly impatient by now, Theo waited until she was finished, then draped a jacket around her shoulders as she came back into the bedroom. He dried her cheeks with a clean handkerchief, settled her on the edge of the bed, patted her knee with avuncular tenderness, and offered her the glass of water from the bedside table. She allowed his ministrations with a few muted gulps of gratitude.

"You must explain," he said gravely.

"It was so ghastly. In truth, it was the most ghastly experience of my life. If anything like that ever happens again, I'll just—"

"What happened, Dorrie?"

"Well, since everyone had gone to bed like a bunch of middle-aged party poopers, Bitsy and I decided to go skinny-dipping in the pool. It's a perfect night—balmy, starry, redolent breeze, the exact sort of thing one reads about in romance novels. Not that I read those trashy things, mind you, but some of the girls in the dorm do and they're always reading the torrid excerpts aloud over dinner. It's enough to destroy whatever appetite one might rally for the cafeteria, better known as carbo city."

Theo bit back what could have been interpreted as an acerbic comment. "Please get to the point," he said with measured calmness. "We can discuss literary preferences at another time."

"I wouldn't call romance novels literature with a capital L, Uncle Theo. But anyway, Bitsy and I crept downstairs and went out to the pool, which was very dark since no one bothered with the lights tonight. We left our towels and things on a chaise and eased into the water so that no one would hear any splashes and come to investigate. We were giggling, of course, but very quietly. I wouldn't have minded if Biff and Sandy joined us, but Trey has both the hands and the morals of a squid, and I certainly didn't want to wrestle with him in the dark.''

"Where is Bitsy at this moment?'' Theo said, resisting an urge to shake the pertinent portion of the story from her. "Is she unharmed?''

"Yeah, I guess. She fainted in one of the chaises beside the pool. She didn't look as if she was going anywhere for quite a while, so I tossed a towel over her and left her there while I came up here to tell you what happened.''

"Which I am optimistic that you are going to do—now.''

"We were swimming around, feeling rather daring in an adolescent fashion—as if we were at summer camp and thirteen years old, zits and all. At one point we thought we heard someone in the driveway, but we decided it was a cat. Then I bumped into something in the pool. At first I assumed it was Bitsy, since it felt like an arm and she does have a pair of those. I poked her and whispered for her to watch where she was going, because I really had no intention of getting my hair wet and being forced to wash it after we finished swimming. Well, she shot back a snippy little remark—from a far corner of the pool.'' Dorrie gulped loudly and again clamped her hand over her mouth. After several convulsive jerks, she gained control of herself and gave Theo a shaky smile. "It scared the holy shit out of me, if you'll pardon my French. I poked this thing in front of me, and it just bobbled away without a sound. Bitsy started hissing to know what was going on, but I ignored her and swam a stroke or two to find out what it was. It was a body, Uncle Theo—a dead body.''

This time she could not stop the upheavals of her stomach, and scrambled for the bathroom. Once she returned, Theo wiped her cheeks, but he kept his hands on her shoulders as he stared into her eyes. "Who was it, Dorrie?" he inquired gently.

"It was too dark to see anything, so I got out of the pool pretty damn fast and ran over to the wall to switch on the pool light. There was Eli, floating face up with his eyes wide open and his face contorted as if he'd had terrible stomach cramps or something. After we determined who it was, I turned off the light. Bitsy was screeching like a Radcliffe coed on a football weekend, so I dragged her out of the pool, slapped her a couple of times, and told her to shut up or she'd find herself eating terrycloth. That's when she fainted. You'd have thought she was Scarlett O'Hara in a twelve-inch corset."

Theo realized he had been expecting to hear Mary Margaret's name, and let out his breath. Not that this did anything to reassure him of her safety, however, he reminded himself with a wince. "Did you notice anything that might indicate the cause of death?" he asked Dorrie, still forcing himself to speak gently.

"No, but he certainly was dead. I could see that much. What do we do now, Uncle Theo?"

"I shall telephone the police. You check on Bitsy, and if she has revived herself, take her upstairs and both of you change into more suitable attire. I'll let the others know what's happened."

Dorrie stopped in the doorway and looked back at Theo, who was already reaching for his trousers. "Earlier you said you had an idea of Eli's true identity, because of the camera equipment and upscale wardrobe, but you didn't want to say anything more until you talked to him. You're not going to talk to him, Uncle Theo."

"I did have a few words with our chum from the CIA, who confirmed my theory that Eli was an undercover policeman involved in a drug operation."

Dorrie's hand tightened around the doorknob as she stared back. After a moment to digest the information, she said, "And he took the job here so that he could observe Count

D'Orsini next door, right? Eli had a lovely view from the balcony, not of the ocean but of the pool and terrace on the other side of the fence. I should have figured it out myself; it's so obvious. Do you think Eli was murdered, Uncle Theo? If someone murdered him, then what does this mean for Mary Margaret? As much as I hate to say it, I am concerned about her.''

''As am I, my dear, but there's no point in hypothesizing at this moment. Eli's death is most likely an ordinary accident, brought on perhaps by a medical condition that caused him to lose consciousness or be stricken by cramps. You run along and attend to Bitsy, who may very well recover and start screaming once more. Her voice is quite piercing, to say the least, and liable to rouse all the villas on the hillside.''

''All the villas on all the hillsides,'' Dorrie amended before closing the door.

Theo finished dressing and went out to the landing. Biff stood in the doorway of his room, a bathrobe draped over his shoulders.

''Is that you, Mr. Bloomer?'' he said, squinting in the dim light. ''I thought I heard a woman scream a few minutes ago. Did you hear it, too? I mean, did someone really scream— or was I imagining things? Did Dorrie just dash out of your room? Why are you dressed?''

''You heard a scream,'' Theo said gravely. ''There's been an accident, and I fear Eli has drowned. Where is Sandy?''

''He must have gone to investigate. I had so much champagne after dinner that it took me a long time to decide I wasn't dreaming.'' He rubbed his temples as he continued to squint at Theo. ''How did Eli drown? Is Dorrie okay? Was she the one who screamed?''

''We'll deal with your questions after I've called the police. Get dressed and go to the terrace.'' Theo went downstairs, but as he turned to enter the kitchen, he saw a figure silhouetted against the doorway of the terrace. ''Sandy?'' he whispered cautiously, sliding his hand along the wall to find the light switch.

"Mr. Bloomer?" Sandy's laugh was shaky. "Thank God. I heard a scream—or at least I thought I did, so I came downstairs to look around." He showed Theo the empty Perrier bottle he was clutching by its neck. "I wasn't sure I could intimidate an intruder with this, but my golf clubs are in a closet down here. Anyway, I looked around and didn't find anybody."

"Did you check the yard and the gate?"

"Yes, sir. The gate's locked. I didn't see anything by the pool, but it seemed okay. Trey's in his room, snoring away like an electric razor. Nobody was lurking in the yard or the driveway. Eli's either still missing or passed out cold; I knocked on his door and had no answer. I guess either I was dreaming or the scream came from another villa down the hillside." He flipped on the light and, with a self-deprecating smile, put the bottle on the dining room table. "Did you come down for a glass of warm milk, sir?"

Theo assured him that there had been a scream. After instructing him to wake Trey, dress, and meet on the terrace, Theo went to the telephone and grimly dialed the telephone number of the police station.

The duty officer listened more attentively this time. Theo admitted he had no idea of the cause of death, the time of same, or any possibly pertinent facts, including proper name, home address, or next of kin. The voice on the other end promised to send officers within a few minutes. By the time two policemen parked at the bottom of the driveway and came through the gate, Theo and his charges were on the terrace. He had related what had occurred and plied them with enough coffee to produce a semblance of horrified comprehension. The pool and its unsavory contents had been left in darkness, and no one glanced in that direction.

Dorrie and Bitsy were both pale. As the two dark-skinned policemen came onto the terrace, Theo stepped forward and quietly related the events that led to the discovery of the body, hoping to head off some of the questions he knew would be directed at the girls. The policemen introduced themselves as Sergeants Stahl and Winkler, both of the Cornwall County Criminal Investigation Bureau, then went down the stairs to the pool to ascertain the validity of the narration for themselves. When the lights came on, those on the terrace tensed, but no one turned his head.

"How do they know it wasn't just an accident?" Dorrie asked. "It seems like they'd send patrolmen out for an accident, not sergeants. And why are they from the criminal branch?"

Biff went over to put his hand on her shoulder. "Maybe this is the only branch they have here. But it doesn't concern us, since he was simply an employee. In fact, he wasn't even our employee; he worked for that real estate woman's firm. Let's all remember to insist on the fact that this has absolutely nothing to do with any of us."

"You didn't crash against a corpse in the pool," Dorrie said, shuddering.

Sandy reached across the table to pat her hand. "It must have been a nightmare, literally. Mr. Bloomer, how long do you think he was in the pool? Could he have come back after we went to bed, or was he . . . well, was he there all along, while we were eating dinner and drinking up here? The thought makes me want to throw up. After all, he was a good chap—a little slow, but always agreeable about running errands, doing little favors. I feel really bad about not noticing him." He ducked his face and ran a hand through his stubby hair. "This is lousy, totally lousy."

"Maybe he heard Dorrie's avowal of revenge and decided to take the easy way out," Trey murmured.

"I didn't say I was going to drown him, you slime," Dorrie said, her face regaining some of its color. "I said he ought to be fired."

"Unless he was dead. I distinctly remember you saying Eli had better be dead. You got that right, Dorrikin. As an oracle, you're up there with the Delphic broad."

"You might consider abandoning this unsuccessful attempt at wit and worrying a little more about Mary Margaret," Dorrie said. "She is your sister, after all, and she's been gone half the night. You do have an ounce of sibling affection somewhere in your perverted little soul, don't you?"

"She's like one of Bo Peep's sheep, darling. Leave her alone and she'll come home, wagging her tail behind her. I'm hardly inclined to lose any sleep over her."

"Do you know what you are?" Bitsy demanded shrilly.

Everyone, including an unrepentant Trey, nodded, saving her the minor effort of forming the word.

Sergeant Stahl came up the stairs. "I need to use your telephone in order to call in a report."

Theo offered to show him the way to the kitchen. Once they were there, he said, "Can you tell us anything regarding the time or cause of death? We're all feeling quite distressed about this, since it seems possible we ate supper on the terrace while Eli was below in the pool."

"The medical examiner will have to make that determination. If you're finished with your questions, I will make the necessary calls in order to start the investigation into the death of the young male in the swimming pool. Then I have questions for you and the others."

"Based on your first impressions, can you tell me if the death appears to be an accidental drowning?"

"It may have been an accident, but he did not drown. I've seen the symptoms of the vomiting sickness too many times here in Jamaica, and although this is not official, I would say with some certainty he had ingested the fruit of an unripened ackee. It is deadly."

Theo glanced at the windowsill above the sink. There were two hard, unopened ackees on one side, both glinting darkly. He found himself wondering how many had been there in the past. The immediate past. Even yesterday, if one chose to be precise.

When the rest of the investigative team arrived, Theo and his charges were sent to the living room to wait until they were needed for questioning. The red velour furniture, although seemingly decadent, proved to be both scratchy and lumpy, and Theo gratefully accepted Sandy's offer to bring a chair from the dining room. The uncompromising back seemed more appropriate.

"He didn't just have a heart attack and drown, did he?" Dorrie asked from a lounge with an elaborate headboard, several satin pillows, and a decorative fringe that resembled thready icicles. "There are about fifty cops out there, which seems a little extreme for an accident."

Theo saw no reason not to tell them what would be common knowledge before the sun rose. "Sergeant Stahl said he recognized the symptoms of ackee poisoning."

"But Eli's a Jamaican, and a well-educated one at that; he ought to know better than to start munching on an unripened ackee. They don't look all that appetizing when they're ripe, for pity's sake."

"Well-educated?" Sandy said. "He was just a pool boy, and I had to write down the words the first time I sent him out for a *Wall Street Journal.* Maybe he was into some island voodoo club where they eat things for a thrill, or maybe he got so drunk the ackee looked ripe. He did have a fondness for cheap rum."

"Well, he ran errands for you all the time. He wasted all sorts of time to find that boring newspaper every morning," Bitsy said, "and half the time you didn't bother to glance at anything but the headlines. You left one on that nasty train today. In any case, you don't have to deal with the memories of finding his body in the swimming pool. Dorrie and I were both blown away." She touched her cheek, then gazed at Dorrie with a thoughtful expression. "Some of us absolutely fell to pieces and began doing and saying all sorts of incredibly crude things. Some of us were inhuman and totally insensitive, like a Nazi soldier."

"While others of us squealed like a chubby little pig," Dorrie responded sweetly. "But, Uncle Theo, Eli wouldn't eat an unripened ackee. Surely he knew all about the effects of one and was trained to recognize the symptoms just like sergeant whatever-his-name-is. Someone who lives in one of those horrid shacks in the mountains might not know any better, but Eli was fairly sophisticated.''

''Are we discussing the same person?'' Biff said.

''Oh, he was an undercover narcotics agent,'' Dorrie said in an irritated voice. ''You must have been too occupied with Mary Margaret's bikini to notice, but those of us with any acumen to speak of could hardly fail to realize it.''

''What about Mary Margaret, sir?'' Biff asked Theo, pointedly turning his back on Dorrie, who responded to the outrage with a toss of her chin and a discreet snort.

''I don't know,'' Theo said. ''When I called earlier, the police dismissed her disappearance as self-induced. The recent tragedy makes her disappearance seem more ominous now, but I don't know what they can do until morning, even if they are more inclined to consider it relevant. She's not next door, she's not under a bush, and—well, I have no theories, myself.''

Dorrie sat up. ''What about Sitermann or Spitzberg or whatever we're calling him? Could he have anything to do with Mary Margaret's vanishing act—some terribly clever CIA scheme to . . . something?''

''Sitermann or Spitzberg? The CIA? Eli an undercover cop?'' Sandy stood up and crossed the room to stand in front of Theo. ''I don't understand what's going on, sir, but I feel that we're all entitled to an explanation. I thought we were here to party, not to get involved in some bizarre business with bodies and secret agents. I wish somebody would tell me what the hell's going on. We deserve to be told the truth.''

''So do I.'' Theo sighed. Unable to offer any rebuttal to Sandy's argument, he provided a brief synopsis of what he knew of Sitermann's true identity and Eli's occupation. Only Dorrie seemed unruffled by the information; the others listened with shocked expressions and a scattering of interjections.

After an enigmatic look at Dorrie, Biff said, ''Surely the local police department doesn't bother with assigning an officer to bust a bunch of tourists for half a baggie of ganja.

Eli didn't strike me as a role model for Eliot Ness, but he must have been on something fairly important. He'd have had a good opportunity to keep a neighbor under surveillance, for instance.''

"I was aware of that," Dorrie said, stretching out her hands to inspect her fingernails. "Anyone not fawning over an overstuffed bikini would have picked it up eons ago."

Bitsy shivered. "I'd sort of like to see that overstuffed bikini stroll through the door right now."

Sergeant Stahl strode through the door. "All of you will have to come to the station for questioning. What has happened is very serious, very serious indeed, and puzzling. But we will get to the bottom of it at some point, even if it requires a lengthy investigation."

Dorrie raised an eyebrow. "You may require a lengthy investigation in order to sort this out to your satisfaction, but we're returning to the United States on Saturday. We're all students and we have classes on Monday morning. I've already had to cut classes in the past, and I simply cannot miss any more this semester. You may call Simmons if you wish. I don't know her number off the top of my head, but she's in the classics department at Wellesley."

"We shall do everything possible to expedite your departure," the policeman said, retreating under the chilly blast.

"I should hope so. Besides these bothersome classes all week, I'm scheduled for a permanent on Wednesday. I doubt you can imagine how difficult it is to get an appointment with Mr. Robert, rather than having to accept some neophyte right out of beauty college, but you can believe me when I tell—"

"Let's go, my dear," Theo said. "You and Bitsy fetch your handbags while I make arrangements for transportation with the sergeant."

The sergeant, looking faintly bewildered, nodded.

The police station had the ambience, if not the vastness, of the airport. Housed in a crumbling gray building on a narrow, rutted street in Montego Bay, it clearly had been in use for several decades, and had received no benevolent attention in its lifetime. A fan whirred gently, stirring the dust but doing little to alleviate the cloying humidity and heat. Flies made lazy circles near the ceiling. An incurious desk officer pointed at a row of wooden chairs, then returned to the thick paperback novel in front of him.

"Shouldn't we call the consulate?" Dorrie whispered to Theo.

"I see no reason to become alarmed," he said, patting her knee for the umpteenth time. "We're only here to assist the police. We really don't know much of relevence or value, but I suppose we ought to do whatever we can. Eli was a pleasant individual, if not precisely what he pretended to be. He was doing his job, however, so we mustn't hold his pretense against him. I feel badly about his death." Theo took off his bifocals to polish them, earning a fleeting, impassive glance from the policeman behind the desk.

"What are you going to say about Sitermann?" Dorrie continued.

"I suspect the officers are aware of Sitermann's presence and involvement, so I think we'd better settle for the truth."

The door opened. Count D'Orsini, escorted on either side by uniformed policemen, gave those on the chairs a bleak nod as he was hurried past them and around a corner.

Bitsy let out a muted yelp. "Oh, my gawd. Do you think Count D'Orsini murdered Eli? After all, he was a dope dealer and Eli was watching him . . . If the count learned that Eli had been spying on him, he might have hired a thug to—to bump him off."

"Come on, Bitsy," Trey said from the end of the row, "you've been watching too much television. Dope dealers and thugs are passé now that 'Miami Vice' has slipped in the ratings. He might have hired a sitcom single parent to be so sensitive that Eli died of boredom, but not a thug. Jeez!"

Before Bitsy could respond, the door again opened and Gerry came into the room. Her hair was rumpled, and her makeup had been applied with haste. She gave the desk sergeant a curt nod, then came over to Theo.

"What on earth is going on?" she demanded in a low, hoarse voice. "The officer who came by my house gave me some garbled story about one of my employees, then told me to be here as soon as possible. While I was parking, I saw Hal being taken out of a police car. I'm trying to convince myself that this is a crazy dream, that I'll open my eyes and find myself in my own bed, but I have a dreadful feeling I'm already awake."

Theo told her about the unfortunate events leading to the discovery of Eli's body in the swimming pool. When she looked as if she might topple, he stood up and insisted she take his seat.

She sank down with a distracted murmur of thanks. "Then this is not some sort of joke? Poor, poor Eli—and his family. I know very little about him, since he only applied for the position a few weeks ago, but he seemed to be a nice young man with a good mind. I believe he has a mother and several younger siblings in one of the villages. Has anyone told them about this horrible accident?"

Theo handed her a handkerchief as her eyes filled with tears. "It does not seem to have been an accident," he said gently. "Eli was an undercover policeman on an assignment, and his death is hardly apt to be a coincidence."

"He was a—what?"

Theo repeated the information, keeping an eye on the desk sergeant. "The police are taking into consideration the fact that Eli was one of them, and the death of an officer while on duty is quite naturally suspicious."

"He was a police officer," Gerry mumbled, shaking her head. "I can't believe it, Theo. It makes no sense. There's no reason why he would take a job at one of the villas. The tourists often purchase a bit of the local product, but not of any significant quantity to merit an investigation. The police quietly overlook this minor sort of indiscretion, since any harassment would have disastrous effects on tourism. You're mistaken.''

"I agree that Eli was not concerned with the small usage in the villas. I must warn you that Count D'Orsini may have been involved in drug trafficking, if not in the disturbing events surrounding Eli's death.''

"And don't forget about Mary Margaret,'' Bitsy added primly. "She's managed to have lost herself in a thoroughly suspicious manner. If Count D'Orsini killed Eli, he might have killed Mary Margaret, too.''

Gerry's face sagged. Then, before Theo could realize the necessity of action, her eyes rolled back, her breath came out in a whoosh, and she slid out of the chair onto the floor. Her straw purse fell beside her, sending out a lavalike flow of wadded tissues, keys, pens, and female paraphernalia.

Dorrie glared at Bitsy. "Well, that was tactful.''

"What did I do?''

"For one thing, you told her that her dear old chum might be a kidnapper and a murderer.''

"That's hardly my fault, is it? I mean, it's pretty obvious that he snatched Mary Margaret and put her someplace, probably so that he could rape and torture her before cutting off her head with a machete.''

"She'd enjoy some of that,'' Trey said.

Theo resisted the very real urge to take each one of them by the scruff of his or her neck, turn same over his knee, and paddle each until he elicited sincere promises that the bickering would end. Dismissing the fantasy with a sigh, he told Sandy to find a cup of water, and then, with Biff's assistance, picked Gerry up and put her back in the chair. The desk sergeant watched wordlessly, offering neither suggestions nor aid. By the time Sandy returned with water, Gerry's eyes had fluttered open.

"Hal is not a criminal,'' she said to Theo. "I've known him for twenty years, and he's simply not the sort to harm anyone.''

"But you must acknowledge the possibility that he earns

his living in a variety of unsavory ways. Although it was quite unintentional, I happened to overhear a conversation from his villa the first night we were here. It was—well, informative in a disturbing way."

Gerry gulped down the water and squeezed her fingers around the cup. "What did you hear, Theo?"

"A male voice making some rather unpleasant remarks about the count being a gigolo, I'm sorry to say. There were also some insinuations that led me to wonder if drug trafficking might be a secondary occupation of the men. It was none of my business, naturally, and I left the terrace immediately."

"I refuse to believe this. You must have misinterpreted what was said. Would you recognize this voice if you heard it again?"

Theo toyed with the tip of his beard as he tried to reconstruct the conversation. "I recognized Count D'Orsini's voice when you brought him over for a drink, but as for the second voice . . . I don't know. I did tell myself that there was something about it that seemed vaguely familiar, which is absurd. It couldn't have been Eli, because he drove up a minute or two later, having delivered Dorrie and her friends to the beach party." He gave his beard a final tweak. "It's nonsensical to think I had heard the voice before."

"Well, it's unfortunate that we can't locate this person in order to find out why these outrageous accusations were made, but I don't see how we could find him." Gerry looked down at the cup clutched in her hand and, with a surprised expression, slowly uncurled her fingers. "What did Bitsy say about Mary Margaret? Has something happened to her?"

"She disappeared somewhere between the terrace and Count D'Orsini's front door," Theo said. He explained what had happened, adding that the police were now more inclined to worry about the girl. "I am at a loss to decide what I ought to do, however. I should hate to alarm her father if she is indulging in some sort of prank, but I should be irresponsible not to do so if she's involved in all this and in very real danger.''

Trey yawned loudly. ''No problem, man. Any danger she's in has to do with diseases that can be cured with a few doses of penicillin.''

The desk sergeant looked up as the group hissed the word ''disgusting.'' Everyone, including Theo, contributed to the sibilance.

8

As Theo and his charges straggled up the driveway the next morning, exhausted by the night of innumerable questions interspersed with frustrating idleness on the hard wooden chairs in the police station, Amelia came onto the terrace. "Mr. Bloomer!" she called, frantically waving both arms as if she were on a desert island and he were a rescue ship. "You have a long-distance telephone call. The lady keeps insisting you're here, even though I told her otherwise."

Theo gave Dorrie a wan smile. "Although this is hardly the time for parlor games, would you care to hazard a guess as to the identity of the caller? I'm not sure I'm strong enough to deal with your mother, my dear."

"Sorry, Uncle Theo, but I'm heading straight for bed. I'm so totally exhausted I'm not going to wash my hair. I may even go so far as to skip the latter half of my skin care routine, but you can bet your platinum card I'm not going to do battle with the dragon lady."

She darted around Amelia and vanished into the villa. The others followed more slowly, since they had not been threatened with the wrath of Nadine. No one stopped to offer any advice. Or sympathy, which Theo felt was more than justly due.

"I'll take the call in the kitchen," he said, resigned.

"That is some crazy lady on the other end," Amelia muttered sourly. She led him into the kitchen and pointed at the receiver, from which squawks erupted periodically. "Emelda and I will wait outside. I can use the fresh air."

Theo put the receiver to his ear. "Yes, Nadine?"

"Well, Theo?"

After a silence thick with tacit accusation, he took a deep breath and hurriedly said, "The villa is as charming as you'd told me it would be, and the view is spectacular. The yard is dotted with all sorts of fascinating flora, including a bougainvillea with a delicate shade of orange not unlike my night-blooming cereus."

"Well, Theo?"

"Ah, yes," he said, increasing the tempo out of some indefinable sense of dread, "and we've been to the beach several times, and we took an excursion on a private train into the interior, where I was fortunate to find a orchid of the family—"

"I do not find these evasive tactics amusing, Theo. On the contrary, they are beneath you, although you've always had an inexplicable tendency toward deception. Even as a child, you often shirked responsibility."

"Did I, Nadine? I fear I don't recall the precise instances to which you're referring, but should you care to elucidate at some time in the future, I shall do my best to analyze them and profit from these youthful transgressions. It was nice of you to call, and I've enjoyed the conversation. If you'll excuse me now, I was on my way upstairs to—"

"Whomever you have answering the telephone in that place said all of you were at the police station. Why were you at the police station?"

"There was an incident last night—nothing that directly involved any of us. The pool boy was discovered in the pool, and—"

"We would hardly look for him in a banana tree, would we? Please stop rambling about the servants and get to the point, Theo. Pookie's picking me up any minute so that we can discuss our bidding system on the way to the tournament. She dropped me in a cue bid yesterday, just stranded me in this idiotic contract, and then had the nerve to sit there pouting—while I went down three. It was so humiliating that I seriously considered feigning a heart attack so that she'd have to play out the thing. I intend to see that it does not happen again.''

''How dreadful for—''

''Even Charles was horrified, and he doesn't know a thing about bridge, much less the more subtle nuances of Blackwood. I don't know what got into Pookie; one would almost think she'd suffered a cerebral hemorrhage at the table. We were third in our section, but we'd have been first had she not made the error.'' Nadine snorted several times as she relived the indignities. ''But that is not the reason I called, Theo.''

''Do I hear Pookie's car honking in the driveway? I should hate for her to become impatient and back over the azaleas. Charles is so fond of them, as we all know, and likely to—''

''Theo, you are once more being evasive, and I simply do not have the fortitude to deal with such childish behavior today—not with two sessions of the women's pairs staring me in the face. Now, we'll overlook this business about the police station and your peculiar obsession with the servants' behavior. Simply explain the ransom note.''

From beyond the kitchen door came the sound of easy laughter. The pipes rattled as showers were turned on upstairs, and a radio played a lilting reggae tune somewhere down the hillside. A doctor bird hummed above a yellow flower. A car backfired as it drove down the street. The light breeze rustled the curtain above the kitchen sink.

''Ransom note?'' Theo was unable to believe the words even as they came out of his mouth.

''I assured Win that it was a mistake.''

''Win?''

''Really, Theo, if I wanted to have my every word repeated, I'd invest in an echo chamber rather than CDs and municipal bonds. We are discussing Winston Andrews Ellison II, the father of those adorable twins. I assured him that the ransom note was a mistake. It was a mistake, wasn't it? I trust you haven't allowed anything to happen to Mary Margaret. The Ellisons are very old and dear friends of ours, and I would hate to think you'd permitted something to befall their daughter.''

''What does this ransom note say?''

''It's an ordinary ransom note. Win was upset, naturally, and brought it over for Charles and me to examine the very minute we finished breakfast. He went so far as to consider calling Corky, but he was too distraught to face the ordeal with the overseas operator, and none of us could determine the time difference. It's either six hours earlier or six hours later, unless it's seven because of daylight savings time. I wish these Europeans would use the correct time instead of insisting on using local time. In any case, the clinic is quite strict about waking clients in the middle of the night.''

''I haven't the slightest idea what you're talking about, Nadine.''

''Corky Ellison is having a series of cellulite treatments at an extremely exclusive clinic in Switzerland. Although the menu is French, the staff are all German and tend to be more than a little authoritarian,'' Nadine said with the slowness and deliberate enunciation used for maximum communication with a non-English listener. Theo knew she had mastered the technique while doing good works at an Episcopalian home for unwed mothers of Mexican-American descent. The home had folded after the girls had fled.

''Thank you, Nadine; I am beginning to understand,'' he said soothingly. ''But what about this purported ransom note?''

''There is nothing 'purported' about it. It came to Win Ellison this morning. It was formed with words clipped from some publication and glued down in a sloppy yet legible fashion. It implied that his daughter was in the hands of unscrupulous people, and that these people would harm her if they did not receive a specified amount of money. You can imagine how he felt.''

''Did he call the police?''

''The note said quite bluntly that it would be unwise to contact the authorities. Besides, what would be the point of calling the police here? Mary Margaret is in Jamaica—under your chaperonage. If this is a joke, then it is tasteless. That's all I can say.'' It wasn't. After a lengthy exhalation to convey the depth of her displeasure, she continued, ''If it is not a joke, then you'd best tell me what you intend to do about it, Theo.''

Theo intended to sink down to the kitchen floor, lean against the refrigerator while gazing blankly at the underside of a table, and hope something would come to mind. ''Ah . . . how much money was demanded for the return of the girl?'' he asked.

''A million dollars, in small, unmarked bills. It was trite, to say the least. One would be inclined to think these people sat around all day watching nothing but old gangster movies. Anyway, I assured Win that the whole thing was poppycock, that he was not to worry one bit more about it—since you would see to it that Mary Margaret was returned in the same condition in which you took her on this self-indulgent, whimsical little trip of yours. I shall be at the airport in person on Saturday to pick you up, Theo, and I expect to pick up all seven of you. Do you understand?''

Before he could respond, the receiver clicked in his ear. He sat for several minutes, listening to the buzz while he tried to assimilate the conversation with Nadine. Mary Margaret's father had received a ransom note. The note demanded one million dollars. The note warned against contacting the police and implied Mary Margaret's welfare was uncertain should there be noncompliance. No one in Connecticut had any intention of compliance. He had been ordered to bring Mary Margaret home. She was to be delivered with all extremities intact.

The floor was hard, but the view not unpleasant. Theo

was still there when Amelia and Emelda came through the back door.

"Are you okay?" Emelda asked, her face puckered in alarm. "Are you having a heart attack or something?"

"I was merely thinking," Theo said with what dignity he could muster. He stood up, brushed off the seat of his trousers, and replaced the receiver. "If it's convenient, I would like coffee on the terrace. I really do believe I shall continue to think out there."

"They's all crazy," someone muttered as he left the kitchen, but he did not turn back to refute the statement.

He was on the terrace, coffee in hand, when several police cars parked on the street below. Sergeant Stahl sent his men into Eli's room below the pool, then came up the stairs and sat down across from Theo.

"Do you think there might be an extra cup?" he asked wearily.

Theo poured a cup of coffee and set it down in front of the sergeant. "You've been up all night, too. The young people are in bed, but somehow sitting out here in peace seemed as appealing as sleep."

"I'll see my bed in about a week," Stahl said. "Sooner if we clear up this mess, but I don't know. The guy next door is involved—that much we know, but it's not as simple as we'd hoped."

"Then you're not convinced Count D'Orsini is responsible for Eli's death? Could it have been an accident after all?"

"It wasn't an accident. I got the initial lab reports back an hour ago. I shouldn't be telling you this, but we found a bottle of rum down in Detective Staggley's room that was laced with pulverized ackee. The only prints on it are his. No, we can rule out an accident; someone went to a lot of trouble to poison that bottle and leave it for him."

"I don't suppose he could have been experiencing some sort of personal problem and decided to . . . take his own life?" Theo asked without much enthusiasm.

"Jamaicans know how the vomiting sickness goes. It's a

painful thing, and nothing anybody would choose. It takes about six hours for the symptoms to begin, but once they do, it's all over. Convulsions, coma, and good-bye.'' Stahl wiped his forehead as he looked down at the pool. ''Staggley must have ingested the rum sometime during the afternoon, although we'll know more once we get the autopsy results. He probably went to the deck to clean the pool, was overcome with cramps, and fell into the water. There'll be water in his lungs, but it doesn't matter whether he died of hypoglycemia as a result of the ackee or from drowning. Someone caused the death. Staggley was a good officer and a good man, damn it.''

''What had he told you of his investigation?''

''Not enough. We hadn't had a report in twenty-four hours, and I was planning to have him come in this morning to give us an update. He said earlier in the week that he had the goods on this D'Orsini and one of his contacts. But we don't know what Staggley had—or on whom.''

Theo told him about the camera lens that had been discovered on Dorrie's balcony. ''I would imagine it would be worth your while to have the film developed as soon as possible. Eli—Officer Staggley, that is—most likely was able to photograph a drug transaction next door.''

''We found a roll of film in a drawer. It's at the lab, but the boys there swore it would be late afternoon before they could get to it, if not tomorrow or the next day. I let it go because we weren't sure that we'd find anything significant, but if it is what you say it is, I'll send back a uniformed officer to tell them to hustle their bureaucratic asses. I sure would like to have some solid proof that D'Orsini was dealing big quantities of cocaine. We've had an eye on him for years. We know damn well where he goes on his yacht, and we have a good idea whom he meets and what takes place. But D'Orsini's a smart chap. He was a big buddy of the governor before independence in 1962, and he still hobnobs with the more powerful political figures on the island. In fact, we're already getting pressure to release him, and we're going to have to do so if we can't find anything concrete to hold him on.''

"Perhaps these photographs will be adequate," Theo said.

"If they prove the drug connection, we can hold him on that. If they're no good, we'll have to let him go. The only thing we've got is possible motive and passable opportunity, although it's a shaky case at best. There's nothing to link him to Staggley's murder.''

"Have you any idea who his associates are?''

"We have a few names of Colombian dealers, but there are some gaps in the overall picture. D'Orsini doesn't bother with small, local dealers. He purchases the cocaine in significant quantities, then has it transported to the States. Somehow.''

"Perhaps on jaunts to Florida?''

"It doesn't seem likely. Your Feds are real serious about what takes place in their water. It could happen, but they've kept tight surveillance on him and he's kept his nose clean. All of his close friends—and even his short-term women acquaintances—are given a thorough search at customs. The cocaine goes out and the cash comes in, just about as predictably as the tide. We don't know how.''

Theo replenished the sergeant's coffee cup. "Why are you telling me all this? As much as I appreciate your candor, I find myself somewhat perplexed by it. I am, after all, a civilian.''

Stahl flashed even white teeth. "That's not what your friend from the CIA says. Sitermann says he doesn't know what the devil you are, but that you've been well-trained. He didn't go into detail about what happened over in the Middle East, although he hinted that you cleared up a messy problem that baffled the police. He also said that it might be worth my while to have a quiet talk with you, Mr. Bloomer. That's what I'm doing.''

"I suspected as much." Theo said with a sigh. "Sitermann has been quite generous in his willingness to provide references. It is certainly beyond the call of duty.''

Sergeant Winkler came onto the terrace. "We're done with the room below the pool, Stahl. The men will be done with the pool in another few minutes. What now?"

"I think we might drive down to the lab and see how they're coming with that roll of film," Stahl said, standing up. He adjusted his sunglasses and looked down at Theo. "Have you had any word from the girl who's missing? I put out an APB on her, but I still think she's out partying and will come home sooner or later to nurse a hangover."

"We haven't heard a peep from her," Theo said, meticulously truthful if not terribly accurate in the present spirit of candor. There was a very real problem concerning the ransom note. He soothed his conscience with a promise that, should the problem not be resolved briskly, he would report the purported abduction and blame the omission on fatigue. In the interim, he could not force himself to bring more trouble on the residents of the Harmony Hills villa. They were in enough trouble as it was.

Stahl gave Theo a grin, then went down the driveway and drove away. After a few minutes, the men by the pool packed up their equipment and left, as did those in Eli's quarters below the pool. Amelia came out of the kitchen to ask about lunch; Theo told her he doubted anyone would appear before midafternoon. They had been up all night, he added in order to divert any unspoken condemnation.

"I heard what happened to Eli," she said, standing in the doorway with her arms crossed. "Those ackees shouldn't have been brought into my kitchen. It was asking for trouble, and trouble's what you got."

"I noticed the ackees on the windowsill. How many were brought in?"

"There was a paper bag with some in it," Amelia said. "I'm not ignorant enough to buy ackees when they're not ripe, but I hated to waste them. I put them aside to ripen. Looks like I should have wasted them."

"How many were in the paper bag?"

"Three, if I recollect. Now there's two."

"Could someone have come into the kitchen of the villa yesterday while we were on the Governor's Coach?"

She shrugged. "How do I know? Emelda and I cleaned up after lunch, folded the laundry, made salads for dinner, and left for the day. We didn't have no reason to stay around here with everybody gone."

"Did Eli come into the kitchen before you left?"

"I already told all this to the police, about ten times by now. Eli came back from the station, helped himself to a piece of fish and some salad from the refrigerator, told Emelda she was putting on a little weight, and generally hung around being a nuisance until we left. I hinted that he could drive us home, but he just laughed and said he was going to spend the afternoon by the pool, pretending he was rich folk."

Theo hesitated, unsure how to pose a particular question without offending the woman. "Ah," he said, wading in timidly, "is it possible that Eli might have helped himself to the liquor supply in the kitchen? I'm not implying any sort of theft, but might he have considered it a mere loan if he were temporarily out of his own supply?"

"I told the police what he said. I can see you'll hound me until I tell you. I got better things to do than to stand here repeating myself, but I guess it won't hurt nothing. Eli took some fruit juice from the refrigerator and said he had a little birthday present he was going to use to make a pitcher of rum punch. Some birthday it turned out to be!"

"Did the police find the pitcher by the pool?"

"Eli knew better than to leave it there, where Emelda or I would find it and have to take it inside the house. I suppose he took it in himself and washed it before . . ." Her expression hardened, but a nerve jumped in her eyelid and her voice was strained. "He cleaned up before the vomiting sickness overtook him. Put the dishes away, the glass to dry in the sink, and the ackee rind in the garbage can out back. His mama must have taught him about cleanliness being next to godliness. Too bad she didn't teach him about the sin of taking your own life.''

"You think he committed suicide?'' Theo asked, surprised.

"He was sure acting crazy early in the afternoon. All excited, and tighter wound up then a dreadlock. He told Emelda he was leaving right soon. She thought he meant he was taking a vacation, but she's liable to get all kinds of things wrong. Like lunch.'' Amelia turned away and marched into the kitchen, leaving Theo to blink at her rigid back.

Once the kitchen door slammed shut, he poured himself another cup of coffee and sat back in the chair. It was a muddle of incredible magnitude, he thought, tugging distractedly on his beard as he tried to sort things out. Things seemed disinclined to be sorted, at least to any satisfactory conclusion. Eli had photographed a transaction involving Count D'Orsini and an unknown figure, who could well be the man Theo had heard when inadvertently eavesdropping. It was possible that the count had learned of the mysterious lens cap and had taken action to see that the investigation was halted. Extreme action. But some of it made no sense, and Theo could find no way to resolve the irritating contradictions.

Mary Margaret's disappearance, although equally irritating and increasingly distressing, could be coincidental. The appearance of the ransom note hinted as much. Theo grimaced as he gave his beard a hard tweak. There was an obvious way to clear up the glaring problem of the note, but it was distasteful at best. He sat for a long while, seeking an option.

At last he ceded and went across the dining room to the kitchen. "I shall be out for lunch,'' he said apologetically. "The others will survive on sandwiches. Please be so kind as to tell them I shall return by the middle of the afternoon and that I hope the absence of the car will not disrupt anyone's plans.''

"You going to drive?'' Amelia asked with a smile that

seemed faintly sardonic. "You ain't in Connecticut, you know."

"I hadn't considered it, but I suppose I shall be forced to drive." Theo went to his bedroom and put on a jacket and tie, repeating to himself that he could handle the drive with minimal peril to his vehicle and his person. If he could just remember to stay on the left, especially when entering the road and turning, he would survive. Two million Jamaicans did it daily. Tourists zipped about on motorcycles, scorning such basic protection as helmets. The local newspapers did not have lengthy lists of those maimed and killed in automobile mishaps, which surely meant most of the drivers avoided accidents.

In the middle of the mental pep talk, there was a tap on Theo's door. "Uncle Theo? Are you awake?" Dorrie whispered. He let her in and invited her to sit down. "I couldn't sleep," she said, twisting her hands together and flicking her foot back and forth in an impatient cadence.

"Are you having difficulties with what occurred in the pool, my dear? It would be understandable if you found yourself dwelling on unpleasant memories."

"Do you think my hair is the tiniest bit too ash? Bitsy said she thought it tended towards brassy, but she can be awfully bitchy when the mood strikes."

Theo tucked his wallet in his pocket and soberly observed himself in the mirror while he confirmed that his tie was straight. "A question of such importance cannot be answered without thought. Allow me to ponder the possibilities before I tender what will be an amatuerish response. Hair color has not been a major issue in my life; hair retention, on the other hand, has rather occupied my idle moments."

"Oh, Uncle Theo, I know it's not all that earth-shattering." Dorrie joined him in front of the dresser. "Besides, Mr. Robert wouldn't even allow me out of his salon if he thought it was brassy. He has incredibly high standards." She pushed back her hair and regarded him in the mirror with appraising eyes. "What did Mother have to say? Was she livid when you told her what happened to Eli?"

"A goodly part of the conversation concerned a mishap at the bridge table. I was prepared to tell her of the recent tragedy, but the conversation took another direction and I simply let it go."

"Oh?" Dorrie murmured. "And where are you going? Aren't you tired after being detained in that nasty police station all night?"

"I thought I might go to a hotel for lunch. All of you seemed apt to sleep through lunch, and I saw no reason to make things difficult for the help. Preparing lunch for one, you know, can be a bother."

"Which hotel, Uncle Theo, and how are you going to get there?"

"Any of them, I suppose; I hadn't really decided. As for transportation, I am going to take the car. I'll be back in sufficient time for you to go to the beach or do whatever you may desire."

"Let me pop on some lipstick and get my purse. I'll meet you in the driveway, Uncle Theo. I cannot imagine anything more exciting than doing lunch in a hotel with my darling uncle."

"But surely you would prefer a nap," Theo said as the door closed on her heels. "Surely you would."

"Now, remember to stay left," Dorrie said as they backed down the driveway and onto the street. "No matter how wrong it feels, it's right, so just grit your teeth and resist the urge to correct things. A head-on will feel très worse. Which hotel is Sitermann in, by the way?"

"The one where we utilized the beach several days ago." Theo tightened his fingers around the steering wheel and peered down the street. No traffic approached—a good omen. "I had not considered the fact that I would be obliged to change gears with my left hand, and that the foot pedals might be reversed. It is most unsettling. I am not sure that this is wise, Dorrie. It is one thing to risk my life with this jaunt, but quite another to risk yours.'' After a bout of fumbling, he managed to find first gear. The car spurted forward, then sputtered to a halt. ''It is clear that this is imprudent, if not reckless. I feel—''

''Just gun it, Uncle Theo. They'll get out of our way.''

Despite the turtlelike pace and the occasional problem with the stick shift, Theo managed to arrive at the hotel. He parked under a palm tree and gave Dorrie an impish grin. ''Quite an adventure, wasn't it?''

''It certainly was. We were almost rammed in the rear about two dozen times, Uncle Theo. Once we've done lunch with Sitermann, I'll drive us back to the villa.'' She twisted the rearview mirror and examined her lipstick, then opened the car door. ''He does expect us, doesn't he?''

''I would imagine he does,'' Theo said under his breath. To Dorrie, he merely shrugged, then trailed her into the hotel lobby.

Sitermann was on a rattan couch, a drink in one hand and a rolled-up magazine in the other. He wore a white jacket over a pink T-shirt, and green trousers. The lobby was dim, but his sunglasses were firmly affixed and he seemed to experience no difficulty in spotting Theo and Dorrie. ''Yo, how are you sports doing? Got time to do lunch? You know, Bloom, this little girl of yours gets prettier every time I touch base with her—and that's no hype. She ought to be in pictures.''

''Can it, Sitermann,'' Theo said wearily. ''It occurred to me that doing lunch with you might be informative, if somewhat hard on the digestion. Let's put it on your expense account, old man.''

''Dynamite!'' Sitermann slapped Theo on the back, then took Dorrie's arm and tucked it through his own. They went into a dining room filled with round white tables, dripping ferns, a central fountain with a discreet waterfall, and a low background of what tourists considered to be island music. Dorrie made an appreciative noise as a jacketed waiter dashed across the room to pull out a chair for her, then snapped a gleaming white napkin into her lap. A menu with the thickness of a telephone directory was placed lovingly in her hands. The waiter, who assured them that his name was François and that he was delighted to serve them, promised to bring cocktails immediately.

"Not bad," Dorrie said. "Is this how spies live all the time, or is this part of your cover?"

Sitermann winced. "Let's not worry about that, you gorgeous thing. Why don't you try this lobster thing for an appetizer and the scallops for an entrée? I had them the other night, and they were out of sight. What looks like the thing for you, Bloom?"

"Let's start with an exchange of information. What's the prognosis for the murder investigation?"

"D'Orsini will be released by the time I eat the olive in my martini, unless that roll of film provides enough damnation to hold him. Half the bigwigs on the island have telephoned the other half of the bigwigs and insisted that D'Orsini is being treated as if he were a common criminal. High society does not acknowledge the possibility that he's a major drug dealer. Too tawdry, I suppose."

"Do you think he murdered Eli?" Theo asked.

Sitermann gazed pensively at François, who was introducing himself and pledging total devotion to a nearby table occupied by three well-baked women. "You know, Bloom, I don't think he did. D'Orsini may not have known Eli was a narc, but Eli sure as hell knew D'Orsini was a crook . . . and not one from whom to accept tokens of friendship. Hard to see the two of them sipping rum beside the pool, isn't it?"

"It is indeed," Theo murmured, having had the same thoughts.

Dorrie looked up over the edge of the menu. "If D'Orsini didn't do it, then who did? It had to be someone who had access to Eli's quarters below the pool. That is key, Uncle Theo."

"It is indeed."

The fickle waiter returned with their drinks and took their orders. Theo waited until he was gone, then said, "Sitermann, there is another little problem that has arisen. This is in conjunction with Mary Margaret's mysterious disappearance."

"I really don't know where she is, Bloom."

"So you say. But we'll let that go for the moment. I was informed this morning that the girl's father received a ransom note that demanded a million dollars in exchange for the hostage. Clipped words, small, unmarked bills, don't call the police—that sort of thing."

Dorrie choked on a mouthful of martini. "Is this for real? You're not making it up? A million dollars for Mary Margaret? Oh, my God, what did her father say?" She took a deep drink from the glass. "What did Mother say?"

Theo ignored her. "You do see the problem, don't you?" he said to Sitermann. "This is not an ordinary case of kidnapping."

"What problem?" Dorrie squawked.

Sitterman nodded. "You've zeroed in on the crux, Bloom. But which one of them?"

Dorrie drained the glass and barked an order in François's direction. "Which one of what what?"

"Which one of your friends is involved in this supposedly professional kidnapping?" Theo said gently. "Mary Margaret disappeared last night at approximately midnight. Her father received a note this morning, not more than eight or nine hours after the fact. It's rather obvious that someone from here contacted someone in Connecticut and had that person deliver the note. There was either a great deal of foresight and planning, or collusion."

"That's the bottom line," Sitermann said.

Dorrie took the martini from François's tray and drank it.

9

"You won't say anything to the others, will you?" Theo said as he chugged up the driveway of the villa. Dorrie had been much too astounded to take the wheel, and Theo had actually begun to enjoy the thrill of driving in such a bizarre fashion. The perpetual peril had been . . . well, invigorating. "I may be wrong about the ransom note," he continued, "in that it may not involve anyone in our small group. But if I am correct, I do not wish to alert this person and cause him or her to do something foolish."

Dorrie gave him a sharp look. "Her? It's unlikely to be either Amelia or Emelda; servants are hardly capable of that level of subterfuge, unless we're discussing padding the grocer's account. I would assume you're referring to Bitsy. Come on, Uncle Theo, she has nothing to do with this. She's straighter than Pookie's nose after the plastic surgeon had a field day with it on Park Avenue—and we're talking straight. Bitsy teaches Sunday school. She's never set foot outside her bedroom without a brassiere. She squeaks when she walks."

"It is difficult to envision. But you're overlooking another distaff player in the game, my dear. It is not unheard of for the kidnap victim to be, in reality, a co-conspirator. Mary Margaret may have misjudged her father's sense of parental duty, or even the extent of his liquid assets, but she may very well be the instigator of the ransom note."

"Why would she do that? It seems like a lot of bother. Her father gives her all the money she wants, and she has enough plastic in her wallet to purchase a small European country and declare herself empress. Catherine the Great could serve as her role model, although I never bought those lurid stories. It sounded so unhygienic."

"I have no idea why she might have agreed to the scheme, much less initiated it," Theo admitted. He realized he was still clutching the steering wheel with white fingers, and forced them to relinquish the death grip. A stray image flashed through his mind, but with such haste he was unable to identify it. "Well, we made it home safely, which I find no small feat. Shall we have a celebratory coffee on the terrace?"

"I've been courting puffy eyelids too long. I'm off to nap, then see if Amelia can produce cool cucumber slices without hyperventilating. She wouldn't survive ten seconds in Connecticut."

Theo went to the terrace and gazed at the Caribbean, his lips pressed in a pensive frown. Sitermann had agreed to see what he could learn about the delivery/deliverer of the ransom note. He had not anticipated much success. They had lunched agreeably and parted on amiable terms, except for a mutter from François that had expressed doubt over Sitermann's ability to calculate in the delicate arena of tipping. "Joik" had not had its origins in a Parisian bistro.

Sandy and Biff were on the deck beside the pool, both stretched out on chaise longues and oblivious to everything but the sun. Bitsy sat in the shade of the umbrella, a magazine in her lap. A radio behind the kitchen door played Jamaican music. Dorrie appeared briefly on the balcony, ascertained Biff's whereabouts with a proprietary smile, and wiggled her fingers at Theo as she vanished back into the bedroom.

It was what he had imagined the trip would be, a peaceful scene of sunbathing, reading, enjoying the idyllic weather and lazy ambience of the island. He had hoped to see the botanical gardens, maybe even to speak to the Jamaican horticulturists about their insights into the cultivation of exotic bromeliads, for which he had a fondness. He had even dared to hope he might return to his greenhouse in Handy Hollow with a few choice cuttings to be nurtured into wondrous things that would be quite the topic of gossip at the local horticulturists' meetings.

But it was not to be, he thought as he sat down. Instead of snippets of plants and enlightening exchanges concerning temperature control and botanical diets, he was in the midst of murder. Of drug dealing, of kidnapping, of adolescent bickering. Of fraudulent aristocracy and . . .

"I say, Bloomer," Count D'Orsini called from the bottom of the driveway. "Could I be so presumptuous as to invite you over for tea or a drink? Gerry is here, and we very desperately want to talk to you."

After a quick appraisal of the poolside and the vacant balcony, Theo went down the driveway. The count was dressed in the same clothes he'd worn at the police station, and his cheeks and jaw were faintly gray with unshaven stubble. Deep lines cut into his face as if done with a blade. He had, Theo decided, rather gone to seed during the last twelve hours.

"This is good of you," he said, putting his hand on Theo's shoulder for a moment. "I know you have a low opinion of me, perhaps deservedly so. Come up to the house and let me get you something to drink, and please excuse my appearance. I was released less than an hour ago, and I must say I've had a particularly trying night."

Gerry was sitting on the patio beside the pool, a glass in her hand and a pitcher nearby on a table. "Thank you for coming, Theo. This is such a ghastly sequence of events— Eli's death, Mary Margaret's disappearance, and the knowledge that the police would like nothing more than to lock Hal up in some dingy cell until they can concoct enough evidence to convict him."

Theo sat down across from her. "But the police have released Count D'Orsini, so one must assume they have no evidence. Surely his local connections will prevent his being framed for something he did not do.''

"One hopes,'' the count murmured as he went behind a small bar and found a bottle of Perrier. He poured a glass and brought it to Theo, then moved a chair next to Gerry. "I didn't do it, you know. Gerry tells me that you believe this rot about my possible involvement with drug traffic, and I wanted to assure you that the police chaps are mistaken. They are convinced I rove the Caribbean in the true bucca-neer tradition in order to engage in wickedness.'' He crossed his legs and gave Theo a comradely wink. "If it were the eighteenth century, I would probably follow in the grand tradition of Edward Teach, who's always been a hero of mine. I'd like nothing more than to board a schooner aswarm with terrified virgins, my black beard flaming and my manhood in full bloom. Alas, there are no virgins aswarm anywhere these days, and the navy takes such a dim view of that sort of adventuresome spirit.''

"Virgins or cabin boys?'' Gerry said drily.

"Both,'' he said with a second wink to Theo. "Admit-tedly I do take friends out on the yacht, but I do so at their insistence. They find deep-sea fishing, or at least the premise of it, as romantic as Hemingway told them they should. The *Pis Aller* is not the *Love Boat*, alas, and most of them end up in the throes of mal de mer and frantic for terra firma.''

Theo nodded. "And while these friends are conveniently below in the cabin, moaning over too many martinis, you have an opportunity to rendezvous with craft of Colombian origin, no? Your passengers subsequently and obligingly pro-vide an alibi, should the narcotics people be so intrusive as to question the purpose of the outing.''

Count D'Orsini had the courtesy to look somewhat abashed. "Touché, Mr. Bloomer. I may have assisted some acquaintances with the exportation of substances not exactly welcomed with open arms in the United States, but I can assure you that I am not the veritable Rothschild of the cocaine industry that the police envision me to be. They do so overestimate my impact on world trade. As for this gigolo nonsense, I have taken lonely women out for a bit of romance, but I have never requested they render payment for my attentions. If they have chosen to reward me, they have done so without any prompting on my part. I am a wastrel; there is no doubt about it in anyone's mind. I am a blackguard, a philanderer, a parasite both on my friends and on society as an entity. Were the profession feasible, I would make a dandy privateer. However, I am not a cad."

"And he's not a murderer," Gerry said. "You've got to believe that, Theo. I've known Hal for twenty years. We met at a time when my life was a shambles. My friends would not speak to me, and my relatives had scratched my name out of the family Bible. Hal helped me find myself, to sort out my life and determine who I really was and what I wanted to do with the knowledge. He is my closest and dearest friend in the world. I believe him when he says he's not a murderer."

"It is clear that you believe in his innocence, Gerry," Theo said gently. "Your faith and loyalty are admirable. I, too, would like to feel equally assured of his innocence, but I cannot. There are too many unexplained events."

D'Orsini rubbed his jaw, exposing a certain softness to his chin that belied his boyish appearance. "Permit me tell you what happened yesterday. It sounds rather damning, I'm afraid, but it is the truth. I was here by the pool all morning, catching up on correspondence and perusing the newspaper. I heard your group leave, and then I heard the car return some thirty minutes later, roughly at two o'clock. I thought nothing more about it until Eli came up my driveway an hour later, strutting as if he had wiped out the bank in Monte Carlo. It was an amazing sight, to say the least. Can I refill your glass, Bloomer?"

"No, thank you, this is sufficient."

"A bit leery of my hospitality?" Count D'Orsini laughed, then turned to look at the driveway. "Eli came up to the patio and threw himself down in a chair as if I'd suggested he wander by for cocktails. He proceeded to tell me that he was an undercover narcotics officer with the Jamaican Criminal Investigation Bureau, that he'd been observing me for several days, and that he had evidence that I'd engaged in a major transaction on this very spot. I naturally quizzed him as to the validity of his statements, and found him most convincing. Once I'd conceded his story, I asked him why he felt it proper to share the information with me—the object of his official scrutiny." He again laughed, but without sincerity. "Eli then brandished a roll of film and offered to sell it to me. He felt it would be of great interest to me—or to his superiors should I decline to purchase it."

"He was blackmailing you?" Theo said, frowning. "Did you tell this to Sergeant Stahl?"

"Ah, not precisely. I said Eli came over to see if the lawn needed attention. I saw no reason to introduce the issue of the film."

"They came across it when they searched his room in the preliminary investigation. It is being processed now, and I should imagine they will have prints at any moment."

Gerry put her hands over her face. "I told you, Hal. It's a matter of time before they come back to arrest you. You know what you have to do."

He pulled her hands away and gave her a smile of great tenderness. "I can't, darling. If they have the film, and if it depicts what Eli said it did, then there's nothing I can do. They'll stop me before I get twenty feet off the island. All I can do is insist that I didn't poison this police chap—and I didn't. After he suggested the deal, I could only laugh and show him an empty wallet. I did tell him that I would see what sort of cash I could lay my hands on, and that I'd get back to him when I was in a position to negotiate some sort of settlement. He was willing to give me a day or two."

"You do have a basis to argue your innocence," Theo said, tugging on his beard as he pondered the count's version of the events. Eli's expensive wardrobe and penchant for imported liquor did nothing to undermine it. "If Eli agreed to give you some time to acquire the money, and it seems reasonable to suppose he would, then you would have been most foolish to murder him in the interim. He wouldn't have given you the roll of film for safekeeping; he would have concealed it in a safe place. He was more dangerous dead than alive."

"That's true." Count D'Orsini stood up and began to pace across the patio. "I pointed out that I was hardly likely to hand over twenty grand until I saw exactly what he had. He said he would develop the film, show me the prints, and pass along the negatives when we concluded the deal. We actually shook hands when he left, as though we'd finalized a merger or contracted to purchase widgets from each other. It was downright eerie, if you ask me."

"It makes sense," Gerry said, suddenly coming to life. "Hal wouldn't have done anything until he saw the prints."

"The prints that show him either buying or selling cocaine to an associate," Theo pointed out drily. "Who was it, D'Orsini? Who's the connection?"

"It's hard to say, since it rather depends on when he took the photographs. He failed to be specific, and I was too unnerved to inquire in great detail." He began to pace again, turning sharply at the pool and coming within inches of a wicker sofa. "Don't you see that, Gerry? He could have caught a fetching likeness of that swarthy Colombian chap with the dirty fingernails, or more possibly my . . . ah, shall we say, entrepreneur friend."

"Either of whom has the same motive you do," Theo said. "Eli may have approached the second person, intending to collect from the two of you."

D'Orsini paused to think, then shook his head. "Not the Colombian. We merely tossed about some ideas for future transactions, and he left the island the next morning to confer with his partners at home. Furthermore, had Eli approached him, our pool boy would have been discovered without a face. The South American business types aren't subtle."

"And the other man?" Theo prompted.

"That would be telling, old chap. If the police have ascertained his identity, then they'll be more than delighted to tell." His face grew more animated; Theo could now see why women were attracted to him. "But," he added, flashing teeth as white and even as the petals of a snowcap shasta daisy, "the police haven't come screeching up the hill, sirens blaring, lights flashing, all that overly done sort of thing. It's perfectly quiet. I do think it's possible that this insidious roll of film was simply a threat on Eli's part." He knelt down in front of Gerry and took her hand, looking like a small, exuberant altar boy. "The roll may be a dud, darling. If so, they have nothing on me—or on anyone else. I'll be home free."

"Then you'll cease this deadly drug thing?" she asked in a hoarse voice. "You'll quit completely? You swear it?"

"And do what—work?" He turned to Theo with a self-deprecating grimace. "Harvard trained me to pull wonderful pranks, to use the correct silverware, to wear the proper clothing and say the proper things. A bit of French opens many a château door. All in all, it was a valuable experience, and I am quite indebted to the institution for that. But I was booted before I finished a degree, due to an unavoidable scandal that not even the dean, a liver-spotted pedant with limited imagination, could laugh away over a cigar and a glass of sherry. I'm not qualified to do anything useful. No, by damn, that's not totally accurate—I am a charming extra man at dinner parties, where I flatter the ugliest of the ducklings until they're so flustered they drink from the finger bowls. I use my talents to make otherwise lonely women feel cherished. I tend other people's houses and am meticulous about watering their plants, supervising their servants, and seeing that the lawn and the pets are groomed on a regular basis."

Gerry gave him a look of exasperated fondness. "You could work at my firm. It's not as exciting as jetting over to Nice for brunch and Paris for le cocktail hour, but it does keep one in groceries."

"But don't you see? I do work. It's not your perception of honest labor, but it really and truly is. Someone has to do this sort of thing. Babysitters do it on a primitive basis, tending to children. Servants do it, too, but for money. I do it for free." He squeezed her hand so tightly she winced. "I provide a necessary service to the idle wealthy, and I ask no payment in return. I accept what is offered, certainly, but for the most part it's a meal, the use of a house or yacht, a trinket of jewelry, a ticket to the theater, a little safari. What I receive is minor in comparison to what I give so freely."

Theo suspected the count was about to wax poetic over the intricacies of providing such a selfless public service to the jet set. He put down his glass and rose. "The police do have the roll of film and are presently developing it. You must be prepared to deal with that, although I do tend to believe you are not responsible for Eli's death."

"I would never murder someone," he said earnestly, still on his knees in front of Gerry. "For one thing, I've had no experience in that kind of endeavor, and I wouldn't have the slightest idea how to go about it. I suppose one could seek suggestions from a mystery novel, but I rarely have time to finish the *Gentleman's Quarterly* and *Town and Country* every month. For another thing, I do have a vestige of loyalty to the family name and I would never do anything to add to the disgrace I've already put on it. Mother was quite right to cut me off, you know; I hardly would have expected her to have done otherwise."

Theo did not point out that a conviction for drug trafficking might be considered a whack to the family tree. He thanked the two for the drink and went down the driveway, keeping an eye on the undergrowth on the off chance he might spot Mary Margaret's foot under the spectacular ferns (Heliconia). He did not.

Theo retired to his room, hung his jacket in the closet, aligned his shoes in the closet, and lay down on the bed with his guidebook to read a section on ferns (Heliconia). When he opened his eyes, more than an hour had passed. He discovered the book astraddle his chest and placed a bookmark in it before putting it on the bedside table. He was, he reminded himself sternly, sixty-one years old and unaccustomed to spending most of the night in a police station. Count D'Orsini had described the ordeal in the police station as "trying." "Trying" was a mild term, but of course the count was at least ten years younger—and had all his hair.

He was peering in the bathroom mirror at the shiny circle on the top of his head when his door opened. "Mr. Bloomer?" Bitsy said.

"Yes?" he said, coming out of the bathroom with a slightly guilty expression. Vanity was not a mortal sin, but he did not wish to be caught in the act.

"That policeman is back, and he's absolutely frothing about the mouth. He brought a herd of men with him, and they're searching the entire house. They actually insisted on pawing through my lingerie, if you can believe it. It's nasty, and probably illegal."

Theo realized he had been hearing some activity for several minutes, although he had not assumed it came from an invasion of the magnitude Bitsy described. "I have no idea if a search warrant is required in Jamaica, but it does seem worth the bother to inquire. Where is Sergeant Stahl?"

"On the terrace. He's drinking our coffee and talking to your friend." The implicit accusation hung in the momentary silence. "I cannot bear to watch them going through my private things, so if you don't mind, I shall wait in here," she added in an indignant squeak.

Theo saw several policemen in the master bedroom as he went downstairs, but he did not linger to discuss the legality of their activity. He stopped in the kitchen to request a glass of water, but the room was uninhabited. Drawers had been pulled open; cabinet doors were ajar. Canisters had been placed on the counter—and searched, if the scattered flour and sugar were valid indications. Cases of beer had been pulled into the middle of the floor, and the contents of the refrigerator were piled on the table. Amelia and Emelda were gone, no doubt in a huff more indignant than that of the occupant of his bedroom.

Stahl and Sitermann were on the terrace, a tray with coffee and cups on the table between them. Trey sat at the far end of the table, his feet propped on the table and his hands wrapped loosely around a beer can. He appeared to be lost in his thoughts, although Theo was beginning to surmise he was merely lost.

Dorrie, Biff, Sandy, and Sandy's golf bag were lined up against the rail. Dorrie was pinker than a foxglove (*D. purpurea*); the boys' faces had the more mottled hues of a rosita lily. Dismayed by the proximity of weapons (irons, woods, and hard white spheres), Theo gave the bag a cautionary glance as he pulled out a chair and sat down. "Looking for something?" he inquired politely.

Stahl nodded with a stony expression, but Sitermann said, "The sergeant was not happy about the results from the photo lab. To be honest with you, he was more than a mite disappointed with the roll of film."

"Overexposed? Too dark?"

"No," drawled Sitermann, leaning back in his chair, "the lighting was pretty damn good for an amateur. Focus wasn't bad, and neither was the composition. One of them might win a prize in a photography contest. Of course it'd have to be sponsored by *Playboy* or one of that ilk."

"And why is that?"

"I don't think I should explain out loud, not with a fine, upstanding young lady present, Bloom." He picked up an envelope from the table and handed it to Theo. "Take a peek and you'll see how awkward it might be to verbalize the problem."

Theo took out the prints and studied them. The first was of Mary Margaret, her eyes closed and a serene smile on her face. Her breasts were bereft of any clothing. The second centered on her buttocks, which were snowy white hills of unimpeded flesh. "Oh, goodness," Theo murmured, primly moving on to the next print. It featured not only Mary Margaret's breasts, but also a totally bewildered gentleman with a balding head and scandalously wide eyes behind bifocals.

"I especially liked that one," Sitermann said. He slapped Theo on the back. "Your peepers are about to pop right out of their sockets, aren't they? That must have been some camera sweep. A right delicate closeup of something most men would kill for, in a manner of speaking."

"Uncle Theo!" Dorrie said in a shocked voice. "You didn't really stare at . . . at whatever Mr. Sitermann is snickering about, did you?"

"Right on, Mr. Bloomer," Sandy said. "You're my kind of guy."

Dorrie swiveled her head to give him a withering look. "I can assure you that my uncle is not 'your kind of guy,' Alexander Whitcombe. I find these tawdry insinuations juvenile and primitive. You may be both, but Uncle Theo is neither." She rotated her head in case Biff felt a urge to contribute his opinion. He did not.

Theo hastily put the prints back in the envelope. "May I assume they are all of a similar nature?" he asked Sitermann.

"Prone and supine. Nude, nuder, nudest, and whatever comes after that. Mary Margaret made a fine model, didn't she? I really ought to arrange a screen test for her."

"Uncle Theo," Dorrie began ominously, "is this—"

Sergeant Stahl banged down his cup. "The entire roll of film consists of this sort of thing, Mr. Bloomer. I personally badgered the lab men for several hours to hurry them along, and will now owe favors for a long time to come. I was disappointed, very disappointed, especially since you had led me to believe we would find something of value to the investigation. I was not prepared for pornography."

"Pornography?" With an outraged expression, Sitermann bounced his hand off his forehead. "This isn't pornography, Stahl; this is art. Why, I'd gladly have one of them blown up to poster size and hung in my living room right over the mantel. Did you see the tits on that girl? Old J. Edgar himself would've had a coronary if—''

''Uncle Theo,'' Dorrie said, her expression as icy as her voice, ''muzzle that man or I shall do it myself. He has no right to expose me to this locker room vernacular.'' She glared at the spy until he wilted into his chair like a dog's tooth violet in a drought.

''Yeah, watch your language,'' Biff said gallantly, if belatedly.

''I understand your disappointment,'' Theo said to Stahl. ''There was reasonably credible evidence that the film was shot from the balcony and that it would implicate Count D'Orsini and an unknown associate.''

''But it seems my top officer wasn't occupying himself with the investigation. It seems he had other things on his mind—and in his expensive lenses. That equipment cost a great deal of money. I didn't requisition it so that Staggley could indulge in voyeurism.'' He snatched up the envelope before Sitermann, whose hand was moving stealthily across the table, could reach it. ''What's more, we don't have a damn thing on D'Orsini now. With the pressure we've gotten in the last eighteen hours, we wouldn't dare give him a parking ticket if he drove through a wall and parked in the middle of the police station.''

Dorrie stepped forward. ''I still don't understand why you've taken it upon yourself to search the villa. We certainly don't have Eli's film canisters tucked in among our panties, although it might be an appropriate place for them.''

''Yeah,'' Biff said, nodding. ''Do you have a constitutional right to do this—or a good old-fashioned search warrant? Dorrie's father has some high-power connections, and he'll be totally pissed when he finds out how your men have—''

''Sir,'' a uniformed officer said, coming from the dining room, ''we found this in the downstairs bedroom.'' He held up a plastic baggie. ''It's ganja, sir. About three-quarters of an ounce.''

Trey flapped his hand. "Oh, that's mine. Be a good sport and put it back where you found it. I promise not to say a word if you want a little toke, but don't make a pig of yourself."

"Possession of a controlled substance is a felony in Jamaica," Sergeant Stahl said coldly.

"I told you to get rid of it," Dorrie hissed.

Trey gave her an indulgent smile. "Yes, you did, darling, and several times if I recall. But I didn't, did I? You may have enough pocket money to squander it; I, on the other hand, have been trained from birth to pinch every penny, since we all know that's why the rich stay richer. Do you think that's the reason I do so love to pinch bottoms, too? A nasty habit learned from dear old nanny?"

The uniformed man had been following the exchange with growing amusement, but he sobered when he caught Stahl's glower. "What shall I do, sir? Do you want me to arrest him and transport him to headquarters to be booked?"

"Tedious, too tedious," Trey said with a yawn.

Theo wanted to suggest tar and feathers, but instead said, "It is a minimal amount for personal consumption, Sergeant Stahl. I hope you won't allow this young man's behavior to influence your decision."

"I think you ought to nuke him," Dorrie said. She marched through the door into the villa. Biff trailed after her, murmuring to the back of her head.

Trey held out his wrists. "Have your way with me, Sergeant. Handcuff me, swallow the key, and drag me to some filthy prison cell populated with lepers and rats. Or, if you prefer, I can trot downstairs and fetch my checkbook. I could make it out to you personally, if you prefer. That way it won't have to detour through the system."

Blinking at Trey, the officer said, "I am impressed with your obviously fervent desire to spend several more years in Jamaica, with room and board provided by the national penal system. However, I fail to understand your motivation to do so. Do you not think life will be pleasanter in your parents' home in Connecticut?''

"It's a toss-up, actually. Hanging around the family mausoleum is boring, especially if Magsy's not about to needle. My parents have always encouraged me to meet new people and try new experiences.''

Stahl sighed. "I won't take any immediate action concerning the illegal possession—but I won't rule out the possibility of doing so in the future. At the moment, I'd rather find a roll of film that will provide evidence of D'Orsini's involvement. Maybe it doesn't exist. Maybe Staggley spent his idle moments photographing the young lady in various stages of undress.''

"But if there is a second roll of film, why do you think it's inside the house, sir?'' Sandy asked. "Wouldn't Eli have been more likely to leave it with his family or with a friend?''

"I have no expectations that we'll find it,'' Stahl conceded in a wry tone, "but it seemed prudent to look around for it. I don't understand why he didn't bring it to the police lab the next morning to be developed. If he had, we would have concluded the investigation, arrested D'Orsini, picked up the associates, and handed the entire thing over to the prosecutor. Staggley knew better, damnit!''

Theo felt obliged to explain why Eli had not taken the roll of film to the police lab. He related the blackmail attempt, D'Orsini's admission of complicity, and the settlement the two had reached concerning a delayed exchange of goods and services. Once Stahl had stopped growling, Theo added, "D'Orsini did not imply he'd actually seen this roll of film, but it seems likely Eli had it in his possession at that moment. However, it is possible that it might be at a private developing service.''

"I'll put Winkler on it immediately,'' Stahl said, standing up. "As much as I'd like to drag D'Orsini right back down to the station, I'll have to wait until we have evidence.'' He jabbed a finger in Trey's direction. "And as for you, you retarded little snot, keep your nose clean if you don't want to learn some of our island techniques for eliciting confessions. A checkbook won't do you any good, and neither will your family's money."

"Yes, sir." Trey made a sweeping gesture with his hand. "And have a nice day, sir. It was lovely to see you once again. Perhaps you and the wife can drop by some evening for a drink."

Theo grabbed Stahl's arm and hurried him down the steps to the driveway. "There's something I'd like to discuss with you, Sergeant."

"Capital punishment? It's not legal, but it can be arranged."

"Forget about the Ellison boy; he is, as you said so eloquently, a retarded little snot. There is a problem about the prints you obtained from the roll of film in Eli's room."

"Yeah," Stahl said, beginning to grin, "they show an old man lusting after a naked girl. Ooh, she sure does have knockers, doesn't she? We're still watching for her. My men are working their way through all the bars and parties, but there are a daunting number of them and it takes time. I don't suppose you've had any word from her yet?"

"No, not a peep. But we both know I was present when at least some of those photographs were taken. The problem is that I'm not at all sure that Eli was."

"You were too busy staring at those big round nipples to see who else was around, Bloomer." He held up his hands in mock defense. "I'm not saying that in criticism, either. I sure as hell wouldn't have been analyzing the bushes for covert camera equipment. My wife could have been standing on her head in a palm tree, along with her mother and my boss; I wouldn't have seen any of them."

Theo gave him a pained look. "I will admit that I was rather taken aback when I first opened my eyes, in that I expected to see nothing more startling than a few of the young people preparing to sunbathe in normal attire. Indeed, I was momentarily at a loss for words. But once I recovered from my initial confusion, the girl apologized and went to the far side of the pool.''

"And stripped? Ooh, ooh, ooh," Stahl said gleefully.

"She did remove her bikini in order to avoid tan marks. However, I was unable to continue my nap, and I did not see Eli anywhere in the vicinity of the pool.''

"Oh, Bloomer, don't tell me you spent the rest of the afternoon watching the steps from the driveway to the patio around the pool. I know damn well what you looked at—and it wasn't some ocean liner out in the pristine waters of MoBay." Laughing, Stahl went down the driveway and drove away in a white police car.

Theo simmered in silence until he could trust himself to return to the terrace. When he did, he found Sitermann and Sandy seated at the table. The coffeepot had been replaced with a pitcher of rum punch, and the two were arguing amiably about the utility of woods on the fairway.

As Theo took a seat, Sandy looked up. "Ah, Mr. Bloomer, the policeman never showed us the actual photographs, but I gathered from what was said that they were of Mary Margaret . . . in the flesh. What do you think that means?''

Sitermann snickered. "What I'd like to know is how we can get our hands on the negatives.''

"I would hate to imagine the look on the obstetrician's face the day you were born," Theo said to the spy. "But as for the odd roll of film, Sandy, I'm not sure what it means. If I hadn't been an unwitting participant, I would have presumed that Eli persuaded Mary Margaret to engage in a private session while the rest of us were occupied.''

"The look on *your* face," Sitermann cackled, thumping Theo on the back. "Lordy, Bloom, you were about as bewildered as a nun in a soap opera!''

"To continue," Theo said, "at least some of the photographs were taken the first afternoon of our trip, not too long after our arrival. Most of you went upstairs to unpack. I went down to the pool, where I inadvertently dozed off for a few minutes. When I awoke, Mary Margaret was nearby, dressed—or should I say undressed—to some extent." He ran a finger around his collar as heat raced up his neck. "I tend to think Eli was not even at the villa at that time, that he had gone to fetch ice or a newspaper."

"Then you think Eli was in cahoots with someone?" Sandy asked.

"You bet your time-share in Bermuda," Sitermann inserted. "And whoever it is ought to be put up for an Oscar for cinematography, or whatever you call fancy camera work."

"And you ought to be put out of your misery," Theo said testily.

10

Sitermann left in a flurry of crude innuendos that Theo might be more of a rogue than one might assume on first appraisal. Sandy picked up his golf bag and started for the dining room.

"I'm amazed you found the energy to play golf after such a difficult night," Theo said, shaking his head at the very idea of physical exertion. "How was the course?"

"When the uniforms swarmed in, I went to the backyard to practice chip shots," Sandy admitted. "I see too many of them at school. Biff and I are going to try to get in eighteen holes later this afternoon." His scalp turned pink under his stubby blond hair. "Is Mary Margaret's anatomy some kind of clue, sir?"

"Go polish your putter." Theo went to the kitchen in hopes that Amelia and Emelda had returned. They had not. With a sigh, he located Gerry's number on a business card taped near the telephone and dialed the number.

"North Shore Property Management," she answered listlessly.

He identified himself, then apologetically mentioned that the residents of the villa did not have a key to the gate.

"I suppose the police have Eli's key. I'll have a copy made and have a messenger bring it over immediately. This terrible mess has left me in a walking fog, and I didn't think about the key. How did all of you get in the gate last night?''

"We managed," Theo said evasively. He went on to report that the staff had vanished, most likely because of a police invasion of the kitchen, and very well might not reappear anytime soon. He did not intend to cause difficulty, but it was—well, somewhat of a crisis, since his young people were not likely to respond well to the proposal that they all pitch in. Any inherent spirit of self-sacrificing volunteerism lay in the arena of charity functions, black ties, large orchestras, and an opportunity to display the family jewels to an audience with appreciative tastes.

"I'll call Amelia and plead," she said in the same flat voice. "You'll be leaving in two days, so I can even offer her time-and-a-half for . . . combat duty. Have you heard anything from the police? Did they show you the prints?"

"Yes," he said, relieved that she could not see the redness creeping up his neck, "and at this point Count D'Orsini may be safe from any kind of prosecution. The roll of film did not contain any incriminating shots of him in the middle of a transaction with this mysterious associate."

"Oh, thank God. Then the police aren't planning to arrest Hal? He would be brutalized in jail, and probably wouldn't last a month. I've got to call him and tell him. Despite his show of bravado earlier today, he was absolutely terrified of what might happen. He will be so thrilled to know he's safe."

Theo interrupted before she could say good-bye and ring off. "There's something you and D'Orsini should consider. The roll of film that the police now have may not be the only one in existence; it's possible Eli left the pertinent one with a friend. The police have searched here and in Eli's quarters, but they haven't given up yet. They're currently checking with the private film laboratories. It very well may surface somewhere."

"Oh," she said, deflating more quickly than a punctured balloon. "Then you think Hal is still in danger of being arrested?''

"I don't know." He gazed at the two ackees on the windowsill. "There is something else which you ought to discuss with D'Orsini, Gerry. This so-called associate of his might have decided to murder Eli rather than deal with the blackmail demands. Now that the film has failed to expose him, D'Orsini is the only person who knows his identity. If he has killed once, then he may decide to do so again in order to lay to rest any possibility that he might be identified in the future."

There was a very long moment of silence. Theo could hear her breath against the receiver as she considered his words. "No," she said slowly, "I think Hal is safe. I'll tell him what you said, and warn him of the possible danger. He'll be cautious until this is resolved."

"The only way in which he can be safe is to tell the police the identity of this associate."

"That would prove a little more complicated than you think. But it is kind of you to be concerned, and I will speak to Hal about taking precautions until the police can solve the murder. Now I'll telephone Amelia and see if she and Emelda can be persuaded to return for the rest of the week. It will take some bribery, but I suspect they'll agree."

Frowning, Theo replaced the receiver. The roll of film was a puzzle. The lens cap had been found on the balcony of Dorrie's bedroom, and it had been plausible to conclude someone had taken a series of photographs of occurrences next door. Now it seemed the camera had been aimed in quite a different direction, although it made little sense. Eli had told Count D'Orsini the film was incriminating. Surely Eli had known which way he was pointed—and at what subject. He had agreed to produce the prints, and it would have been more than whimsical to hope to collect any blackmail money by flourishing the study of unclad flesh. Neither art nor pornography would motivate D'Orsini into paying twenty thousand dollars.

So where was the roll of film that Eli valued and D'Orsini feared? It was not in the villa, Theo decided as his frown deepened, and not in Eli's quarters. Eli had, however, shown it to D'Orsini around the middle of the afternoon, then returned to the villa, mixed a pitcher of rum punch, and gone up to the pool to celebrate his anticipated windfall. By that time, Amelia and Emelda were already gone. The gate had been secured. There had been no hint that Eli was working with someone else.

"Drat," Theo said to himself, permitting a euphemism for a more volatile word. The situation warranted as much. He spent a few minutes cleaning up the kitchen, then went upstairs and knocked on Dorrie's door. He flinched only a bit when she opened the door, her hair hidden under a terrycloth turban and her face smeared with a pea green paste the precise shade of the foliage of the Carolina allspice (*Calycanthus floridus*). Although he was unsure of the chemical basis of the substance, he had encountered it in the past and been informed it did something quite astounding to her complexion. Of that, he had no doubt.

"I wondered if I might interrupt you long enough to engage in a small experiment," he said. He entered the room and carefully closed the door. "I'm still pondering the mystery of the film."

A slit formed in the pea green mask. "It's not in here, Uncle Theo. Those beastly policemen searched every nook and cranny, not to mention every cosmetic bag, beach bag, suitcase, lingerie drawer, and bottle of shampoo. Bitsy was an absolute basket case by the time they were finished. It was almost—but not quite—worth it."

"I presume the police would have found it if it were in the villa. What has been bothering me is that set of prints. I cannot believe Eli would be murdered over such photographs."

"Yeah," she said, smoothing the paste along her nose with a practiced swoop of her index finger. "Mary Margaret's not all that hot. So what's this experiment? In six minutes I have to scrub this off and move on to the moisturizing base. If I'm delayed, the consequences may be devastating."

"It will take only a second. I was wondering about the camera angle from the balcony." He went across the room and out onto the balcony. Shading his eyes with a hand, he looked down at the terrace immediately below and the pool beyond it. Bitsy was seated in the chair he'd taken that first afternoon, when Mary Margaret had caught him by surprise. Although he had a clear view, the angle was clearly wrong. He then glanced at the side of the pool where Mary Margaret had retreated to continue her sunbathing. The edge of the terrace extended into his view, blocking off most of that area of the deck.

Dorrie tapped him on the shoulder. "Four minutes and counting. What's the conclusion, Uncle Sherlock? Did Eli shoot that roll of film from my balcony?"

"No, he did not," Theo said pensively. "Sergeant Stahl was behaving in such an adolescent manner that he would not listen when I tried to make the point that Eli could not have been on the balcony at that time. I certainly would have seen him. Bitsy was upstairs changing and would hardly fail to remark on the intrusion. And in any case, the angle is wrong." He swiveled his head to look over the fence at D'Orsini's pool and patio. The area around the bar was visible, as was the grouping of rattan furniture and most of the pool. "This does offer a reasonable view, however. Under cover of darkness, one easily could creep out here, set up a tripod, and take all the photographs one wished of activities next door."

"Three minutes and counting. Maybe Mary Margaret went over there to sunbathe. She seemed terribly possessive about dear Uncle Billy's old school chum—and he is male, over fifteen, titled, and wealthy. Any one of those qualifications could have sucked Magsy over the fence like a two-ton magnet."

"But I was on our deck," Theo reminded her. "And although D'Orsini is indeed male and over fifteen, I'm not at all sure his title is credible. I doubt he's wealthy."

"Poor Mary Margaret's in for a shockeroo, then. First

believing Sitermann was a hotshot Hollywood producer, and then salivating all over Count D'Orsini and his yacht. Did he rent it from Hertz for the day?''

"He's tending it for friends, along with the villa. And he is involved in the transportation of cocaine, although he claims only in a small fashion. He admitted it to me early this afternoon.''

"Two and one-half minutes. Then did he murder Eli when he learned he was a narc?''

Theo related the highlights of the blackmail attempt and the reasons why he felt fairly certain D'Orsini had not poisoned Eli. He was in the midst of stressing the necessity of finding the notorious roll of film when Dorrie glanced at her watch, shrieked, and ran toward the bathroom. The slam of the door was followed by the splash of water in the sink. The conversation, for all intents and purposes, seemed to be at an end.

Theo went out to the landing and started toward his room. But after a single step in that direction, he turned on his heel, marched the few feet down the hall, and rapped on Biff and Sandy's door. Biff, dressed in boxer shorts and socks, opened the door. "Yes, sir?''

"We need to talk, my boy," Theo said. "I think we will realize more enlightenment if we do so in private.''

"Sure, sir. Sandy's in the shower, and I was waiting my turn. I don't understand why there's this urgent need for privacy.'' When Theo continued to regard him through unblinking eyes, he stepped back and held open the door. "I am totally in the dark, Mr. Bloomer, but, sure, come on in. Sandy won't be able to hear anything while the water's running. He takes incredibly long showers, because he's only allowed a minute or two at the academy and he swears hot water is almost as nifty as cold beer. Would you like to sit down, sir? We have some ice if you'd like a drink. The potato chips are stale, but—''

"I would like to look out your window," Theo said firmly. "I am interested in the potential camera angles.''

"Wow, sure, help yourself." Biff's face turned scarlet as he busied himself with the ice bucket and glasses. "Ah, does this have anything to do with Dorrie, Mr. Bloomer? I mean, you're her uncle and I know she really dotes on you, but you don't have to get involved—"

"A charming view, charming. Why, you can see the Caribbean, the tops of the villas below us, the street, the yard—and the patio around the pool. The view is amazing, if somewhat unexciting at the moment. A nude sunbather would add an element of interest, don't you think?"

"Yeah, the view's super." He gave Theo a glass of Perrier, then sat down on the bed and sighed noisily. "You're not going to tell Dorrie, are you? She'll work herself up to such a snit that she won't speak to me for a month. I'll have to send flowers, buy presents, call her ten times a day so that she can hang up on me, and literally crawl around on my knees until they bleed. We have a really good shot for the mixed doubles title in the Labor Day tournament at the club. God, I'd hate to let Akinson and his sister win it for the third straight year. Akinson is such a prick."

"It may occur to her without any assistance on my part. However, I won't say anything, in that I am also aware of her probable reaction to the news that you took a series of photographs of another woman. The additional fact that your subject lacked clothing will not help you plead your case. But how did your roll of film end up in Eli's room below the pool?"

"Beats me, Mr. Bloomer. Dorrie always insists I take the film to one of those one-hour places so that she can see the results as soon as possible. Somehow, I figured it might be smarter to wait until we got home to take that roll to some little hole of a place where they don't know me. I just stuck the film in my camera case and started a new roll. Until I realized what those prints were, I had no idea it wasn't in my case."

"Have you examined the case? It's possible someone exchanged the two rolls, thinking it would be a safe hiding place. Poe did that sort of thing with a letter once, and it worked well.''

"I was here when the police searched the room. I was floored when they found no used film in the camera case, since I was preparing to explain why they didn't want to confiscate that roll. You know,'' he said, bristling a bit, "someone must have taken that film.''

"Very good, Biff. The most obvious suspect is Eli, who did prowl in the villa when we were gone, but I cannot imagine why he would take a roll of film from your room. Although in reality the subject matter was less than ordinary, he would have anticipated nothing more interesting than palm trees and beaches, with Dorrie smiling in the center.''

"Yeah, it's totally mind-boggling.'' Biff went to the window and looked down at the pool. "What have the police found out about Mary Margaret? Do they have any theory about what might have happened to her? I mean, it's been less than twenty-four hours since she vanished, but something could have happened to her.''

"I have the feeling that they're not especially worried about her, that they continue to believe she disappeared for her own reasons,'' said Theo. He noted the tautness of Biff's shoulders as he added, "I have not yet told them that her father received a ransom demand this morning.''

Biff spun around, a shocked expression on his face. "Holy shit! She's been kidnapped? What does that mean, Mr. Bloomer? Shouldn't we do something? Is she in danger?''

"Kidnap victims are usually in some danger,'' Theo said, wondering how Biff had made it through the entrance exams for his school—or even primary school. Nursery school. "I have some doubts that she was taken against her will, however. We were all sitting on the terrace, and we would have heard something had she been grabbed from behind. Count D'Orsini would have heard a scuffle, or even a muffled cry. He claims to have heard nothing, and Sitermann says he saw no traffic along the street.''

"But, wow, a ransom note . . .'' Biff sank down on the

bed and stared blankly at the small pink hearts sprinkled on his shorts. "How much? Did old Win have a coronary when he saw the figure? Has he sent the money?"

"Dorrie's mother told him to ignore the demand, and she would not have tolerated a coronary in the breakfast room. She told me to deal with the situation from this end, and to bring Mary Margaret home intact."

"Have you figured out what you're going to do, Mr. Bloomer?"

"Not with any sense of direction. Any suggestions?"

"No, sir. This is just an absolute mess, isn't it? I think I'm going to start locking my door at night. But now that Eli's dead, we won't have anyone to keep the gate locked. It could be dangerous without any security system."

"Are you proposing to take charge of security?" Theo asked curiously.

Biff gave him a bewildered look. "Me? No, sir. But I will call the police and tell them to station a man at the gate. If they're toads about it, we can have that real estate woman send over a new man. After all, we're paying for a full package of servants. There's no reason why we ought to settle for anything less than that."

"Of course not," Theo said. He put down his glass and went downstairs to see if Amelia and Emelda had returned. They had not. He considered calling Gerry, but opted instead to retreat to the terrace and let things proceed of their own accord. They seemed to be doing so despite his best efforts.

When Dorrie joined him, he pointed to a photograph in one of the brochures Gerry had left for them. "I am thinking about taking the tour of Rose Hall," he said. "It's not far, and it promises to be interesting. Would you care to join me?"

"A guided tour of an old house?" Her complexion, charmingly radiant, paled. "Uncle Theo, you know how much I detest being led around old places with a herd of sweaty tourists right off the street. I always get tired, and those guides absolutely expire if you so much as glance at a chair. It's not as if I haven't sat on Chippendale since I was a toddler. My high chair was Regency.''

"This house has quite a legend, my dear. It seems the mistress murdered three husbands, took numerous lovers, had slaves beheaded, and generally spilled a lot of blood until her slaves revolted and murdered her in her bed.''

"Really?'' Dorrie said, covering a yawn.

"Rose Hall is a restored plantation great house, built in the late-eighteenth-century Georgian style. Also, it is rumored to be haunted,'' Theo persisted. "Annie Palmer's grave is in the East Garden. I would like to catch a glimpse of a garden, even one marred by a grave.''

"Oh, I am being beastly! I swore I'd go to all those gardens, didn't I? You were a dear to come with us, and I ought to be a good sport and go with you.'' Her lower lip crept out in a delicately girlish pout. "It's just that I've made no progress to speak of on my tan. With all these policemen stomping around, I haven't had any time at all to relax and work on that hideous white line across my back. But I will go with you if you wish, because you're my very favorite uncle.'' She studied him through her eyelashes as she produced a coy smile intended to disarm him.

"Good,'' Theo said, picking up the brochure and tucking it in his coat pocket. "Get your purse; I'll meet you at the car.'' He went down to the driveway and bent over to examine the air pressure of the tires, being careful to avoid any glances in the direction of the terrace. He did hear a sharp exhalation of breath, followed by a despondent word or two, and footsteps that seemed to drag across the surface of the terrace and ultimately into the dining room beyond.

"How long will this take?'' Dorrie asked as Theo parked behind a tour bus.

"The tour lasts only half an hour, unless we chance upon a ghost or two. You can compare the furniture here with that of your mother's, or simply sit in the shade while I explore the garden.''

Dorrie eyed the group of tourists coming around the corner of the house. "Schoolteachers from Iowa," she said under her breath. "I'm going to spend hours and hours and hours in the company of schoolteachers from Iowa. I should have made Biff come along, but he was acting very odd when I went by his room. He was as nervous as a junior golfer at his first tournament. What on earth could be wrong with him, Uncle Theo?"

"He might be upset about the murder of someone he knew," Theo suggested as they walked toward the house.

"We're all upset about that. I'm hardly accustomed to spending the night in dreary, grimy police stations, or having my lingerie pawed by policemen in Bermuda shorts. But I haven't allowed that to cast a nasty shadow on my spirits, have I?" She caught Theo's arm and stopped him. "Do you think he's all distraught about Mary Margaret's disappearance?"

"I told him of the ransom note," Theo said, nudging her back into motion as a tour bus bore down on them. "It's quite normal to be concerned when one of your friends may be in danger."

"Friend," she muttered under her breath, sending a malevolent look at the group spewing forth from the bus.

They followed a guide dressed in a print skirt through the great house, obediently eyeing the furniture when instructed to do so, then went to the East Garden to ponder the grave of the Witch of Rose Hall. Dorrie had been quiet the entire time, and Theo was not surprised when she suggested they find a place to sit in the shade for a serious conversation.

"What do you think is going on, Uncle Theo?" she asked once they were perched on a low rock wall. "Who left the poisoned rum for Eli? If Count D'Orsini didn't, then someone else did. I can't imagine either Amelia or Emelda having any reason to do him in, but it has to be someone with access to the villa. Do you suppose that real estate woman is involved?"

Theo tugged at his beard for a moment. "She is a very

good friend of Count D'Orsini and might do almost anything to save him from the clutches of the police. But the murder of Eli increased D'Orsini's peril, rather than alleviated it."

"But it alleviated someone's peril. The exchange of the film protected the identity of D'Orsini's so-called associate. Don't you think it was the same person?"

"We have at least three unknown factors. Someone took an ackee from the kitchen and used it to poison a bottle of rum. We shall assume, for simplicity's sake, that the same person then either presented it to Eli as a gift or left it in his room. That's one person." Theo held up a finger. "Someone exchanged the film from Eli's camera with another. That's two." As he held up a second finger, he caught her sudden frown. Hurriedly, he added, "The mysterious business associate was implicated by the film Eli shot and might have chosen extreme measures to avoid blackmail. That's three—unless any of the said factors are one in the same."

"Let's go back to number two," Dorrie said. "Eli couldn't have taken that film; you yourself said as much earlier this afternoon. He was probably on my balcony that night to photograph the goings-on next door, but he didn't take the shots of the unclad walrus." She took a deep breath and let it out slowly. Her voice grew icy as she continued, "There's only one other person at the villa with a camera, Uncle Theo. That person has been behaving very strangely lately. That person—"

"Hey, could you do us a favor?" A woman in shorts, a T-shirt, and a straw hat approached them. "I hate to interrupt, but we're dying to get a group shot of all of us, so we can show it to our colleagues in the teachers' lounge when we get back to Boise. Would you take a picture of us in front of the witch's grave?"

"I would be charmed," Theo said, standing up to accept the proffered camera. He abandoned his niece, who was now growling with the vehemence of a pit bull terrier, and trailed the woman across the garden. He waited patiently as the group, identified through their chirps as Carolyn, Mo, Belinda, Angela, and Esther, jostled each other into position. When they had satisfied themselves, they produced bright smiles and Theo took the shot.

"Let's do a really goofy one," one of them suggested. "After all, this witch was a first-class murderer, and we ought to go for the drama of the locale. How about if I'm strangling Esther in front of the house, while the rest of you cringe in the background? Mr. Wooten would love it."

"You're perfect as the witch," another said, laughing, "but I'm not sure I can play one of your husbands. Let Belinda do it—her voice is deeper and she does have that darling little mustache."

"I beg your pardon! I do not have a darling little mustache. I spent a fortune on electrolysis, and you couldn't find a hair on a bet."

"How much do you want to bet, sweetie?"

"How about your pension, honey?"

With a vague smile, Theo returned the camera to its owner and went to find Dorrie. She was in the same position, as if made of marble, although he could detect a faint line across her forehead. Her expression was as stony as the wall on which she sat.

"Biff took those photographs, didn't he?" she said as Theo sat down beside her. "He took a whole roll of Mary Margaret in the flesh, so to speak."

Theo nodded. "Once I examined the angle from your balcony, it became obvious the photographer was stationed in the center of the upstairs story, rather than the corner. I confronted your young man, and he admitted it."

"And you didn't tell me?"

"He asked me not to," Theo said apologetically. "He did not want to upset you any more than necessary."

"How totally considerate of him." Dorrie snatched up her purse and began to stalk toward the parking lot. "I wouldn't be surprised if he had kidnapped Mary Margaret and stashed her in a love nest in some seedy hotel," she added as Theo caught up with her. "They arranged for the ransom note to

be delivered to dear old Daddy, hoping to take the money
and elope to South America or some such primitive place.
Eat tamales and watch the sun set over the ocean. Servants
to bring those icky drinks with umbrellas in them. Silk sheets
and—'' She broke off with a gulp, then ducked her head to
wipe her eyes with a trembling hand.

"Now, Dorrie," Theo said, alarmed at the un-Caldicottish
public display of emotion. "It was a boyish prank, very typ-
ical of the mentality. Boys do buy magazines with photographs of . . . of women in disarray, but it hardly implies
they're sex maniacs or conspirators in kidnap schemes.''

"Right." She got in the car and slammed the door. "I'd
prefer to return to the villa now, if you don't mind."

"How about a nice drive along the coast? It might give
you an opportunity to cool off before we go to the villa."

"Why ever would I want to cool off, Uncle Theo? I'm
perfectly composed at this moment."

In that her words had been spat from between clenched
teeth, Theo was less than convinced. He saw no way to divert
her, however, so he put the key in the ignition and turned on
the engine. He was fumbling with the gear shift when a hand
rapped on his window. A florid face loomed over the wind-
shield, grinning gleefully.

Theo reluctantly rolled down the window. "What, Sitermann? We were about to leave, and it's too warm for idle
discussions."

"I saw you with those lovely ladies with the dimpled knees
and luscious rumps, you old Romeo, you. Are you trying to
set a record for wooing women in paradise?"

"They requested that I take a group photograph. I did.
Now, if that's all, we're leaving. You may follow us if you
wish, since it seems to be your favorite hobby these days.
Perhaps it will help you to know our destination—the villa."

"Me following you?" Sitermann put his hand over his
heart as he gave Theo a pained look. "Is it not possible that
I am visiting the touristy highlights of the island, attempting

to soak up some sense of history and culture, exploring the traditions and life-styles of the natives?''

"No." Theo began to roll up the window, risking a glance across the car at his niece. She still resembled a marble statue, her face frozen and her jaw extended to an ominous angle that forbode ill for Biff. If she had heard any of the previous remarks, they had not interested her.

"Well, Bloom," Sitermann yelled through the glass, "I guess I'll see if your lovely lady friends over there need any technical assistance from a real, live Hollywood producer."

Theo rolled down the window a cautious inch. "What they need is a male to portray a husband being throttled. Would you like me to scribble a recommendation for you to play that part? I would be more than delighted to arrange for your death scene, mock or real."

"If I didn't know you better, I'd let my tender soul be wounded by that, old man. But I know you have a genuine fondness for me, so I'll let your petty little ripostes go right over my head."

"I would like to leave now," Dorrie said.

"A wonderful idea." Theo rolled up the window, gave Sitermann a small wave, and backed around the tour bus. They bumped down the rutted road to the highway, also rutted, and drove back toward Harmony Hills. The name seemed increasingly incongruous with each hour that passed.

11

They drove to the villa in cold, cold silence. Once Theo had parked, Dorrie got out of the car and swept inside, her expression the essence of Caldicottian fury. Theo hesitated for a moment, wondering if the walls were apt to come tumbling down, then eased through the side door and listened intently. Nothing. He checked the kitchen, but it was exactly as he had left it and still quite unpopulated. He returned to the dining room and listened once again for sounds of conversation or violence from upstairs. It was, he thought soberly, very much like the calm before the storm. If he had judged Dorrie's mood correctly (and he feared he had), then the storm would be a full-blown hurricane, worthy of both name and notoriety in the annals of meteorology.

Feeling a little silly, he tiptoed across the dining room and went out to the terrace. Bitsy was occupying the chair under the umbrella, the magazine replaced by a paperback novel. The boys were nowhere to be seen, and Dorrie was likely to remain upstairs, sharpening both her tongue and a fingernail file.

"Are you enjoying the sun?" he called as he went down to the pool. "Would I be disrupting your solitude if I joined you?"

Bitsy glanced up with only a flicker of annoyance. "No,

I'd love some company, Mr. Bloomer,'' she said as she closed her book and put it in her lap. "Sandy and Biff walked down the hill to the golf course, although Biff didn't look very excited about the prospect of a round of golf. Now that I think about it, the poor baby looked rather distraught. Sandy must have been desperate for company. Some man from the real estate office came by with a key; it's on the dining room table. Where did you and Dorrie go?''

He told her about the jaunt to Rose Hall and a synopsis of its legend. He mentioned the group of schoolteachers who had asked him to take their picture, but his voice trailed off before he finished the story. He was staring at the wall beyond the pool when Bitsy tapped him on the shoulder.

"Are you okay, Mr. Bloomer? Would you like a glass of water?''

"No, thank you," he said, still perplexed by a surprising . . . a thoroughly bewildering idea. Heretical. No, not heretical. Hard to believe, but not impossible. That sort of thing did happen. Not in the ordinary daily progression of life, of course. He caught himself wishing he could find the schoolteachers and hug them, but instead he turned to Bitsy. "Where is Trey?''

"I have no idea. For that matter, I couldn't care less if he has been dragged off by Rastafarians to be sacrificed over a barbecue spit. I'd gladly chip in for the sauce.''

"They don't do that anymore," Theo said drily. "Do you think he might have gone to his room to change for dinner?''

"Are we having dinner? The kitchen is rather bare, and I'm not about to whip up ackee quiches for everyone. I'm on vacation. I doubt you can convince Trey to carry so much as a glass of water to the dining room table; he's so stoned these days he can't find the dining room, not to mention the table. It's simply disgusting, but exactly what one would expect from his sort.''

"Dorrie mentioned that you and he were once engaged. If you'll excuse the curiosity of a snoopy old man, what did he do to cause you to terminate the relationship?''

She snatched up her book and opened it. "I really don't care to discuss it, Mr. Bloomer. I can assure you that it was disgusting. The very thought of it makes my skin crawl to this day."

"Goodness," Theo murmured. "It wasn't anything illegal, was it?"

"Just disgusting." She flipped a page and pointedly began to read. Several pages flipped by at an improbable rate. Then, with a martyred sigh, she closed the book and looked at Theo. "I came back to my dorm room one evening and found him there. He was prancing around the room in . . ." She gulped several times, and her eyes filled with tears. "He was wearing my underwear, if you can imagine such a thing. My new black bra and panties, both trimmed with lace, panty hose, a half-slip, and my best black pumps that I wore all the time. They were stretched hopelessly out of shape. I put all of it in a bag and threw it away in the trash can behind the dorm."

"What did Trey say when you caught him?"

"He said it was practically a family tradition," she said, beginning to sniffle. "He said almost every male in his family did it. Not his father, of course, but all the black sheep branches." The sniffling increased, until she was forced to blot the tip of her nose with a towel. "It's one of the reasons he's forever being booted out of school." The sniffling evolved into a deluge. "It was so humiliating," she sobbed. "What if one of my friends had caught him? I would have died, literally died, right there on the dorm floor. My parents would have had to bury me in a pine box out behind the stables. The obituary wouldn't have made the *Penny Saver*, much less *The Times*. It was just so totally icky."

Theo waited quietly until the sobbing had run its course and her composure had returned, at least to some extent. He then said, "Some men do like to dress in women's clothing. It's rare, but perhaps not as rare as we presume. It doesn't mean that he's a homosexual, however."

"I just couldn't go through with the marriage. What if he

wanted to wear the garter at the wedding? A bridesmaid's dress rather than a tuxedo? My analyst and I agonized for days over it, but he agreed that I would never overcome my phobia that Trey might be a homosexual—or at least a bisexual. There's no way I could deal with that; my analyst says I have a very fragile ego due to a lack of parental warmth during my formative years. I don't intend to rear children who can't tell Daddy from Mommy without a scorecard.''

Theo reached across the table to pat her hand. ''I understand your reaction to the disturbing scene and your decision to break off the engagement.''

''When I gave him back the engagement ring, he had the nerve to ask for my half-slip. He said it was awkward to shop for that sort of thing, especially in the finer stores, and that he adored silk. It was so disgusting that I almost barfed.''

''I truly do understand. However, my dear, you might do well to put that behind you and continue with your life. There are many other men in the world; I'm confident you will encounter a more conventional one—if you cease this obsession with Trey's behavior.''

''Like Sandy?'' She let out a short laugh. ''He may be Biff's best friend, but he's hardly a suitable match. Once he graduates, he'll have to do some dreadfully tedious stint in the navy, on an aircraft carrier or a submarine. After that, he'll stay in the navy as his father did. The best he can aspire to is admiral; the prestige is not unpalatable, but the salary certainly is. Sandy does not come from a wealthy family, and there is no possibility of a trust fund from some obscure relative. He's forever scrambling about for mere pocket money. He even works in the summer doing unskilled labor. Biff almost has to kidnap him to have him crew at the regattas.''

Theo could sense it was not a match made in heaven. ''There will be others along the road, but you must be careful not to judge them too quickly.''

''You're absolutely right, Mr. Bloomer. I'm going to ask for transcripts, credit references, bank account statements, potential trust situations, and prenuptial contracts. I fully intend to protect my personal and family wealth. My father worked hard for our money; I am not going to allow some callous fortune hunter to take advantage of my naïveté.''

"So I see. Well, please don't let me disturb you further. I suspect we'll go out to dinner tonight, since the servants haven't returned. I suggest we meet on the terrace in an hour to discuss where we might want to go.'' He went around the pool and tapped on the sliding glass doors of Trey's bedroom. After a muffled grunt that he assumed indicated permission to enter, he opened the door and went in to be met by an acrid cloud of smoke.

The figure sprawled on the bed flapped a hand in greeting. Theo opened both windows, remaining near one in order to savor the air. Trey pulled himself up partway and aimed a finger in the direction of a chair. "Have a seat, Mr. Bloomer. Have a toke, for that matter, or a martini if you prefer the more staid vice of alcohol.''

"I shall stay where I am, thank you. I thought the police had confiscated your marijuana.''

"They sure did, the arrogant bastards. I had to go all the way across the street to buy some from the gardener. It's pretty good, but not nearly the quality of the stuff those damnable policemen stole from me. They're probably higher than kites by now—on my designer ganja.''

"From whom did you make your original purchase?''

"From Eli. No problem, he kept telling me. He got hot and bothered the day I flashed it on the street, but other than that he was a real cool dude. We mustn't speak ill of the dead, you know.''

Eli was seeming less and less the ideal policeman, Theo thought with a grim smile. Selling ganja, blackmailing the neighbors. One could only speculate where his career might have headed, had his career had the opportunity to head anywhere. "When did you purchase it?'' he asked.

"About ten minutes after we arrived. Service with a smile. Old Eli had a damn discount store in his room, although his quantities weren't impressive. He offered to put us in touch with major retailers. He was a real sport—humble, polite, eager to serve in any capacity. Damn shame he kicked off like that.''

''Did he subsequently put you in touch with major retailers?''

Trey rolled his eyes. ''No. I figured he would double-cross us. Dealers have been known to pocket the money from the sale, then report their clients to the customs officials and make a little more change. And,'' he said, wiggling a finger through the smoke, ''I figured that out before we found out he was a narc. I really have no intention of passing a few years in some tropical dungeon. I think I'll do the Grand Tour this fall, see how many European women I can lay in seventeen countries, seven days, ground transportation and gratuities included.''

''While shopping for lingerie in Paris?'' Theo said softly.

''Ooh la la, the fancy silks and satins of Paris. I suppose Bitsy has been spilling her icy little heart to you? How like her to confide in any male who remembers her name for more than fifteen seconds. She's just a little kitten waiting to curl up in her daddy's lap and purr out all her troubles.''

''I'm not interested in your private amusements. I am curious about your Uncle Billy's fond memories, though. What did he tell you of his antics with D'Orsini during their days at Harvard?''

''Uncle Billy didn't much go for dressing in drag,'' Trey said pensively, lighting what Theo prayed was a conventional cigarette. ''Not to say that he didn't have a certain fondness for polyester pants suits, but he was a mere youth and we must forgive him his minor sins. He made it through without the big boot, but only by the seat of his skivvies. D'Orsini wasn't as fortunate. Both of them were caught in bed, but at different times and with decidedly different people. Uncle Billy was with a dean's wife, which is why it was hushed up. D'Orsini was, if I remember correctly, coupling on a regular basis with the janitor's son. He was booted across the state line. That's what one deserves if one insists on coupling with the lower classes.''

''I wondered if he might be a homosexual,'' Theo said. ''Despite the implication that he lavishes love and attention on single women, I suspected it might be of the platonic variety. Not that it alters much of anything. It does lend credence to a somewhat fanciful theory, though.''

''A fanciful theory? I am impressed, sir. My theories are no better than mundane, idle, hazy fragments of speculation.''

Theo told him to be prepared to go to dinner in an hour, then escaped from the cloying miasma of smoke and bitterness. After he showered and changed into a light gray suit, he went to the terrace to enjoy the pinkish hues of the clouds as the sun began to set. A foursome of strolling minstrels wandered by the house, laden with their island instruments. Theo shook his head when they called to him. As they moved along, he heard them call to Count D'Orsini next door, who apparently also declined a private performance.

It was not difficult to understand why D'Orsini was in no mood for music, Theo told himself. The pertinent roll of film was still missing, but might well surface at any moment, followed by flashing blue lights, sirens, handcuffs, and a lengthy session in the hot, grimy interrogation room at the police station. His associates would be identified and included in the unpleasantries. And Theo was beginning to think he knew the identity of one of them—the one he'd heard the first night.

But that individual was not apt to have murdered Eli. D'Orsini had admitted that he had entertained a Colombian businessman. He also had claimed that the same had departed the next morning—and would not have stooped to poison in any case. That implied the existence of yet a third person, someone who had negotiated a drug deal beside the pool. Someone who might have objected to being blackmailed and had been willing to take extreme action to avoid it.

Trey was a candidate. He had a fondness for drugs and a disinterest in either the legality or the morality of using them. But the police had searched the villa most thoroughly, uncovering Trey's baggie along with Bitsy's lingerie and Dorrie's skin conditioners. None of the young people could have hidden a significant quantity of cocaine in the villa, and they had no contacts outside the villa with whom to leave a package.

Except for Mary Margaret, Theo amended with a frown. She seemed to have made quite a few friends in the few days they'd been in Jamaica. Male friends. He glared at the driveway, down which she'd vanished. He glared at the pool, in which Eli's corpse had been discovered. He glared at the fence, behind which D'Orsini had conducted illegal business. When he again glared at the driveway, he found himself glaring at Sergeant Stahl. Which wasn't at all friendly, although somewhat appropriate since the sergeant appeared to be in an equally foul mood.

"No film, Mr. Bloomer," Stahl said as he sat down. "We checked every place on the island; no one had the roll of film we're looking for. I know D'Orsini's a dope dealer, but I don't have a damn bit of evidence. I know somebody murdered one of my men, but I don't have the faintest lead as to the identity of the murderer. I'm still getting calls from the ex-governor and the island elite assuring me that D'Orsini is a splendid chap." He banged his fist on the table. "I don't have shit."

"Officer Staggley was a bit more of an entrepreneur than we'd realized," Theo said, repeating what Trey had told him about the so-called discount store below the pool. "His offer to put Trey in touch with a major dealer leads me to think he might have been encouraging his investigation by providing his suspect—D'Orsini—with a purchaser. It is not entertaining to run surveillance on someone who's failing to do anything worthy of said surveillance. Eli must have decided to recruit a purchaser in order to facilitate progress."

"And did he succeed?" Stahl asked.

"I don't see how it could be anyone from this villa. Your men searched every inch of it and found nothing beyond Trey's small bag of ganja." Theo glanced up at the balcony, then added in a lowered voice, "I do know the identity of the photographer who took the shots of the . . . ah, the nubile sunbather. It seems one of our young men noted the opportunity from his bedroom window. He claims he put the used film in his camera case, and was flabbergasted when your men did not come across it during the search."

Stahl took out a notebook and flipped through the pages. "Yeah, I have a notation that Bedford Hartley has a camera and a case. So he put the film in his case . . . and someone put it in Staggley's room. It certainly threw us off the track. This Hartley doesn't have any idea who stole his film?"

"He claims no knowledge whatsoever," Theo said, still keeping an eye on the balcony. "He is a rather oblivious type, unaware of anything that doesn't directly concern his immediate personal well-being. Egotism is a common malaise within this group. Of epidemic proportions."

"So I noticed," Stahl said in a rueful voice. "I've never before taken down so many statements that centered on hair conditioners, wardrobe changes, and manicures—from both sexes. What about the Ellison boy? What's his problem?"

"It is deep-seated and complex, but I'm not convinced he has anything to do with this muddle. As one of the girls commented, he's been too stoned to do much of anything. You don't seem surprised to learn that one of your officers was selling dope."

"I wish I were surprised. We found some stuff in his room, but we were assuming it was evidence, that it had something to do with the investigation. Hoping, anyway. But a lot of my officers—most of them, to be frank—smoke ganja in their time off. It's readily available, cheap, and grown in most every backyard. We discourage them from showing up high or dealing, but that's the best we can do. It's the island."

"Have you done anything about the missing girl? I realize

it's been less than twenty-four hours, but I am increasingly concerned about her.''

"I had the patrolmen check the beaches, the hotels, and the bars for her. There're about a hundred private parties at any given hour, though, and she's likely to be at one of them— or on a boat, or shacked up in a hotel room, or in a private residence, or in a jeep, or simply moving around. Jamaica's got more than four thousand square miles, man. Maybe she went to Kingston to prowl or to the Cockpit country to look at those crazy folks. Or maybe she's next door in D'Orsini's hot tub. As you said, it's been less than twenty-four hours— and I've got a murder on my hands.''

Theo considered the wisdom of relating the existence of the ransom note, but decided once again to delay the revelation. Sitermann might come up with information from his Connecticut cohorts. The information was apt to be damning for one of his sextet. And there wasn't much Stahl could do about it, anyway, Theo concluded with an admittedly minuscule edge of justification. "Have you had an autopsy report?''

"This is Jamaica, not Los Angeles. We won't hear anything from forensics for weeks. We're assuming Staggley came back from the railroad station in MoBay, ate lunch and teased the women, visited D'Orsini, then came back over here. He made a pitcher of rum punch, went to the pool, drank the lethal stuff, and eventually collapsed and fell into the pool. Several of the boys who do yard work in the neighborhood swore they didn't see anyone go in or out of the gate here. That means the rum was laced with ackee pulp and given to Staggley sometime before noon yesterday. He had the pertinent roll of film when he visited next door, and he didn't go anywhere else after the visit. Someone made the exchange before we searched his room this morning.''

"D'Orsini couldn't have climbed the fence or come through the back?''

"We thought of that, but the Greeley woman said she was there all afternoon. She swears she drove up just as Eli came down D'Orsini's driveway, and she didn't leave until almost seven o'clock. Even though we're aware of the friendship between the two, we're operating on the premise that she wouldn't lie to cover a murder.'' Stahl's teeth flashed for an instant. "It's not to say that we didn't check out her story. The boy across the street saw her famous flamingo wagon arrive, and he saw it leave about the time she told us. There's no gate in the back, no way to force a path through the thicket of thorns and overgrowth there. The vines on the fence haven't been disturbed.''

"D'Orsini could have given the rum to Eli during the blackmail attempt,'' Theo said, yanking at his beard hard enough to pull out a hair. "I don't think he did, though— since Eli didn't have the film in his possession. He could have talked his way out of verbal allegations, but not out of black and white evidence.''

"Which we don't have.''

"The film is missing,'' Theo agreed. "Mary Margaret is missing, evidence of D'Orsini's criminal activity is missing, and the identity of his associates is missing. As are the cook and the maid, for that matter. The real estate agent is trying to persuade them to return, but seems to have had no success thus far.''

"I'm missing dinner. I'll be missing an ear if I don't get home and apologize to my wife. If you run across a roll of film, give me a call.''

Stahl went down the driveway, nodded to Sandy and Biff as they came through the gate, then drove away. Sandy had his golf bag over one shoulder, and his face was pink from the exertion of carrying the weight. Biff was also carrying a golf bag, but his face, in contrast had the milky whiteness of a hibiscus Diana.

"Has Dorrie said anything?'' he asked softly.

Once again Theo prudently glanced at the balcony. "She arrived at the correct premise over an hour ago. She did so with no hints from me.''

"Is she totally pissed off?''

"That would be a mild description of her initial reaction and present mood."

"Did she resemble her mother?"

Theo nodded. Biff ran his fingers through his hair, peeked at the balcony, and then, with a shudder, went through the dining room and up the stairs. To the lion's den.

"Wow," Sandy said, "what was that about? Old Biff looked as if he might roll over and die."

"Dorrie has determined the identity of the photographer who took the shots of Mary Margaret beside the pool. She was not amused."

Sandy leaned his golf bag against the rail and joined Theo at the table. "And she's gone into melt-down mode over that? God, we thought it was a stitch. Biff said he was going to pin up the prints all over his room at school, and tell everybody how hot she was for him. But it wasn't totally serious or anything. He knows which side of the toast the caviar's on, and he was just using Mary Margaret to make Dorrie jealous."

"The sergeant and I were discussing the girl's disappearance. The police are somewhat more concerned, and have gone so far as to make a desultory search of the public beaches and bars, but they seem to continue to treat it as a lark on her part. I am still perplexed and more than a little worried. Count D'Orsini was extremely agitated when he returned with you. Think back to the trip, Sandy. When you first went to his villa, was there anything at all that struck you as the slightest bit peculiar?"

"Well, he did have company. Some guy was sitting on the sofa in the living room. I only got a glimpse of him, because D'Orsini closed the door when he came out on the porch."

"Although he didn't actually say so, he certainly implied he was alone," Theo said thoughtfully. "Perhaps he was agitated because he did not want anyone to know about this midnight visitor."

Sandy's eyes narrowed. "Do you think D'Orsini and this guy grabbed Mary Margaret and stuffed her in a closet? Neither one of them looked like he'd been in a struggle. I think Mary Margaret would have struggled, don't you? She's a healthy sort; I sure as hell couldn't wrestle her down unless she cooperated.''

''Mary Margaret is indeed a healthy, robust girl with functional lungs and very long fingernails. Can you describe the man you saw?''

''Not really, sir. Ordinary height, short brown hair, regular build, middle-aged, dressed in normal clothes. Like I said, I only had a glimpse of him, and I wasn't paying much attention. I was worried about Mary Margaret.''

''He had brown hair? You're positive it wasn't a swarthy man or someone with white hair, along the lines of our pet CIA agent?''

''The guy was normal,'' Sandy said apologetically. ''He sort of jumped when he saw me in the doorway, but he didn't yell or pull a gun or anything. That would have made me suspicious. As it was, I forgot about him until you asked me.''

''What precisely did D'Orsini say when you asked him if he's seen the girl?''

''He looked as though I'd pulled up to the door on the U.S.S. *Constitution*, sir. I mean, his jaw dropped and his eyes got really wide. He asked me to repeat the question, then he shook his head and said he hadn't seen or heard anybody at his door.''

''Did you believe him?''

''Yeah, he really seemed floored. He told me to wait while he went inside for a minute. As we walked back over here, he made me tell him once more what had happened. He kept staring under the bushes and glancing over his shoulder all the way over.''

''It sounds as if D'Orsini was indeed surprised by your question. I doubt he and this friend had time to deal with the girl, mix drinks, and appear composed in the few minutes from the time she left until the time you knocked on the door. If her disappearance is voluntary, her motivation is impossible to determine." Theo felt like throwing up his hands in despair, but he instead put them in his lap and sighed. "One would almost wonder if the White Witch of Rose Hall had swooped down to carry the girl away. It makes as much sense as anything I've hypothesized."

"What did the police say about the murder, sir? Have they made any progress?"

"No, they seem stymied by the missing film. Eli had it in his possession yesterday afternoon. He remained at the villa, and no one was seen visiting. Therefore, the rum was already poisoned and the film has to be here somewhere. You and Biff are sharing a room. Do you have any idea how someone might have taken the film from Biff's camera case?"

"It's creepy, isn't it? The police found it in Eli's room, so I guess I thought he'd taken it for some obscure reason. He did go into the girls' room and onto the balcony. He might have sneaked into our room, too, although I don't know why he'd take a roll of used film."

"Someone did," Theo said peevishly. "Someone also mashed up pulp of the ackee plant, mixed it in a bottle of rum, and either gave it to Eli or left it as an anonymous present. The means are not insurmountable, but the motive escapes me—unless our poisoner was D'Orsini's associate."

Sandy looked nervously at the fence between the villas. "Was he really dealing dope right over there? The authorities are pretty lax, but I'd be more cautious than that. I thought he used the yacht for that sort of thing."

"He went out in the yacht to make the transfer on the open seas. He saw himself in the role of a twentieth-century buccaneer, I suspect. But he couldn't use the yacht to take the cocaine to Florida, where he would receive the best return on his investment. He knew he was being watched very carefully by the DEA agents, so he had to make other arrangements to export the cocaine."

"What about the real estate woman?" Sandy asked in a hoarse whisper, as if the bougainvillea vine were a telegraph cable to the opposite side of the fence. "She said something about going to New York for travel fairs, and she seems really chummy with Count D'Orsini.''

"The authorities are aware of their friendship. I would imagine her possessions are searched thoroughly each time she enters the United States.'' Theo finished his coffee and stood up. "We're going out to dinner in forty-five minutes or so. Would you be so kind as to relay the information to those upstairs? I think I shall take a walk.''

Sandy looked less than delighted, as though torn between an instinct for self-preservation and an unwillingness to disobey an order, no matter how politely couched as a request. "I was going to practice a few pitch shots in the yard before I change for dinner. I managed to find every sand trap on the course earlier this afternoon, along with the egrets, cows, cow patties, and other assorted hazards. The PGA players don't have to putt around livestock. Biff didn't survive the first three holes; he went down the road to a hotel and hung out in the bar for a couple of hours.'' He glanced at the balcony. "I hope the drinks helped calm him down. He's been in a flap ever since you nailed him, because he knew a confrontation with Dorrie was inevitable. At least she hasn't thrown him through the window—yet. Do you really think it's wise to interrupt them, sir?''

"Just relay the message before too long,'' Theo said with a jaunty wave. He went down the driveway and walked along the curving road, admiring those yards that were particularly tidy and looking up when the occasional jet roared across the distant water to return sunburnt tourists to their homes, offices, factories, and schoolrooms. He had little time left before he would be obliged to pack up his charges and put them on such a jet. Six of them.

All the villas had fences and gates. Mary Margaret could not have darted up a driveway to hide in someone's yard. D'Orsini had said he noticed no unfamiliar cars parked along the street. Sitermann had noticed no suspicious activity in the neighborhood—or so he'd said. However, Theo thought for not the first time, Sitermann did lie.

And why was Sitermann so interested in the comings and goings of the occupants of Harmony Hills? He'd claimed it merely offered an opportune cover to observe D'Orsini in the next villa. That might explain why the spy had popped up like a dandelion in the market the day they'd taken the yacht back to the local pier. It did not explain why Sitermann had been lurking in the area the previous evening, when Mary Margaret had vanished and Eli's body was discovered. Theo began to stride more rapidly as irritation stirred within him. He studied each villa for signs of illicit behavior, but saw only plastic flamingos (a symptom of yuppie influx), lush foliage, manicured grass, and a handful of residents moving about their patios.

By the time he returned to the villa, he was quite as red-faced as Sandy had been. Sandy's condition had been the result of lugging a golf bag up the hill from the golf course. Theo's was the result of a desire to throttle the man from the CIA. At that moment in time, given the opportunity and despite his distaste for violent interaction, he very well might have.

12

They had gathered on the terrace for dinner, the boys in suits and the girls in dresses. When Theo arrived, he found them sitting around the table. Glasses of untouched rum punch were grouped near the pitcher; a plate of cheese attracted the attention of only a fly and a sprinkling of gnats. No one spoke as he pulled out a chair and sat down. Theo realized he had attended tax audits more jovial than the present scene.

"Does anyone have a suggestion for a restaurant?" he asked.

Dorrie stared at the Caribbean in the distance. Biff cleared his throat, then looked at Dorrie for a second, shrugged helplessly, and opted to study his feet. Trey produced a dazzlingly blank smile. Bitsy glanced at him, sniffed, and began to twist a ring on her finger. Sandy slithered farther down in his chair and shook his head.

"I have a travel guide," Theo continued valiantly. "Does everyone think seafood sounds good? Or barbecue? If no one has a preference, we could try one of the hotels or just pick a place out of the book."

"It does not matter to me," Dorrie said.

"Yeah, any place will be swell." Biff tried to smile, but conceded defeat when Dorrie gazed through him at the pool.

"Yeah, any place," he added weakly. Bitsy and Sandy nodded without interest. Trey nodded without comprehension.

Theo managed to herd them into the car, drive to a hotel, unload them, and get them all into the restaurant, feeling as though he were the trainer of a circus of zombies. Everyone mumbled a selection from the menu, sat until the food arrived, and ate. The few attempts at conversation were briskly squelched.

At least they had ceased the incessant bickering, Theo told himself as he drove them back to the villa. The silence was not disagreeable, although the tension was thick enough to be served on crackers. He was relieved when each announced he or she was going to bed, thank you for dinner, it was lovely, good night. Social amenities were too instinctive to be overlooked. Theo soon found himself the sole occupant of the terrace.

He heard a low murmur of voices from D'Orsini's villa, much as he had the first evening he'd been in Jamaica. He now was confident he knew the identity of the male speaker who'd sounded vaguely familiar, but for the moment he could devise no way to use the knowledge.

Sitermann hailed him from the bottom of the driveway. Theo went down to the gate and stopped. "What's new?" he inquired through the bars.

"I thought I'd come by and have a drink, Bloom. Why don't you unlock this contraption?"

"I think not. I'm having a lovely time alone on the terrace. Dorrie and her friends have stopped quarreling, in that they've stopped speaking to each other for various reasons. We had a peaceful dinner, and they've all retired for the evening. It's remarkably nice to have a period of serenity; I see no reason to mar it with your loquacity, most of which is mendacious and without the redeeming virtue of wit."

"There you go again—pretending you don't love me. Open the gate and I'll tell you what I learned about the Connecticut connection." Sitermann took out a handkerchief and wiped his neck. "I walked all the way up the hill, and I can tell you it's steamier than a casting couch. I could use an icy martini while we talk on the terrace.''

"I can hear you quite well here, and there's something comforting about seeing you behind bars. What did you learn?"

"I'm too thirsty to remember, old boy."

"You mean you can't lie without a drink in your hand," Theo said, taking the key from his pocket to unlock the gate. He locked the gate behind Sitermann and trudged up the driveway, adding, "No, that's not true. You could lie while dangling from one foot upside down from a mango tree. You spies study prevarication in your freshman year at spy school."

"Required course," Sitermann agreed. "But you have first-hand knowledge of the curriculum, don't you?" When Theo merely smiled, he plopped down at the table. "As Bond, my boyhood hero, would say, shaken—not stirred, my good man. You might as well make a pitcher while you're at it."

For lack of anything better to do, Theo went to the kitchen and mixed a pitcher of martinis. After stirring it to his heart's content, he returned to the terrace and set the tray in front of the spy.

"May I presume you have learned something of value?" he asked.

"Maybe, maybe not. The ransom note was in an envelope, the words cut out of *The New York Times*. That narrows it down to ten or twenty million people right there. If some of them didn't have access to scissors and glue, then we can narrow it down even further." Sitermann poured the martini down his throat and refilled his glass. "And if we exclude all the folks that didn't know Mary Margaret Ellison dropped off the face of the earth last night around midnight—why, that shoots down most everybody."

"You are a veritable cerebral machine. Did you discover anything concerning the identity of the deliverer of the note?"

"We did, and we didn't. Do you have any olives?"

"I have no idea, but if we indeed have olives, I would rather roll them down the driveway in a primitive version of bowling than offer them to you. Would you please continue?"

"Holy major studio release, you are testy this evening. Here I am, offering to tell you information gleaned by the largest covert agency in the world—except for the KGB, since they're on the same scale as the readership of *The New York Times*—and you won't give me a measly olive. I swear, Bloom, I'm likely to get my feelings hurt once and for—"

"Would you please continue?"

"Okay, okay. Well, the note was stuck in Ellison's mailbox about seven o'clock this morning. The cook was just coming in to fix breakfast, and she spotted this suspicious character darting up the road."

"How suspicious?" Theo said, resigned to the necessity of playing straight man to Sitermann's self-perceived wit.

"Dressed in navy blue sweats and a knitted cap. Wearing designer sneakers, wrist and ankle weights, and one of those portable radios with a headset. The cook said that the figure looked mighty suspicious."

"Why did the figure look mighty suspicious?"

"Jogging is passé these days. It's considered more civilized to exercise at one's health club, where one will not be assaulted by dogs, bird droppings, motorcyclists, swerving BMWs, or the possibility of sweat. One can go directly from the low-impact aerobics session to the whirlpool and the sauna, where one will be in the company of the right sort of people. The sidewalks are public, you see, and the clubs are exclusive."

"How kind of you to explain the intricacies, Sitermann. I suppose this was gleaned from a yup-spy in a spandex trenchcoat? Please get to the point. Is there any way to identify this jogger?"

"Nope. The cook wasn't even sure of the gender, much less anything more descriptive. There could have been a crewcut under the cap, or waist-length hair pinned up. The

sweats were baggy. Youngish, but that's not extraordinary.
In good shape. Designer outfit, standard issue in that neighborhood. Sorry, Bloom."

"For this I mixed a pitcher of martinis? And you had the
audacity to request olives? You are a treacherous devil."
Theo poured himself a martini and leaned back with a sigh.
"There's been no sign of the girl for almost twenty-four hours
now. Sergeant Stahl had his patrolmen check beaches and
bars, but he listed several dozen places she might be. Un-
derstandably, he is more concerned with the murder investigation, which seems to be galloping toward a brick wall."

Sitermann's expression sharpened. "I spoke to him a while
ago. He said the film is not to be found anywhere on the
island, and that it's his only hope to solve the murder. What
do you think?"

"I've thought about it quite a lot in the last few hours,"
Theo admitted. "It seems logical to assume the film is here
at the villa, but the police surely would have come across it.
This joint is clean, as they're inclined to mutter in old movies."

Sitermann nodded. "Whoever swiped it might have simply tossed it out a window or buried it under a banana bush.
There's no reason to think the police'll ever find it. It's challenging to hide a busty young woman, but it's easy to dispose
of a cylinder less than two inches long." He paused long
enough to refill his glass. "So it looks like D'Orsini's going
to get away with his drug trafficking for the time being, and
the murderer's going to get away with murder. Hardly seems
sporting, does it?"

"I hope the kidnapper doesn't get away with kidnapping—
if that's what happened," Theo said in a discouraged voice.
"I have not yet mentioned the ransom note to Stahl, but I
shall feel obliged to do so tomorrow if the girl does not
return. We may well be in Jamaica for Memorial Day, if not
Thanksgiving. My tomato seedlings will not plant themselves in the garden without assistance. I am relying on my
sister to water them and see that they are not burnt should

there be an unseasonable warm spell, but she is less concerned about their welfare than about her performance at the bridge table and might forget to drop by my greenhouse. Were I at home, I would be planting beans and potatoes by now, but instead I have been thrown involuntarily into all sorts of distasteful events. I am not a happy man, Sitermann.''

"Finish off the pitcher," Sitermann said graciously. "It'll do wonders for the old spirit. We're plowing through the island telephone records, but it's needle-haystack stuff to think we can isolate one call from the entire island to the state of Connecticut. No international calls from here, by the way.'' He wiped his neck with a handkerchief, drank the last few drops in his glass, and rose. "You don't have to walk me to the door, Bloom. I'll let myself out.''

"I locked the gate.''

"Picking locks, sophomore year. Have you forgotten already?'' Laughing, Sitermann went down the driveway, paused in front of the gate for a few seconds, his bulk blocking the view of the formidable lock, then exited and strolled down the hill. His laughter drifted back in the now cool breeze from the Caribbean.

Theo ascertained that the gate was secured. He carried the tray to the kitchen and rinsed the glasses and pitcher, locked doors, checked windows, turned out the downstairs lights, and went upstairs to bed. He was in the midst of a most complex dream, in which Mary Margaret was the mistress of Rose Hall and Biff a husband with a limited future, when the ring of the telephone awakened him.

He grabbed his bathrobe and hurried downstairs, praying he would not stumble in the dim light. He switched on the light in the kitchen and snatched up the receiver. "Yes?''

"It was beginning to become quite tedious waiting for you to answer the telephone, Theo. I considered hanging up.''

"And how are you, Nadine?''

"Not well, Pookie played the second session with all the acumen of a trustee at a psychiatric facility. She then refused to listen to a single word about the string of ghastly errors she made, although I did make every effort to temper my criticism with a few kind words. It was not easy to find those kind words, and I was most irritated when she abandoned the table to dance with that orthodontist who thinks he's the Charles Goren of Hartford.''

"Oh, really?'' Theo said, having learned in sixty-one years that his sister could not be diverted once she had been launched.

"I told Pookie that if she insisted on dancing half the night with Mr. Straight Teeth, then she would have to find another partner for the team event tomorrow. Of course, Betty Lou and Adele will be livid if we cancel on such short notice, but I shall tell them it is entirely Pookie's fault. She has not been stable since her last divorce; I don't know why I attempt any serious bridge with her. She is adolescent, at best.''

"Indeed. Was there anything else, Nadine? It is well past midnight, and I was asleep.''

"I am aware that it is nearly two o'clock in the morning. The evening session was not over until after eleven, and we stayed to have a drink and discuss the hands. I did, anyway. Pookie seems to have stayed in order to gyrate on the dance floor with the kingpin of orthodontia. I simply left her there and drove home alone. I cannot repeat some of the things I said to myself along the interstate; I simply cannot.''

"Has Ellison had any word about his daughter?'' Theo hazarded.

"Why else would I call? This is not an inexpensive conversation, Theo. I had to deal with all sorts of operators whose enunciation is less than crisp, and Charles will expire when he sees the telephone bill next month. If you will cease chattering, I will tell you what Win said when he came over during the cocktail hour this afternoon. There has been a second demand.''

"You waited nine hours to tell me this? Really, Nadine, it is vital that the girl be found—''

"I could hardly call you during the second session of the

women's pairs, could I? Tournament bridge is a timed event, and I am not the egotistical sort to demand that everyone sit in limbo because I need to make a personal call. Yesterday afternoon a woman from Philadelphia had a coronary at the table, and the game was halted only long enough to allow the paramedics to wheel her out of the room. Pookie completely forgot the bidding and leapt to six spades, then proceded to go down three."

"What was the substance of the demand?"

"A muffled voice on the telephone instructed Win to place fifty thousand dollars in small bills in a suitcase and leave it in a Salvation Army collection box in the shopping center. He was to do so by midnight. If he refused to cooperate, all sorts of dreadful things would be done to Mary Margaret."

"Did he follow the instructions?" Theo asked, blinking.

"He asked me for my opinion. I told him it was absurd, that you were seeing to the situation down there, wherever it is. Besides, the banks were closed and the idea melodramatic and utterly preposterous. Win doesn't know a Salvation Army box from a hat box. One has a maid call them to come along in their battered truck to pick up whatever one is discarding; it's their responsibility, after all. Win would have had a sporting chance had the demand involved safe deposit boxes or even cigar boxes."

"Oh, dear," Theo said. He sank down to the floor and leaned against the refrigerator, which rumbled against his spine in a comforting way. "Did Ellison tell this muffled voice that he intended to comply with the demand?"

"I really couldn't say, Theo. Pookie and I had to leave before he finished the little story. You have found Mary Margaret, haven't you? Although her monetary value seems to be decreasing, this ransom business is still disturbing Win."

"I am looking for her," Theo said, looking at the baseboard. "I have every hope I shall find her soon. If there is another communication from the kidnappers, I would like to be informed immediately. Is that possible?"

"The first session of the team event begins at eleven tomorrow morning, and the second at five. If I hear from Win either before or after the sessions, you may rest assured I shall spare no expense to call you, Theo. I am not heartless.''

She hung up before Theo could offer an opinion. He remained on the floor, this time fairly certain he would not be caught by Amelia and Emelda, should they ever return. The floor was cool. The view was almost as familiar as the verdant sweep from the terrace to the Caribbean. He had done a reasonably competent job of tidying up after the police search, although from this perspective he could see a wisp of flour underneath the table. ''Tut, tut,'' he said dispiritedly.

The kitchen door swung open. ''Who's here?'' Dorrie demanded as she came into the room, a golf club clutched in her hand. She looked around wildly.

''Down here, my dear.''

''What on earth are you doing, Uncle Theo? I heard a noise and came down to investigate, but I hardly expected to find you on the kitchen floor.''

''I've been on the telephone to your mother. Once we got through the latest adventures at the bridge table, she told me there'd been a second ransom demand. Midnight—or else. It seems we got 'else,' for better or worse.''

Dorrie propped the golf club (a five iron, Theo noted) in a corner and sat down beside him. ''You mean something has happened to Mary Margaret? You don't believe someone would actually do . . . something to her, do you? But that's terrible—totally terrible. I know I said some catty things about her, but she's one of my best friends, for pete's sake.''

''I don't know. I would have hypothesized that the situation was losing momentum, since the film has not been found. The police seem discouraged and rather at a loss to determine the next move, but for some reason the pressure has intensified for our unknown player—or players. Mary Margaret is now worth only fifty thousand, although it was to be paid within a matter of hours after the demand was made.''

''She's down to fifty thousand? She'll be furious when she

learns that.'' Dorrie gulped several times. ''She will learn that, won't she? Uncle Theo, we've got to do something. This is no longer amusing, and I want you to get her back immediately so that I won't have to worry about her.'' She held out her hand for his inspection. ''Look at that. I've chipped two nails since this morning.''

Theo found himself wishing he had not sworn off cigarettes thirty years ago; it was the perfect time to light a cigarette, blow a cloud of smoke at the ceiling, and ask his niece what precisely she thought he ought to do. About Mary Margaret, about the murderer, or even about her manicure predicament. He was about to inquire when the door opened and Sandy, dressed in pajamas dotted with red and blue sailboats, came cautiously into the kitchen, a golf club in his hand.

''Who's here?'' he demanded in a fierce whisper.

''We're down here,'' Dorrie said, fluttering her fingers.

''My God, are you okay? Did Mr. Bloomer fall? Did he break his hip? Can I get him a glass of water or something?''

''Uncle Theo didn't fall and he didn't break anything. He's just sitting here thinking about what to do next.''

''Are you sure he's not dizzy or weak? He's an old guy, Dorrie.'' Sandy put down the golf club (a seven iron) and bent over to peer at Theo. ''He looks pale, too.''

''He's not that old,'' she said in an indignant voice. ''Well, he's not all that young, either, but he's not so gaga that he wouldn't know if he were dizzy or weak-kneed.''

The dizzy, weak-kneed, gaga topic of conversation patted the floor beside him. ''Have a seat, my boy. If I feel a sudden compulsion to drool, I'll give you ample warning. Dorrie and I were discussing Mary Margaret's whereabouts.''

''They want fifty thousand for her,'' Dorrie added, her eyes wide. ''They might do something totally awful to her if her father doesn't pay.''

''Wait a minute,'' Sandy said. ''Maybe you're the one going gaga. What the hell are you talking about?''

Dorrie related the tale of the ransom demands. ''So,'' she

concluded, patting Theo's knee, "Uncle Theo and I were trying to figure out what to do in order to rescue Mary Margaret from the clutches of the kidnappers—if there really are kidnappers. Right, Uncle Theo?"

Theo had been pondering the criteria each of them used in the selection of a golf club. "Yes, indeed," he said, "we are pondering which course of action would prove most beneficial to the girl."

Sandy scratched his chin. "Do we have options, sir? I mean, do you have any idea where she might be? I don't see how we can snatch her away from the kidnappers if we can't find them."

"A keen observation," Theo said. "We cannot retrieve her if we don't know where she is. Have you any theories?"

"She could be anyplace on the island. It's a big island."

"What if," Dorrie said slowly, "she really is a conspirator in the kidnap plot? I doubt she's met any strangers crazy enough to help her, so it's liable to be someone she already knew. I can't see her working up a scheme with the cook or the maid, and Eli's dead. That leaves Count D'Orsini and the real estate woman."

"The real estate woman has a name," Theo said, trying not to sound irritable.

"Everyone has a name, Uncle Theo; I simply do not clutter my mind with names of short-term employees. Heavens, we had a chauffeur for six months and I never could remember if he was John or James. He could still drive."

Sandy leaned forward, his expression animated. "If Mary Margaret cooked up this disappearance with D'Orsini, then she might be hiding in his villa. We could go pound on the door and demand that we be allowed to search every room. He's not a big guy; I could hold him while you—"

"The police have already searched his villa," Theo interrupted before Sandy could leap to his feet, grab his seven iron, and storm the neighbor's bastion.

"Oh," he said, sinking back against the refrigerator. "I guess they would have found her."

"One would assume so," Theo murmured.

Now Dorrie leaned forward. "But did they search the yacht? Knowing Mary Margaret, she'd absolutely die to hide out on a zillion-dollar yacht stocked with champagne and caviar."

"Wow," Sandy said, "she really might think that was a riot. But wouldn't the police have searched the yacht?"

"They didn't mention it," Theo said. He absently took off his bifocals and polished them on the hem of his bathrobe. "I suppose it is possible, but we shouldn't get our hopes too high."

"I think it's a totally wonderful theory," Dorrie sniffed, offended by his lack of enthusiasm. "I think we ought to go right down to the marina and see if she's there. We ought to do it this very minute, before the kidnappers have a chance to . . . to do things."

"We might call the police," Theo said.

Sandy shook his head. "If the kidnappers see the police, they'll panic and shoot Mary Margaret. Dorrie's right. We can sneak up on the yacht and try to determine if anyone's on board. The captain gave me an extensive tour the other day, and showed me all the staterooms and the equipment belowdecks. I can get us on board, then we can explore the rooms where Mary Margaret might be a prisoner."

"Calm down," Theo said. "The theory that led to all this was that she is a conspirator, rather than the hapless victim of kidnappers. According to Dorrie, Mary Margaret is guzzling champagne and munching caviar, not hog-tied in the bilge. We don't need to dash down to the pier, brandishing golf clubs and tiptoeing across the deck. We—"

"Good idea, Uncle Theo—we'll take the golf clubs. I'll meet you two by the car in five minutes. I have on no makeup whatsoever." She glanced at Sandy's pajamas and Theo's bathrobe. "You might want to change into something more appropriate yourselves." She picked up the five iron as she left the kitchen.

"It's a genetic problem," Theo said. When Sandy looked

bewildered, he sighed, stood up, and went upstairs to change into something appropriate for yacht skulking and kidnapper bashing. Two of his least favorite hobbies.

They met by the car. Theo gave Sandy the key and told him to open the gate at the bottom of the driveway. With Dorrie breathing heavily beside him, he let the car roll to the street, then waited until Sandy had locked the gate and climbed in the backseat before starting the engine.

"I am not at all sure we ought to do this," he said as the car lurched forward. He started the engine again and reminded himself of the necessity of using left when right felt—well, right. He drove down the hill and turned toward the city of Montego Bay, where they would, with luck and a certain amount of divine guidance, find the harbor.

Dorrie turned the rearview mirror to examine her lipstick. "Come on, Uncle Theo, we're rescuing Mary Margaret, not holding up a bank. If she's on the yacht, we'll bring her back to the villa and call Mother. If she's not, then we'll just slip away and admit defeat."

"And if we're arrested for trespassing?" Theo asked.

Sandy patted Theo on the shoulder. "Just think of it as a school prank, sir. We'll tell the police that D'Orsini told us we could use the yacht whenever we wanted to. The captain explained all the equipment to me; I could take us out for a moonlight cruise."

"Could you really?" Dorrie asked. "You know enough to operate the yacht after one quick tour?"

Theo realized the situation was careening out of control. "We are not going to steal the yacht for a moonlight cruise," he said firmly. "We are going to take a quick look for Mary Margaret while praying we are not spotted by the harbor security men. If we are arrested, I can assure you that Sergeant Stahl will not be amused and will not release us with a little slap on the wrist. There has been a murder, you know. It was not a school prank."

He kept up the lecture, although he could see Dorrie was

craning her neck to search the sky for moonlight. He suspected Sandy was envisioning himself at the helm of the *Pis Aller*, the wind ruffling his crewcut as he opened the throttle or whatever one did in the nautical sense.

The streets of the city were dark, the last of the tourists safely abed at their hotels and the natives abed at their homes. There were no cars, no motorcycles, no pedestrians wandering from bar to bar. The stores were black boxes. A dog came out of an alley to stare at them as the car lurched by, then ducked back into the shadows to root through garbage cans.

A streetlight gleamed dimly over the gate to the marina. Theo parked across the road and cut off the engine. "Well," he said, trying to sound disappointed, "there's no way we can get inside the fence, so I suppose we ought to go home and call the proper authorities."

Dorrie eyed the fence. "I am not about to climb that thing. I have on new jeans, and I have no intention of ripping them on barbed wire."

"I can open a regular lock with a credit card," Sandy said from the backseat. "The guys at school are getting locked out of their dorm rooms all the time, and I charge a buck to get them in. But that's a padlock."

"A shame," Theo said. He reached for the ignition key, but Dorrie's fingernails cut into the back of his hand.

"You can open that padlock, Uncle Theo. We'll wait in the car until you've opened the gate, then I'll drive the car through and park where we can't be seen by a patrol car." She gave him a beady Caldicott look. "Go on, Uncle Theo. I'd hate to be arrested now, since we haven't even accomplished anything. Just imagine what Mother would say."

It was not a difficult chore to imagine Nadine's reaction. Nor was it difficult to open the padlock, swing back the metal gate, and wait while Dorrie drove through and found an inky shadow in which to park. She and Sandy joined him, both armed with golf clubs and determined smiles.

"That wasn't too bad, was it?" Dorrie said, slipping her

arm through Theo's. "Now we'll simply find D'Orsini's yacht, slip aboard, and search for Mary Margaret. I find this rather exciting; it's like pouring detergent in the fountain by the library, or drinking wine in the dorm."

Sandy pointed at a long pier lined with boats of all sizes. They were rocking silently, their masts and wires etched against the dull matte of the sky. Things creaked like unseen tree frogs. Water slapped softly against hulls.

"Ooh," Dorrie whispered, "this is straight from some creepy movie, isn't it? All we need is for some hulk to leap onto the pier in front of us, lunging and snarling. Sandy bashes him with a golf club, Mary Margaret stumbles out from the yacht, her eyes glazed from dope, and the credits roll while she babbles gratitude and hugs everybody."

Theo could not find the precise words to convey his reaction to her scenario. It did bring to mind Sitermann, however. Theo was unable to resist a quick peek over his shoulder, prepared to see a flash of white hair and a glowing red nose. He saw only a flurry of insects around the streetlight and a solitary cat ambling along the top of the fence.

Sandy pointed his golf club at the boat at the end of the pier. "That's D'Orsini's yacht. We'd better hurry. I think I saw a flashlight on the far side of the building; it could be a security man making rounds."

The three went down the pier and stopped in front of the *Pis Aller*. It was dark, as to be expected at three in the morning, Theo thought with a sigh, and its deck smooth and glinting. Sandy helped Dorrie scramble over the rail and onto the deck, then turned to Theo with a hesitant look.

"Shall I give you a hand, sir? The deck should not be wet, but it might be slippery and I wouldn't want you to fall."

"I shall be careful," Theo said. He joined Dorrie, who was giggling, and they waited as Sandy stepped soundlessly over the rail in his rubber-soled shoes.

Sandy looked around for a moment, then pointed at a doorway. "She's likely to be asleep in one of the staterooms,'' he hissed. ''Follow me, and watch your head. Keep a hand on the wall to steady yourself, sir.''

Before Theo could point out that he was hardly in the doddering stage, Sandy ducked through the doorway. Dorrie followed, leaving Theo alone on the deck. No, he told himself, Nadine would harp well into the twenty-first century if he simply returned to the car and drove to the villa. He ducked his head and went down the stairs.

13

As the yacht rocked gently under their feet, Theo, Dorrie, and Sandy began to ease open doors and peer into the dark staterooms. Tunnels of dull reddish light streamed through the portholes, allowing them to ascertain the vacancy factor, which seemed to be a tidy one hundred percent.

"This is the dining room," Sandy whispered. "The galley's beyond it, but I can't believe Mary Margaret would be there. She's not in any of the staterooms. Maybe your theory was crazy, after all."

"My theory?" Dorrie hissed. "It was your theory, buddy. Uncle Theo and I just came along to be polite." She put down her golf club in order to fold her arms and stare at him. "You were the one who knew how to find the yacht and how to creep aboard like a wharf rat. You and Biff seem to feel you know everything, as if the two of you have a direct line to God. But you're just little boys, snickering over Mary Margaret's boobs and taking silly little pictures out the window. Did you punch each other on the shoulder while you giggled and goggled?"

Theo looked down at the golf club, which threatened to slide down the wall and hit him on the foot. In a metaphorical sense, it did. Taking Dorrie's arm, he tugged her backward. "Let's save the vituperation for another time, my dear. Sandy is not responsible for Biff's conduct in the minor issue of his choice of models. Mary Margaret is not here, so we really ought to leave before a security guard comes to investigate."

"Minor?" she said, her lip curled and her eyes glittering. "Biff gave me a locket, Uncle Theo, and intends to give me an engagement ring as soon as he inherits money from some comatose old aunt in Boston. We've spent entire afternoons together in Tiffany's. He is supposedly above pubescent, slobbery voyeurism now that we're practically engaged."

"Of course, of course," Theo said. He tugged at her arm again, but it was much like trying to nudge a mountain into motion. "But there's no reason to rail at Sandy. Let's return to the villa; you can awaken Biff and rail at him for the rest of the night, if you so desire."

"I am no longer speaking to him. I do not rail at anyone, including servants, children, and shopkeepers. It is unforgivable to be rude to those less fortunate or in less desirable circumstances."

"Indeed, my dear. Shall we leave now?"

Eyeing her with trepidation, Sandy picked up her golf club and handed it to her. "Are we going to call it a night and split? Your theory was reasonable; it just didn't pan out. As they say here, no problem."

The Caldicott jaw inched out. "The theory was more than reasonable, Sandy. I would like to point out that we have not yet searched the storage rooms or the facilities below this deck. The theory may be proven correct. Now, which way do we go?"

Theo wondered if they had a problem—a very big problem—but he could see no way to extricate his niece without literally jerking her down the corridor to the door that led to the deck. Somehow, it was Biff's fault, he thought grimly as he followed the two through the dining room and galley. Had Biff kept his camera aimed in the proper direction, Dorrie would not be in such a mood. Her moods were written in stone.

They reached another door. "This is a pantry," Sandy

said. "It's locked, though—I guess to keep the crew out of the booze. It's stuffy in here; I could go for a cold brewski right now. Too bad the door's locked."

"Uncle Theo can open it."

Theo gave her an exasperated look. "My dear, we're operating under the premise that Mary Margaret came here willingly, as a conspirator in this ransom business. She would hardly lock herself in a cramped little storage room. I truly think we should leave before we're arrested for trespassing or burglary."

"I am not going to be dragged all the way down to this yacht and then not make a proper search, Uncle Theo. What if she's in there, tied up or drugged—or worse? We'd feel pretty silly, wouldn't we? You've already unlocked Eli's door, the gate at the villa, and the gate at the marina. I fail to see why you're being so mulish about one more teeny little lock."

Cursing Biff's perfidy under his breath, Theo took the metal strip from his pocket and moved toward the door. Sandy suddenly flinched, then peered over Theo's shoulder at the galley.

"I think I heard something, sir," he said, frowning. "And the boat seemed to rock as if someone had come aboard. Do you think I ought to investigate?"

"Oh, stop dithering and go see who it is," Dorrie snapped.

"It might be a good idea," Theo said, still intent on the pantry lock. "If it's a policeman, tell him we'll be there in a minute or two."

Sandy tiptoed through the galley and around a corner. Dorrie began to hum, although to Theo it sounded more like the drone of a hornet than a melody. He inserted the metal strip in the lock and twisted it, allowing his fingertips to sense the ridges of the tumblers. Whoever selected the lock had spared no expense to keep the crew out of the caviar, he thought testily.

"What is taking so long?" Dorrie said.

"It's a delicate procedure. By the way, there's something

you need to be told, and Sandy's absence provides a propitious moment. I fear he's involved in this situation.''

"Of course he's involved. He came with us, and if we're arrested, he'll be singing hymns in the back of the paddy wagon with us.''

"Yes, but more deeply than that. There—I do believe I've got it. Here, Dorrie, go in and see if you stumble over an inert body on the storeroom floor.''

"But what about Sandy?'' she said, staring at him.

"We need to complete our search as quickly as possible and return to the villa. Once we are there, I shall take you aside and explain a few puzzling things that have occurred to me. Speed is of the essence.''

Something in his voice stirred her into action. Clutching the golf club, she edged past him and stepped across the threshold into the dark room. "I don't see anything, Uncle Theo. I actually don't much like this anymore, but I'll look behind the shelves and then we can go.'' She vanished around the ceiling-high metal shelves stacked with cases of supplies. "It's really rather dark back here,'' she added in a small voice. "This is dumb; I wouldn't find anyone unless I tripped over—''

There was a thud and a muffled shriek, followed by a great deal of rattling, clanking, and banging. A metal bucket skidded across the floor and rolled out the door. Brooms fell one by one, clattering like drumsticks against the metal edges of the shelves.

"Dorrie?'' Theo hesitated in the doorway, aware his vision would improve as his eyes adjusted to the darkness. Falling over his niece would not improve the situation. "Are you harmed in any way?''

"I skinned my knee,'' she wailed. "I hit my head on one of these damn cases of champagne, and who knows what my chin will look like in the morning. Good Lord, I broke a nail!''

"What caused you to stumble?''

"I don't know, but it had better be worth a fingernail. I'll have to crawl over and . . ." There was a moment of silence. "Oh, Uncle Theo," she added, her volume increasing until the wailing seemed to be of banshee origin. "It's Mary Margaret. She's dead!"

Abandoning caution, Theo flipped on the light and hurried around the end of the shelves. Dorrie was on her hands and knees, crouched up against a wall and as far as she could move away from the body on the floor. Tears streamed down her cheeks. Her teeth were chattering as she said, "I—I stepped on her, Uncle Theo. I didn't mean to. I really couldn't see. I really didn't mean to step . . . to step on her like that."

"I know," he said soothingly, as he dropped to his knees and bent over Mary Margaret. He touched her face, which felt warm, then felt the side of her neck for a pulse. "She's not dead, Dorrie. Her pulse is quite regular and strong. I would surmise that she's been drugged."

Dorrie took a frayed napkin from a box and wiped her nose. "Are you sure? You're not just saying that to make me feel better?"

"No, my dear. There are needle marks on her arm, which would make it most probable that she was given some sort of sedative. Other than that, she appears to be unharmed."

"Really?" Dorrie crawled forward to join Theo next to the body. "I lost my head, I guess. Finding Eli's body like that did me in to the max. I'm fully expecting to have nightmares for the next year. Then to feel flesh again, and not hear any breathing . . ." She began to cry, more quietly now.

Theo put his arms around her and waited until she broke off with a series of hiccups. "There, there, you had a horrible experience and it would be perfectly normal to panic when encountering what you assumed was another corpse. Mary Margaret is alive, however."

Dorrie dried her cheeks with the napkin, unaware of the black smudges she was applying simultaneously to her face. "What's she doing here, anyway? I was being whimsical earlier when I said all that nonsense about drugs and all. I didn't think I was hitting quite so close to reality.''

"I would think that she was lured down here by someone, but came freely. Once she was here, perhaps hiding in a stateroom with champagne and caviar as you suggested, the game turned ugly. Her co-conspirator decided to increase the urgency of the demands while making the sum low enough so that Mary Margaret's father had a fighting chance to arrange for the cash.''

"Who?" Dorrie whispered.

"Sandy is the most likely suspect." Theo took Mary Margaret's hand in his own and lightly slapped her wrist. Mary Margaret's Rubenesque proportions would make it more than a little difficult to carry her out of the yacht and to the car—if they were permitted to attempt it. "Sandy was the leader of the impromptu search party. He and Biff were the only ones in the villa who were out when the telephone call was placed to the girl's father this afternoon. Biff is hardly the type to arrange this sort of thing. I was worried when Sandy had no problem identifying D'Orsini's yacht in the darkness.''

"But why, Uncle Theo?''

"For money," Sandy said as he came around the corner of the shelves. His golf club had been replaced with a nasty-looking revolver. "I'm dreadfully sorry about the weapon, sir. I found it in the master cabin. Mary Margaret and I thought this little ruse might be an amusing way to earn enough money to do something really wild and crazy. The idea of the yacht did appeal to her, as you said, and it seemed like a harmless little scheme. The captain mentioned that he and the crew were off-duty for the week. It seemed like a heaven-sent opportunity.''

"How did she vanish in the driveway?" Theo asked, trying to avoid looking directly into the barrel of the gun, which seemed to be aimed at the center of his forehead.

"She crouched under a shrub in the backyard and waited. When you sent Biff and me to search for her, I told him to check the front while I checked the back. He's not exactly a candidate for Mensa. Once he and I came back to report, Mary Margaret walked down the road to a hotel and called a cab to bring her here. I happened on a stray key the other day while being given a tour, and it almost leapt into my pocket when the captain turned his back to explain the computerized navigational system.''

Dorrie raised an eyebrow. "I thought Biff was your best friend.''

"He's been useful. He introduced me to the right people and funded a few trips when I was broke. My father is not a generous man; he's very big on discipline and erect posture and all that military malarky. I did enjoy those summers on the Cape, the snooty rich kids, the food and wine, the mindless hospitality. I never had to spend a penny for anything. But when Mary Margaret and I cooked up this scheme, we were talking real money for a change. Good-bye academy, hello Rio. The only flaw in the plan was that we've missed Mardi Gras this year. A year's a long time to wait for a party of that magnitude, but we had to be flexible about some things.''

"What a tragedy you were found out,'' Dorrie sniffed. She stood up and brushed at the stain on her knee. "At least you won't have to pay for prison food.''

Theo jabbed an elbow in his niece's calf. "Let's not discuss prison, Dorrie. I doubt Sandy and Mary Margaret have done anything too serious thus far. No money has passed hands. Her father can hardly prosecute her, which means nothing is likely to happen to either of them.''

"He drugged her, didn't he?''

"Yes,'' Theo conceded, wishing Dorrie would consider the wisdom of her words, "but she'll recover with no ill effects. The entire affair can be kept quiet, I would imagine.''

Sandy waved the gun at them. "To be candid, sir, I'm still hoping that Mary Margaret's father will cough up the money. This is a nice, well-stocked craft, and the navigation system is state-of-the-art. I'm seriously thinking about taking it to Rio.''

"Oh, that's totally darling," Dorrie said. "Just run up the Jolly Roger and slap on a gold earring. Maybe you can overtake a garbage scow and board it, Captain Hook. When you're caught, you'll be hanged from the mast, but you'll have had so much fun playing pirate.''

"It may be entertaining," he said coolly. "I really must do something with you two while I wait to hear from my partner in Connecticut. The drop was to be made by midnight, but I'll give Ellison an extra twelve hours to scoot down to the bank and pack the cash.''

Dorrie studied her broken fingernail. "What does that mean? I don't have twelve hours to sit around while you make devious, guttural telephone calls to Connecticut. I've faced the fact that I cannot get a decent manicure on this island, but I shall presume they've heard of adhesive nails for emergencies like this. I need to try a few stores in the downtown area.''

Sandy blinked at her. "For the moment, I think you and your uncle ought to stay here and take care of Mary Margaret. She became restless this afternoon and implied she was ready to forget the plan and work on her tan. I'm afraid I was forced to insist she continue to participate." He began to back away from them. "Help yourselves to caviar and champagne; I'm sure D'Orsini would not begrudge you a few bites.''

"How totally gracious of you," said Dorrie. "You do realize any champagne in here will be hot, don't you?''

Theo grabbed her ankle as she started forward. "Sit down," he commanded in a low voice. "We'll be fine for a few hours. We don't want to panic the boy. He has a gun; it would be foolhardy to presume he wouldn't use it.''

"You're absolutely right, sir. I don't wish to do anything to hurt either of you, but the game is afoot and we must all obey the rules. I learned that much at the academy. Also, if it's not too much of a bother, would you please let me have that little thing you use to unlock doors? It rather defeats my purpose if you unlock the door in ten minutes.'' Theo obliged. Sandy then backed around the metal shelves. Seconds later the door closed and the lock clicked into place.

"Congratulations, Uncle Theo. Now we're locked in here for who knows how long, and expected to survive on hot champagne and tins of caviar. We don't even know if there's a can opener in here.'' She looked down at Mary Margaret, who was stirring. "Oh, keep your porch lights out. This is aggravating enough without having to deal with you.''

Despite Dorrie's request, Mary Margaret opened her eyes. Theo and Dorrie helped her sit up and explained several times where she was before a flicker of comprehension flashed across her face.

"So Sandy drugged me,'' she said through a yawn. "That boy is something, isn't he? Why, he'd steal the arch supports out of his grandmother's orthopedic shoes. Did Daddy deliver the money?''

Theo gave her a grave look. "No, and I fear he has been instructed by a well-meaning third party to ignore any further ransom demands.''

"Maybe Sandy will reduce it again,'' Dorrie said. "You're already more a selection from a Bloomingdale's sale rack than a Saks designer outfit. If it continues, you'll be ransomed as a blue light special.''

Mary Margaret observed her through heavily lidded eyes. "Whatever have you done to your face, Dorrie? You look like the coal miner's daughter.''

Dorrie took a silver tray from a shelf and held it up to examine her reflection. 'Oh, my Lord,'' she said hollowly. "I look dreadful.''

Theo handed her his handkerchief and watched with only a few winces as she scrubbed the black smears off her face. Once she finished, he suggested they partake of a bottle of champagne. They all agreed there was no reason not to, in that it was Dom Perignon and the room was warm. During the second bottle, the engines below them rumbled to life and the yacht began to move.

"Now what's he doing?" Dorrie demanded from behind the metal shelves, where she was making a casual inventory of their potential rations. "Does anyone want to try a can of pâté? It's French and real goose liver."

"No, thank you. I would guess Sandy's moving the yacht to a different location while he awaits word from his cohort in Connecticut," Theo said. He looked at Mary Margaret. "Who is it, by the way?"

"The cook. She pasted up the original note for a five-hundred-dollar-fee and agreed to say she saw some mysterious sort at the mailbox. At eleven o'clock she was supposed to hide in some charity box and wait for a suitcase to fall on her head." Mary Margaret yawned once again, still fighting the last vestiges of the drug in her system. "I hope she doesn't get canned for it; she does a divine chocolate mousse."

They sat for some time as the floor vibrated beneath them. Dorrie opened a tin of caviar and a packet of crackers, but no one did more than nibble. When Dorrie asked Mary Margaret about possible destinations, the red-haired girl yawned a disavowal of knowledge, leaned back, and fell asleep against a case of very good scotch.

"If he dumps us on a deserted island, he'll be sorry," Dorrie said, breaking off a corner of a cracker to scoop up some caviar. "I am not the sort to find it romantic. Beaches are fine when there's a bar with iced drinks and perhaps a small band playing native music, but basically they're sandy. I absolutely hate sand between my toes. Doesn't that drive you dotty, Uncle Theo?"

"Quite dotty," he agreed in a distracted voice. The girl was found, and that mystery resolved, although the conclusion to the drama was still unknown. Sandy was a greedy sort. Mary Margaret was simply too self-centered to consider the repercussions of the scheme, or to deal with the complications that were inevitable at some point in time. But how did any of it relate to Eli's murder?"

"I do wish we had found the roll of film," he said. "Its disappearance is more troubling than Mary Margaret's, in that I had suspected some degree of collusion on her part. The film, however, did not walk down the hill and call a cab from a hotel."

"Did you ask D'Orsini about it?" Dorrie gnawed on the broken fingernail.

"I did, but he refused to discuss the identity of his associates. One he described as a Colombian businessman who left Jamaica before the murder occurred. He has chosen to protect a second visitor, but for other reasons. The third is likely to be our poisoner. D'Orsini has every reason not to identify the person, since this person, once charged with first-degree murder, will have no reason not to implicate D'Orsini in the drug dealings. Until either the murderer is caught or the film found, there is no evidence against him."

"Surely Count D'Orsini would put personal considerations aside to help solve a murder. He's not all that bad. He prepped at Andover."

"Eli admitted to being a narcotics agent and then attempted to blackmail him. D'Orsini was not devastated when Eli was removed from the scene. Were I in a similar situation, I might feel that way myself."

"Maybe he did poison Eli," Dorrie said, still occupied with her fingernail. "Maybe he got the film and used it for a champagne cork or a golf tee. He probably has ackee trees all over his yard and a cabinet full of rum. Damn, I've got a hangnail now; it's going to drive me wild until I get back to my manicure kit at the villa. We are going to get back to the villa, aren't we? He isn't going to dump us on some mosquito-ridden lump of sand in the middle of the ocean. I really can't face the idea of twenty years on an island with both a hangnail and Mary Margaret. I don't know which would be worse."

The engine roared and the yacht began to roll back and forth. Dorrie grabbed at the champagne bottle before it fell on the canapés. Theo eased Mary Margaret to the floor and placed his jacket under her head as a pillow.

"This is too much," Dorrie snapped. "I have a delicate stomach, and all this rolling about is liable to make me feel quite ill. You're going to have to make him stop, Uncle Theo. You know how I hate to barf." The rolling stopped. "That's better," she said, taking a drink from the bottle. "It's one thing to be kidnapped, but another to be abused in the process. I should have told Sandy that I'd write him a check for however much Magsy's worth these days."

Before Theo could comment on the likely reaction, the lock clicked on the door. He took the champagne bottle by its neck and gingerly rose, doubting that the weapon would be effective against more modern techniques. He crept to the edge of the metal shelves and raised the bottle above his head. The door opened. Theo stepped out, prepared to wreak what havoc he could with an empty bottle of Dom Perignon.

"Holy Metro-Goldwyn, Bloom!" Sitermann said, leaping back as the bottle swung near his head. "You're supposed to drink it, not attack with it. Do you know how much that stuff costs?"

"It would be worth every penny of it," Theo said with a twinge of regret for having missed his target. His fingers tightened around the neck of the bottle as he watched uniformed men swarming through the corridor of the yacht. A second swing would not be politic, he warned himself.

"Did you have a nice cruise?" Sitermann continued, grinning at the tray of canapés.

"It was hardly my idea of a jolly outing. I presume you came aboard earlier, while we were still at the marina. At one point Sandy suspected he heard something and went to investigate. The only thing he stumbled into was a gun in the master cabin. Did you consider the possibility of overpowering him before he locked us in here and set sail?"

"Of course I did, Bloom. But I was just following you three out of idle curiosity, and I was by my lonesome. I lurked on board long enough to figure out I needed assistance, then hopped off and went to make a couple of telephone calls. The locals do like to be included, especially in the dramatic stuff. Makes 'em feel important."

"You forgot your gun, didn't you?"

Sitermann gave him a pained look. "As a matter of fact, I did. I spent most of the evening with an enchantress from Idaho, and I left my weapon in my hotel room so's not to unduly harm the little lady. I wasn't prepared for you and the two youngsters to go charging into the night, waving golf clubs and looking just a mite silly."

"Because of your dalliance, the girls and I were subjected to several hours of unpleasantness," Theo said coldly. "Sandy was clearly desperate enough to do something irrational in the name of self-preservation. Then you pop up like a clump of crabgrass and tell me you could have prevented all this, but you left your gun at home. Really, Sitermann, you CIA boys ought to take lessons from the Boy Scouts. Or even the Cub Scouts."

"As long as you still love me, Bloom." He began to bark orders in a very un-Sitermannish voice. Theo and Dorrie were escorted to the dining room for questions from a grim-lipped coast guard officer. Mary Margaret was carried to a stateroom, where she might sleep more comfortably. Sandy was led past the doorway to another room; he gave Theo a mock salute and Dorrie a polite nod.

The sun had risen by the time they arrived at the marina. Mary Margaret was transported to a hospital to be examined for any residuals from her ordeal, although Dorrie pointed out several times that the kidnap victim was most likely faking sleep to avoid questioning. A uniformed man drove Theo and Dorrie to the villa in their car, and left in a police car that had escorted them. Bitsy, Biff, and Trey were on the terrace, the remains of breakfast on the table. Theo left Dorrie to explain as best she could and went to the kitchen, where he was heartened to find Amelia and Emelda washing dishes.

"How kind of you to return," he said.

"Weren't my idea of a good time, not with all the murdering and stealing and searching going on,'' Amelia said with a shrug. ''Missus Greeley is paying double-time, and I've had my eye on a compact disc player in a store in MoBay.''

Emelda chuckled. ''I need a new television set. I love 'Dallas' on Friday evenings, but the reception's bad.''

Their loyalty was touching. Theo again thanked them for returning, then went upstairs to shower, shave, and find clean clothes. He was very tired, he realized as his knees began to quiver. First the night at the police station, and now a second night on the kitchen floor and in the storage room of D'Orsini's yacht. He was, he thought glumly as he studied a gray hair in his beard, too old for such things. He toyed with the idea of a telephone call to Nadine, but decided she was by this time flinging cards and vitriolic comments across the bridge table.

He laid out a clean shirt and his pin-striped pajamas and was indecisively studying both when there was a tap on the door. ''Uncle Theo?'' Dorrie called. ''Sergeant Stahl is here and he wants to talk to us about what happened. He's frothing again.''

Theo picked up the folded shirt and replaced it in a drawer. ''Please tell him that I will discuss this entire business at five o'clock this afternoon,'' he said through the door. ''He needs to bring Sandy, D'Orsini, and Gerry Greeley with him, so that we can explore all the nagging little details of the last week. In the interim, I shall sleep.'' Theo put on his pajamas, closed the curtains, pulled back the covers on the bed, and slept.

14

꧁ ꧂

"Can I offer you a glass of punch, Uncle Theo?" Dorrie said as he came out to the terrace. "It's a little bit crowded out here, but we'll find room for you to sit at the table, and I've asked the maid to serve hors d'oeuvres. Nothing complicated, mind you—just crackers, cheese, and a tin of pâté." She gave him a bright smile as she pulled back a chair and gestured for him to sit down.

The terrace was indeed a little bit crowded. Count D'Orsini and Gerry sat at one end of the table, both solemn and wary. Sandy sat beside Sergeant Stahl; the presence of several uniformed men at a discreet distance seemed adequate to deter any attempt to escape. Stahl's eyes were narrowed and his lips pressed together in a tight line. Trey, Bitsy, and Biff stood against the railing; the former was smiling but the latter two were cautiously observing the stage, waiting for the drama to begin.

Dorrie sat down and filled a glass from the pitcher. "There you are, Uncle Theo—unless you'd prefer something from the kitchen?"

Theo shook his head. "No, this will be fine, dear. How is Mary Margaret? Has she not recovered from the sedative she was given?"

Stahl glanced at Sandy. "No, she's doing fine, but the

doctor wants to keep her in the hospital overnight for observation. I don't know what'll happen next. Her father's thinking about pressing charges for attempted extortion. I've told D'Orsini what happened on the yacht. He can decide if he wants to file charges for trespassing and theft.''

"How delightful." Trey chortled. "If Daddy has Magsy thrown into prison, I shall move into her bedroom at home."

"And her closet?" Bitsy said, edging away from him to the far end of the railing.

Stahl gave her a perplexed look, then said, "I haven't had any final word about the charges from that end. What D'Orsini does is up to him."

"No harm done, my good man," the count murmured. "I'm relieved the gal was found and is now safe. That was my only worry, although I shall have to fire my captain for negligence. He's a reliable sort, but altogether too eager to give guided tours and leave keys lying about."

Smiling indulgently, Gerry patted his shoulder. "He's not precisely your employee, you know. He came with the craft."

"So he did, so he did." D'Orsini crossed his legs and gazed at Theo. "I understand we're all here to find out who murdered Eli. I don't want to rush you along, but I have a dinner engagement and I need time to change into proper evening clothes."

Theo ignored the low rumble from Stahl. "Yes, I think that if we all cooperate, we'll be able to produce an explanation for the various mysteries that arose in the last few days. The situation is this: Eli Staggley posed as a pool boy in order to observe certain transactions that took place beside D'Orsini's pool. Eli had good reason to suspect these transactions were illegal, and indeed they were. One evening, while we were out at a hotel, he drove back here. He then went upstairs and through the master bedroom to the balcony, where he had an unobstructed view of the pool area next door. Using a camera equipped to take photographs under limited lighting conditions, he shot a roll of film he felt was most incriminating."

"We know this," Stahl said. "Are you going to tell us he ate the film and it'll show up in the autopsy?"

"Patience," Theo murmured. "Two days ago we went on an all-day outing on the Governor's Coach, which gave Eli a golden opportunity to go next door and discuss the possible sale of the film to one of its featured stars. Negotiations were begun and further discussions planned once D'Orsini determined how much cash he could put his hands on. Eli was pleased with himself. He returned here, made a pitcher of rum punch from a bottle given to him, went to the area beside the pool, and eventually died. Therefore, he was not available to pick us up at the train station."

"Now that would have been disgusting," Trey said, lighting a cigarette and tossing the match over his shoulder. "A ghostly driver appears from the fog, his white teeth—"

"Will you shut up!" Bitsy hissed. "You're what is disgusting."

Theo took a deep breath. "To continue, in the middle of all this, Sandy and Mary Margaret cooked up a scheme to extort money from her father. The girl took the first opportunity to wander next door with a fanciful invitation, then simply hid until she could walk down the hill to the relative sanctuary of a hotel. She called the cook in Connecticut and made certain arrangements, then took a taxi to the marina and made herself comfortable on the yacht. A ransom note demanding a fantastic amount of money was delivered to her father yesterday morning."

"I'm surprised it wasn't stuck in chocolate mousse," Dorrie sniffed. When Biff smiled at her, she gave him a look withering enough to damage the hardiest perennial, and turned away. "We're waiting, Uncle Theo."

"Ransom note?" Stahl inserted in a mild voice. "I don't recall anything about a ransom note. Seems to me I asked if there'd been any word on the girl. Seems to me I asked a couple of times, while sitting in this very same chair."

Theo began to polish his glasses. "Yes, you did, and I apologize for keeping the information from you. I told you we hadn't had a peep from the girl, and that was basically true. The communication came second-hand from my sister, who's a friend of the Ellison family, and it was obvious from the beginning that the kidnapping was more complex than it appeared to be. I was waiting to see further developments before I took any action."

"Oh, Mr. Bloomer," Stahl said sadly, "and to think I trusted you with all of my confidences."

Count D'Orsini tapped his watch. "It's inexcusable to keep a lady waiting, chaps. The good sergeant has told us what occurred early this morning, and we now seem to know everything there is concerning this mock extortion. Are we or are we not to discover who murdered the policeman in the swimming pool?"

"We are," Theo said. "I initially assumed the two events were related in some obscure way, then I began to wonder if they were indeed entirely separate. But let us return to Eli's last afternoon. When he mentioned blackmail, he had not yet developed the roll of film, had he?" When D'Orsini nodded, Theo added, "Nor did he specify on which night he took the incriminating shots. Those of us living on this side of the fence knew, because Dorrie found the lens cap the next morning. You, however, were not privy to that knowledge and Eli saw no reason to mention the precise night. Am I right?"

Count D'Orsini removed a slender cigar from his pocket and took what seemed like several minutes to clip the ends and light it to his satisfaction. "That's right. There were many evenings that might have provided photographs which would cause me a certain amount of disagreeableness with the authorities. I did stop to wonder which evening he found so ominous, but I didn't have a chance to inquire. He was dead by then, you see."

"The first night we arrived, I heard you having an argument with a man whose voice sounded familiar, although I had met only four people at the time. Three were women—

Gerry, Amelia, and Emelda—and one a male—Eli. Would you care to tell us with whom you argued that night?''

"I see no reason to do so,'' D'Orsini said through a cloud of smoke. "It has nothing to do with anything that happened afterwards. Nothing at all. My lips are sealed with epoxy; I shall carry his identity with me to the grave, should subsequent revelations indicate I'm headed in that direction.''

Theo gazed at Gerry, who gazed back with a level expression. Now that he was confident he knew her secret, he could see the mannish aspects of her features—the face too large, the jaw too broad, the cheekbones too flat, the forehead too wide. The hint of a mustache on the upper lip, the insidious blue tinge of her cheeks where whiskers lurked even after the most methodical session with a razor.

"But,'' Theo said slowly, "it does have something to do with the problem of exporting illicit substances to the United States, I fear. Neither of you nor any of your known associates, such as Gerry or a swarthy Colombian, could pass through customs without a rigorous search. A man with whom you are never seen would not have such problems, would he?''

Count D'Orsini's expression grew alarmed. "This hypothesis of yours may have had some validity in the past, but I can assure you it is no longer remotely true. The courier service has been terminated.''

Dorrie produced an emery board and began to file her nails. "Well, who is it, Uncle Theo? We're all simply expiring of curiosity.'' Across the table, Stahl was nodding.

"Let's move on for the moment,'' Theo said. "Count D'Orsini has assured us that this particular associate had nothing to do with Eli's murder. On another night, he claims to have conducted business with a Colombian who promptly left the island. On yet another night, we must presume there was a third visitor. Who was that?''

Twirling the cigar between his fingers, D'Orsini smiled. "But surely you see, Bloomer, it's not in my best interests to tell you that.''

"It was the night Eli took the photographs," Theo said in a cold voice. "Whoever was with you was also approached to purchase the film."

"Well, you can't pin this one on me," Trey inserted. "I was dancing, although I'm sure I was disgusting, too. Whatever I do, I do disgust."

Theo turned to look at him. "Yes, you were at the hotel, as were Dorrie, Biff, Mary Margaret, and Bitsy. Sandy remained here, and slept so soundly he heard nothing—not the car come up the driveway nor Eli come upstairs and enter the adjoining bedroom."

"Yeah, I was blitzed," Sandy said. "All that booze did me in."

Theo shook his head. "No, I don't think you were sleeping so soundly that nothing disturbed you. I don't think you were in the villa."

"Sure I was," he said, his freckles darkening against his suddenly pale face.

"Part of the time, perhaps. Before you went next door to discuss a major cocaine transaction, and afterwards, when you wanted to be found asleep should we have returned at an early hour from the hotel."

"Where would I get that kind of money? I can't buy a kilo of coke with my allowance, sir. Maybe Biff or the others could, but I sure as hell couldn't."

"Not with your allowance, no. We might conjecture that you went over to discuss a minor purchase. Larger quantities were suggested as a possibility. You suddenly realized you could make a major deal—if you could get your hands on some cash. Is that when the extortion scheme came to mind? Were you led to believe you would receive a substantial sum of money from Mary Margaret's father, especially if you kept the pressure up and were amenable to compromise? I doubt you expected a million dollars, but a fifty-thousand investment might result in a fortune via resale, would it not? And with Mary Margaret involved, it would seem a stupid prank if it fell apart and the two of you were caught. You might be able to talk your way out of serious charges."

"Dear old Magsy is such a good sport," Trey said, smirking. "Promise her oodles of booze and a round of hankypanky, and she'd think it was a stitch and a half."

"She may have found it amusing at first," Theo said. "But after twelve hours of solitude and idleness, she was apt to grow bored with the game. Sandy was worried that she might back out of the scheme, and he couldn't let that happen. With a fortune dangling within reach, he was determined to continue—with or without her compliance. He needed to get to the marina without incurring suspicion, so he coerced Biff into a game of golf and then encouraged him to go sulk at a hotel bar. Those unencumbered hours resulted in a quick visit to the yacht, a needleful of sedative, and a once again cooperative co-conspirator."

"Until I figured out where she was hiding," Dorrie pointed out modestly. "Poor Sandy must have thought he had everything under control, but I intuitively put the pieces of the puzzle together and insisted we go to the yacht. He had no choice—either he took us, or Uncle Theo would telephone the police and they would go. He even tried to hurry us past the storeroom door by belittling my intellectual abilities. Despite everyone's lack of faith in me, I persuaded Uncle Theo to unlock the door. Voilà. Mary Margaret, unconscious but alive."

Theo managed not to wince during the narrative. "Where did you locate the sedative?"

"Eli had a few downers for sale, and I bought the needle at a drugstore. He was quite a pharmacist."

"For the lesser purchases, anyway," Theo said. "You had to go elsewhere for larger quantities, didn't you?"

Sandy shrugged. "He said to try D'Orsini for that. Initially, I went over to see what I could buy for a thousand dollars. I intended to buy ganja as a favor for the guys at the dorm, who all chipped in what they could."

D'Orsini glanced over his shoulder at the policemen in the

driveway and the police car parked on the street. Clearing his throat, he said, "I'd like to contribute to this, if I may. The young man did come over to discuss a purchase. Once terms were agreed on, he said he wouldn't have the money for several days. Nothing changed hands. It was merely fanciful talk; I was amusing myself at his expense."

"You said you'd have the coke by Saturday morning," Sandy said, knocking over his glass as he jabbed his finger at D'Orsini. "Eli told me you were one of the biggest dealers in Jamaica, and you didn't deny it. In fact, you said you'd arrange for the shipment the next night. I'm not taking a fall alone. I'm just a misguided kid who wanted a few kilos of ganja; you asked me if I might prefer something with more potential."

D'Orsini held up his hands. "All we did is talk, my boy. Sticks and stones and so forth. Had I known that Eli captured that innocent conversation on film, I would have laughed off his blackmail attempt. I was . . . protecting someone else."

"Indeed," Theo said. "But Sandy suddenly found himself in serious trouble. The lens cap was discovered on the balcony the next morning, and he quickly deduced its significance. Although the film might not prove anything that would stand up in court, he could not allow himself to be implicated in the drug bust. Any association with a drug dealer would be enough to have him kicked out of the naval academy and cause a serious rift with his parents. He did not intend to be called as a witness, or to even have his face in a photograph."

"Not even on the cover of *People* magazine?" Trey interrupted. "Magsy would have killed for less."

Theo silenced him with a look. "In order to eliminate the possibility, Sandy purchased several ackees at the market and left them in the kitchen. During the night, he mashed one and put the pulp in a bottle of rum. He often went to Eli's room to send him out for a newspaper; it would not have been difficult to leave the bottle in an inviting place and cross his fingers. He did so the morning of the trip on the Governor's Coach, which distanced him from whatever happened later that day. It was an alibi of sorts, I suppose.''

Dorrie fluffed her hair. "And while on the train, he and Mary Margaret finalized the bogus kidnapping scheme. I wondered why the two were so cozy. She sat in his lap for half the trip back; I was deeply concerned about the circulation in his legs.''

Theo nodded at her, then turned back to Sandy. "After sending Eli on an errand, you left the bottle in his room. You did not, however, have an opportunity to search for the roll of film, since Gerry and I were on the terrace. Dorrie heard you later that night, when you crept down to Eli's room and crawled through the window to search for the film. Biff assumed the screams had awakened you and that you'd subsequently gone to investigate. In reality, you were already in the driveway when the girls encountered Eli's body in the pool. When I saw you by the terrace door, you were on your way back upstairs, the film safely tucked in your pocket.''

"I can't believe it,'' Dorrie said, staring at Sandy as if he were a lab specimen. "You heard the screams, but you went right on with your little mission. You probably guessed that we'd discovered a dead body in the pool. For all intents and purposes, you put it there, didn't you? And then let us find it! That is unforgivable.''

"Disgusting,'' Bitsy sniffed.

"Yeah,'' Trey said with a laugh. "Now look who's Mr. Disgusto.''

Biff opened his mouth to say something, but a look of pain crossed his face and he hastily stared down at his shoes. After a moment, Dorrie moved next to him and put her hand on his arm. He covered her hand with his, and they moved closer together.

Stahl cleared this throat. "Then what about this damn film? We can assume he replaced the film with a used roll from his friend's camera case; that's not all that tough. But we searched every inch of the villa and didn't find it. Did he throw it away?''

Theo looked at Sandy, who was sitting with a politely interested smile. "I think he's too much of a businessman to dispose of something with potential value. He might have wanted to have the film developed so that he himself could use it against D'Orsini.''

"So where is it?'' Stahl demanded. ''It's still our only real evidence. We'll make a case once we have proof he was at D'Orsini's villa.''

"In the one place your men didn't search—his golf bag. He had it with him during the search, and in fact stuck it under our noses while we sat on the terrace yesterday and lamented its disappearance. You might send a man at this time to investigate the contents of the bag.''

"So develop the film; it will prove that I went over for a chat,'' Sandy said, shrugging. ''I don't see how it proves anything else.''

Theo waited for a minute, then in a soft voice said, ''But how do you explain its presence in your golf bag? You really should have thrown it away, young man.''

"Well, that's settled,'' Dorrie said, clasping her hands together. ''Who would like some crackers and pâté?''

It took a while before hors d'oeuvres could be served. Stahl told D'Orsini and Gerry to come to the station the next morning for further discussion, then took Sandy and his golf bag away. Biff and Dorrie went to one side of the pool to talk, their heads bent close together. Trey ambled down to the opposite side and stared into the distance; after a moment, Bitsy joined him.

D'Orsini winked at Theo, then excused himself to change clothes. Gerry moved to the chair beside Theo and filled her glass with punch.

"Given a choice, this would not have been my life-style,'' she said, smiling ruefully. ''A conventional life-style would be much simpler, but there's something within me that necessitates the pretense. I stopped fighting it a long time ago. After some horrid things happened in New Jersey, a conservative place where men don't eat quiche and women don't pump gas, I fled down here, where the sun is constant and the trade winds cool. Should I ever come into a great deal of money, I'll pack my bags and find a clinic in Switzerland to have extensive surgery. Thank you for not exposing my private situation to these young people.''

"I shall be obligated to discuss it with the authorities. Sergeant Stahl will be discreet, I hope, and there is no hard evidence concerning your participation in the drug smuggling. I simply guessed at that. If you desist, I should imagine nothing will happen to you or to D'Orsini.''

"Hal realizes that the only reason he's not going to prison is that the young man had to wait for his money to be wired. Hal made arrangements to acquire the cocaine the following night, but that had not been completed either. I think he'll turn to other occupations, now.''

"Escorting single women?''

Laughing, she stood up. "It keeps him busy, and for rather obvious reasons, it does not threaten me.'' She went down the driveway and drove away in her flamingo station wagon.

Amelia came onto the terrace. "I'm glad that's over with,'' she said, eyeing the clutter on the table with a disapproving look. "I never did trust that boy—he was too polite to be real. You want me to serve dinner?''

Theo looked at the twosomes on either side of the pool. "No, they can dine at a restaurant tonight. I'll fix myself something.''

Dorrikin and Biffkin were enthusiastic about the opportunity to dine at a hotel and dance until dawn. Bitsy agreed to go along with Trey and even swore not to say the word "disgusting'' unless the group agreed it was justified. They drove away in the beige car.

Humming a reggae tune, Theo fixed himself a cup of tea and took it out to the terrace, where he sank down to watch the lights of the jets cutting across the sky.

"Yo," Sitermann called as he came onto the terrace. He wore fuchsia-colored Bermuda shorts and a shirt that threatened to either bloom or explode. "You got everything worked out, I hear. Nailed the boy, pussyfooted around certain folks' private lives, and told Stahl where to find the film. Scared D'Orsini into cleaning up his act in perpetuity. Not bad for an old guy, Bloom. I must admit I was impressed."

"Thank you," Theo said, sipping his tea. "I suppose you followed us to the marina last night. Sandy heard you come on board. You're lucky he had not yet fetched the gun, or he would have caused you grief."

"No, not this old boy. I had a transmitter on my person, and the coastal police were tagging along behind us all the way. I just wanted to hear what all he said to you and that sweet little niece of yours." Sitermann snorted as Theo picked up his teacup. "How about a pitcher of something with a little more oomph?"

"If you want to fix yourself something, please do," Theo said. He accompanied the spy to the kitchen and opened the cabinet where the liquor supply was kept. While Sitermann prepared a martini, Theo said, "Mary Margaret walked down the hill the night she opted to disappear. Could the worst-dressed movie mogul on the West Coast have failed to see someone of her proportions—even in the dark?"

Sitermann slapped his forehead. "Oh, yeah, I remember now. She practically knocked me down. While I was steadying her with a grandfatherly hand, she begged me not to tell anyone that I'd seen her. You know me, Bloom—I'm just a lamb when some future starlet bats her eyelashes and whispers in my ear. But I didn't know where she was going, so I didn't lie to you."

"Sitermann," Theo said, "you are—"

The telephone rang, interrupting what might have been a diatribe of astounding length and depth. Theo picked up the receiver. "Yes?"

"I would like to be kept informed of the situation, Theo.

Apparently Win received all sorts of absolutely bizarre telephone calls and communiqués from wherever it is you are. Considering the tribulations I was forced to endure during the second session, I feel I deserve a full explanation.''

With a smile, Theo handed the receiver to Sitermann. "It's for you.''